Devil
in a
Red Kilt

Devil in a Red Kilt

Elysabeth Williams

Black Lyon Publishing, LLC

DEVIL IN A RED KILT
Copyright © 2010 by MARY E. WILLIAMS

Our books may be ordered through your local bookstore or by visiting the publisher:

www.BlackLyonPublishing.com

Black Lyon Publishing, LLC
PO Box 567
Baker City, OR 97814

This is a work of fiction. All of the characters, names, events, organizations and conversations in this novel are either the products of the author's vivid imagination or are used in a fictitious way for the purposes of this story.

ISBN-10:   1-934912-29-8
ISBN-13:   978-1-934912-29-4
Library of Congress Control Number: 2010928022

Cover Model: **Brannon Charles**
            Sword courtesy of Dutch Fahrney and
            kilt courtesy of Wade Foersterling of the
            Eastern Oregon Celtic Society,
            www.BakerHighlanders.org.

Written, published and printed in
the United States of America.

Black Lyon Historical Romance

To Mom.

*Forever in my heart you will be
snuggled on the ancient brown couch,
reading and sipping coffee in the
stillness of the morning.*

Chapter 1

The fluorescent lights of the office were blinding. Evan stood from behind his large desk and walked to the wall switch to turn them off, and stopped by a sideboard to turn on a smaller lamp. He opened the cabinet where it sat and stared at the crystal decanter. Another long night at the office would be a lonely one. Evan rubbed his tired face. Sighing, he picked it up and poured the honey colored whisky into a nearby glass. He opened a small ice chest and dropped in two cubes for good measure.

Returning to his desk, glass in hand, Evan paused to look at a framed picture on the wall; his wedding picture, radiating with love and a promising future. It seemed like such a long time ago, judging by the smiles and lack of stress lines crowding their faces. His wife, Evie, had been so full of joy. It was a far cry from their current state. He traced her face with a finger, pausing to remember the day. After a brief moment he looked away, too pained to focus. He pulled his cell phone from his pants pocket and text messaged his wife. *Working late. Don't wait up ... Forever & Ever, Evan.* He paused and backspaced over the *Forever and Ever*, and sent it through. He hadn't said those words in almost a year. He didn't want to start anything tonight. Returning the phone to his pocket, he sat down.

The glow from his laptop haunted him. It would be another night of book-keeping; another night of numbers and figures no one but himself would care about. He took a long drink from the glass and placed it next to his computer, ready to pull an all-nighter. He sat for hours going over the bank's figures, trying to finish the end of the month reports before he took vacation. This was the time of year, near Halloween, which he would have to spend with his family no matter what stress kept them apart. Evan would work doubly hard to finish all projects before he was able to leave. This meant, of course, more meaningless man-hours at the office.

There came a soft knock on the door, pulling Evan's thoughts from the figures. The door opened and a waif of a young woman in her early twenties smiled from the hall outside. With her eyes soft and her mouth set in a full pout, she leaned in and spoke quietly. "Mr. MacDonald, would you like anything else before I leave?"

Evan frowned at her. "No, Ms. Smith. I'm fine. You can go home." He ducked his head behind the laptop screen again, hoping she would go away. The girl was notorious for following him around the office at all hours with glassy eyes. Rumors flew around about how she wanted him and he attempted to avoid her at all costs. Yes, she was a decent assistant, but for the most part, she was more annoying than helpful, especially since she seemed distracted by his very presence.

He focused his eyes on spreadsheets and heard the latch click. He exhaled in relief and looked up. Ms. Smith was still standing in his office, her back pressed against the door. Her sheer white blouse was unbuttoned to her navel, showing off her lacy, cream-colored bra barely holding her breasts. Evan huffed. She wasn't unattractive. She was young, single, and willing. It was that he was married, no matter how unwilling his wife seemed. Evan's frown deepened and he swallowed hard.

"Ms. Smith, this is inappropriate. Please leave." He glared at her, forcing himself not to let an eye wander from her smoky, doe-eyed gaze.

Instead of complying, she walked closer. "Mr. MacDonald. Evan … I need to tell you something," she whispered, leaning over the desk, her cleavage directly in Evan's face. The heat from her skin made Evan's body react in ways in which he was immediately ashamed.

"There is nothing you need to tell me with your shirt off, Ms. Smith. This is your last warning. Get out or be terminated." He stood up and moved away from her. He opened the door to his office and held it open. The light from the hallway filled the room, illuminating his towering form.

Ms. Smith was breathless as she looked up at him. Evan was over six feet tall, his shoulders wide and barely contained in the suits he wore, tailored down to the very last centimeter. There wasn't a woman in the building who didn't notice his allure, yet he was a stone to them all. Everyone at the bank knew his marriage was straining. Ms. Smith was the only one gutsy enough to make a move. Emboldened by the thought, she sauntered across the room to him and crushed herself against his body. Splaying her hands across his stomach, she pushed his suit jacket aside. Her tiny fingers worked swiftly on his shirt buttons and she sighed at the sight of his muscled chest. "Mr. MacDonald. I can't stand this anymore. I want you so bad it hurts."

Evan's jaw clenched and he caught her wrists in his grasp. He scowled down at her, causing her courage to wane. Her breath came in shudders as she saw the anger amplified in his blue eyes.

"Pack your desk and leave. Do not return in the morning," he growled as his grip on her wrists tightened. He wanted to throw her across the room, but managed to just hold her there to let his anger subside. The last thing he needed was a lawsuit for assault.

The clicking sound of high heels caught his attention. Evan's eyes tore away from the young woman's face and he glanced down the hallway. His anger turned to horror as he saw his wife. Evie stopped walking as she saw her husband and his assistant, their bodies still pressed together. Evan pushed the girl across the room, sending her tumbling over a chair and into the floor. Evie watched, mortified, as she saw the assistant's state of undress and her husband's bare chest.

"Evie, wait. This isn't what it seems," he gasped, trying to stop her. He caught her by the waist and she turned, splashing the hot coffee she held into his face. Without uttering a word, she turned on a heel and left the office.

Chapter 2

"Will you at least talk to me? I want to explain." It was the fifteenth time Evan tried to call Evie and the third message he'd left. He stood in his office staring out the window into the parking lot, wishing for the days when answering machines would let people sit until the other person finally picked up the receiver. "Please call me, Evie. I want to talk." He flipped the phone shut and sat down at his desk, rubbing his face. The desk phone rang almost immediately and he picked it up, hoping to hear his wife's voice.

"MacDonald."

"Dad, hey … Um … I don't know what's going on, but you need to come home," his oldest child, Mason, sounded nervous, which was very uncharacteristic of his usually level-headed son.

"What's happened?"

"Mom's gone crazy."

"What do you mean?" Evan stood and closed his laptop, yanking out the power adapter and shoving it all into a leather case.

"Let's just say … you're going to have to replace a lot of clothes—and—do we have a fire extinguisher?" The tone was concerned, but it also held just enough amusement to annoy his father.

Evan bellowed into the phone. "What the hell do you mean, Mason? What is going on?"

"Just come home." The phone went dead and Evan ran out of the office, not caring of the nearly trampled people standing in his path.

∞

Evan raced home, going over all reactions he expected from Evie in his mind … and they all terrified him. When he finally pulled down the long gravel driveway leading to the farmhouse, he was still clueless as to how Evie was taking what happened at the office or how he would ever explain.

He threw the car in park and jumped out, running to the front door. He ran through the house looking for anyone. Finding it empty, he darted through the kitchen and out to the back patio to see if anyone was in the back yard. As he stepped out into the brisk night, he stopped abruptly. There was a huge bonfire in the middle of the field behind the house and Evie was standing next to it. His son, Mason, and younger twin daughters, Keiran and Leeann, walked toward Evan.

Mason waved casually as he approached the patio and stopped to talk. "What happened, old man?"

Evan blinked his attention away from the glowing vision in the field and focused on his son. "She saw something at the office she shouldn't have. It was a big misunderstanding." He looked back to the field, and watched as Evie sprayed what he assumed was lighter fluid onto the pile, watching flames lick the sky. He groaned. "Should I even ask what she's burning?"

"Your clothes, right now. She's got a few pictures and some trophies down there too," Leeann responded. Mason looked at her. She refused to make eye contact. He walked closer and hugged her. She hid her face in his chest and sniffled. He put his finger under her chin and raised it to look at him.

"Hey, listen to me. This is what happened. My assistant has a crush on me and she made a pass earlier tonight. Your mom walked in and saw the tail end of a bad situation I was trying to diffuse. She didn't stick around to hear me out. "

Leeann sniffled again. "Is that why you smell like Starbucks coffee?"

"That's why I smell like Starbucks coffee."

Leeann giggled and wiped her nose. "Are you going to leave us?"

"No," he said definitely.

"Mom said she's kicking you out," Keiran said quietly.

"Yeah? I'm not going anywhere. We've all been stressed out since your grandmother died and I'm not giving up." He looked at the field again. "Go in the house. I'll be there shortly. Let me get this under control." Evan kissed his daughters on the head, patted Mason on the back and sent all three of them into the house as he walked out into the field.

"Nice night for a bonfire," he said, standing next to Evie. He took his suit jacket off and threw it into the flames. He faced Evie and crossed his arms across his chest.

"Yep," she said, not looking at him. She squirted the lighter fluid into the flames again and watched the glow brighten.

"Bring any marshmallows?"

"Nope. I thought I would just start with your clothes. Then work my way into the wedding photos."

Evan ground his teeth and nodded. "All right then."

They stood in silence for a few minutes until Evie pulled a handful of clothes out of the pile next to her and threw them into the fire. He groaned inwardly.

"Do you want to talk at all?" Evan took a step closer to her.

Evie breathed deep and looked him in the eye. "I can't concentrate on what I want to say while you smell like a cheap hooker."

Evan took off his shirt and threw it into the fire. "I smell like a pumpkin spiced latte, actually. But if this helps you talk, I'm okay with that." He propped his hands on his hips and grinned crookedly. Evie stared as his bare chest and then narrowed her eyes on his face. "You're an arrogant ass."

"This is news? We've been married for over a decade."

"You didn't cheat on me before."

"I haven't ever cheated on you," he said, taking her by the arms and attempting to make eye contact. She searched his face, her expressions wrenching into different emotions. "I want a divorce, Evan," she whispered, looking away. She pushed his hands from her and started to walk toward the house.

"No. I'll never leave you. I'll never sign a single sheet of paper, Evie. Never. We're Forever and Ever. Remember?" He followed her for a few steps until she stopped and faced him with tears in her eyes.

"Evan, please. Just give me some space. Don't come back in tonight."

He stopped, held his hands up in surrender and let her walk back into the house alone. Defeated, he went to get the water hose and returned to the bonfire to put out the flames. As he stood watching it dwindle, a breeze blew by, causing him to shudder with chill. He started to kick dirt over the remaining embers and washed them down once more and heard a drum in the distance. Evan quizzically looked toward the woods, wondering who would be out at this time of night, drumming. As suddenly as the breeze and rhythmic noise came, it disappeared. Assuming he was hearing things from inside the house, he shut the water off and coiled the hose. He gathered what clothes were left dry and unburned, and retreated to the barn to set up a bed for the night.

Chapter 3

Evie stared blankly at her cell phone's calendar wondering how she could ever keep up this pace. With football practice for Mason, gymnastics for Keiran, and piano lessons for Leeann, she wondered if science figured out how to clone people to make it possible to be in three places at once. Standing in the kitchen of their ancient Virginian farmhouse, she wondered to herself if her great-grandmother who built this old place, did this much in one day. With a slight chuckle, she thought to herself she would have known better if she had paid any attention to her mother, who had incessantly told her stories about growing up here and the oddities that surrounded the land.

After her mother's death, Evie was also surprised she inherited it and managed to convince her entire family to move here. Evan hated it, so instead of taking time to grieve for her mother, he talked her into putting the entire estate up for sale. She gazed out the window to the scorched field beside the house and wondered how it looked back in her mother's time, even her grandmother's and great-grandmother's time. More importantly, she wondered if the family propensity to insanity was genetic.

They lived in Atlanta before moving to this little town. At first, it was to take care of her ailing mother with what the doctor's believed to be dementia, but now, it was just a pass through as they sold her childhood home and returned to the city. The only thing tying them to the area now was Evan's off-the-wall idea of opening up a gym to keep his martial arts skills honed. Beyond that, they were not permanent residents, as far as Evan was concerned.

Evie hated Atlanta. It was too big and too crowded for her. She enjoyed being able to walk down to the gas station for her monthly copy of Vogue, sit on the old wooden bench outside the store and daydream she was a runway model. Never did she think she would end up catering such shows in London after dropping out of college. There she would meet Evan, a southern gentleman on a post college excursion. They were married shortly after they returned to America and had three beautiful babies who grew up to be wonderfully behaved teens.

Somewhere over time, it fell apart. He was spending more and more time at the office or at the gym, and she wasn't talking, especially not since what she witnessed with his assistant weeks ago. Not since she'd asked for a divorce.

A terrible rendition of The Clash's "London Calling" zapped Evie out of her thoughts as the song rocked from the little device in her hand. She shook off her anger as she took the last swig of her now lukewarm coffee. Grimacing, she answered the phone.

"Evie MacDonald, how can I assist you?" she drawled with a honey-thick southern accent.

"Mom, you're late again. You were supposed to pick me up thirty minutes ago."

Evie clenched her eyes shut at the stern male voice on the phone and quietly whispered curses capable of making a stripper blush.

"I'm sorry Mason; I got caught up checking my emails here at home. I'll be there in ten minutes."

"Whatever. Just get up here. It's starting to rain like hell."

"Fine, but you shouldn't talk to your mother that way," she started, but Mason had already disconnected. She stuck her tongue out at her phone and shoved it back into her pocket, grabbed her keys, and headed for the car.

Mason had the hardest head in the family. At sixteen years old, he topped out at six foot four and weighed two hundred, thirty pounds. Built like a "brick outhouse," as her mother would have said just to cause a riot in polite company. He worked out and played football most of his life. Evan always made sure his boy was going to be big and tough and play all kinds of manly sports to be like him, or so Evie surmised. However, the cost of having such a rough schedule was that Evie endured all kinds of sports talk she cared nothing about, when she thought Mason could be paying at least a little attention to some of the girls who always flitted about around him like … *Like what? A swarm of gnats?* she thought.

As she drove up to the school's curb, Evie giggled at the thought of gnat-like girls as she saw a couple of the cheer team around her son. He was scowling, as always, and she unlocked the SUV door to let him inside. He bounded for the car with a faint look of gratitude as he slammed the door behind him.

"Rough day? Must have been tough weathering out there with those two," Evie asked, still giggling at the vision of winged teens flitting about around his head.

Mason simply turned his head to his mother and glared. Immediately, Evie took more joy knowing she got to him and she snorted with laughter. His scowled intensified. She leaned over and gave him a peck on the cheek. She was greeted again with the scoff and grumble that in her heart she knew was love.

"Well, back off to the house to clean. We've got the Halloween party tomorrow night as always," Evie sighed, knowing that since her mother's death after last years' Halloween party, it wouldn't be the same. Mason said nothing as he stared at his mother, his scowling features relaxing a bit.

"Is Dad coming to help?" he asked quietly.

The smile faded from her lips as she turned to face the road.

"I don't know," she managed. The whole family knew what happened at the office. Since then, Evan lived in the barn loft behind the main house, refusing to leave the premises other than to go to work or the gym. It became the longest weeks of her life. Her thoughts switched to the packet of papers in her backseat in an unmarked manila envelope. They were only a few sheets of uncontested divorce papers, but they weighed a ton on her mind.

As she drove from the parking lot, Mason took her hand from the steering wheel and squeezed. She fought back tears knowing it was probably the most affection she had received from her family since the morning in the woods when she found her mother.

∞

Evan closed the front door quietly and laid his only remaining suit jacket on the nearby bench. His fifteen-year-old daughter, Keiran, greeted him with a hug around the waist. "Hey Daddy-o," she said, smiling up at him with ice blue eyes identical to his own.

"Hey Kiddo, what's up?"

"Mama's fixing dinner. Mason's in the barn working out and Leeann is on the phone."

"So it's been a typical day with the MacDonald clan, then, eh?"

"Yep. Oh, but hey, I've got a gymnastics class after school tomorrow and the money is due for our meet next spring."

"So you're hitting me up for cash before I can get both feet in the door?"

"Yep. Don't know when they'll be in the door again, so I might as well do it while I can." She flashed another winning smile at Evan. He grumbled and reached around to his back pocket and pulled out his wallet, ignoring the dig. "How much is it this time?"

"Two hundred."

"Ouch." He handed her two hundred dollar bills, which she took and happily shoved into her jeans.

"Let's go say hey to your Mom," Evan said, beginning to walk toward the kitchen.

Keiran looked uncomfortable and backed up toward the stairs. "You go. I'm gonna go kick Leeann off the phone. She's been on there for an hour. It's my turn." She bounded off up the stairs, her flaming red curls bouncing off her shoulders as she ascended.

"Good luck," he chuckled as he wandered down the hall to the kitchen. He knew the last couple of weeks were difficult on them all. He wanted badly to explain the situation to Evie, but she wouldn't hear of it. The subject would change like the wind, and she seemed to want to repress it all. The kids wanted to be normal, but having their father live in the barn was hardly unnoticeable.

He leaned against the door frame and watched Evie cook. It smelled wonderful as always. Cooking, to Evie, was an innate skill, even if it was just over the evening dinner. He took note of tonight's meal as she had her back turned to him. Country fried steak and gravy. Mashed potatoes and fresh green beans from the last harvest of their garden. Biscuits readying to bake as Evie bent down to put them in the oven. Evan tilted his head sideways, enjoying the view of his wife's behind.

"Evenin', lady," he said, startling her. Yelping a curse, she almost dropped the pan of biscuits, catching them before they hit the floor. "Dammit, Evan, that would have sucked," she grumbled, not looking at him.

"Sorry," he said simply, knowing he just set the tone for the rest of the night. He turned to leave and went in search of solitude until dinner was ready. He walked up the stairs and heard Leeann and

Keiran fighting over the phone. He sighed and hung his head as he turned around and went back down the stairs and out the door.

He wandered toward the barn, taking note of things around the old farmhouse needing repair. "It's not the only thing that needs fixing around here," he muttered to himself. He looked toward the woods and paused, noticing the colors of the leaves beginning to change. He listened to the wind and focused on a faint noise coming from the woods. He had heard the same drumming noise weeks earlier when Evie threw him out of the house. Evan started to walk toward the sound when it dissipated. Looking around, Evan was more than a little annoyed at its presence again. The high school was at least ten miles away, he thought. Band practice wasn't heard this far out. He looked toward the house windows. They weren't open. However, that wouldn't make sense either. The girls weren't into loud music. Assuming he was merely hearing things, he walked on to the barn. As he got closer to the dilapidated building, he noticed music blaring from the inside and decided to go check on his son. "Ah, this must be what I'm hearing," he decided. Evan opened the barn door to hear even louder music and saw Mason lying on the weight bench doing presses. Evan walked to the stereo and turned it down so Mason could hear him.

"Need a spotter?"

"Sure," Mason replied, not moving. "Add twenty more?"

"Sure," Evan replied, turning to grab two more weights to add them to bar.

He stood at Mason's head, watching over his son. He watched as the boy lifted the now two hundred, seventy-pound bar once, paused, and then returned it to its starting position. He sat up and glared at it in disgust.

"Maxed it out, huh?" Evan said.

"I think so. I thought I could do it," Mason said, taking off his gloves and tossing them on the bench beside him.

"My turn," Evan said, shooing him off the bench.

"You're just going to piss me off."

"Probably. Add thirty," Evan grinned, taking off his button down suit shirt and tossing onto the stereo, exposing a white tightly fitting undershirt molded to his muscular chest.

Mason added another thirty pounds of weight to the bar as Evan lay down underneath it. With Mason watching, Evan did twenty presses with the now three hundred-pound bar and put it back, completely unaffected by the exertion.

"I told you. Now I'm pissed."

Evan laughed and sat up, throwing a glove at his son. "Kid, I've got a few years, a few pounds, and am still a few inches taller than you. You'll get there."

"Two inches, Dad. Two. That doesn't make a hill of beans."

"You'll get over it. And if you ever get tall enough for me to look you in the eye, we're gonna be in trouble."

"You're already in trouble, old man," Mason said trying to grab him around the neck in a chokehold. Evan flipped his son's arm around and reversed the move in the blink of an eye.

"Too slow," Evan chuckled, flicking Mason in the ear with his fingers.

"How do you do that?" Mason grumbled to his father.

"Ancient Chinese secret," he laughed as Mason elbowed him in the gut with an "Oof!"

They stopped wrestling around as they heard Evie yelling in the background to come eat.

"Let's go," Evan said with his smile fading. Mason noticed the difference immediately. Evan's shoulders slumped and he breathed deep.

"Is she mad today?" Mason asked.

"Who the hell knows anymore?"

Evan looked at his son's beaten down expression. Too much stress showed on the boy's face. "Are you guys going to split up?"

Evan shook his head. "Never. I'll live out my days in the barn before I'll leave." Mason's face relaxed in relief.

Evan picked up his shirt and put it back on without buttoning it. He turned off lights as they left the barn. Mason walked ahead while Evan fastened the lock on the door. The faint drumming returned with the breeze.

"Mason, did you turn off the stereo?"

"Yeah, why?"

The hair on the back of Evan's neck stood and he felt oddly drawn to the woods. He stopped and looked into the trees. Something or someone was there. The drumming faded away again as the wind shifted.

"Nothing. I guess I'm hearing things." He shook off the weirdness and caught up with his son.

They arrived in the house and both girls were already eating; still bickering about the phone. Evie stood next to an empty plate on the counter as she cleaned.

"You couldn't wait for the rest of us?" Evan asked.

For the first time since he got home, she looked directly at him, her brown eyes accusing.

"I've got too much to do. The party is tomorrow night and I still need to clean everything."

"Do you need any help?" he offered.

"Oh, I think you've helped enough," she gritted through her teeth.

"Okay," Evan said, putting up his hands in surrender. He refused to fight in front of the kids, no matter how old they were. He grabbed a full plate and sat down at the kitchen bar without another word. The kids finished eating and left while Evan and Evie merely existed near each other in silence. Evie eventually cleaned herself out of the kitchen and Evan put his dishes in the dishwasher. Sighing, he went upstairs to take a shower and get ready to make his retreat into the barn, even though the sun was just setting.

Evie dusted the same spot for ten minutes, obsessing about the party. She hid in the living room and faked cleaning while the rest of the household went about their evening. And she knew that's what she was doing; hiding ... *Everybody is always so happy all the time and I'm not allowed to be. Especially with Evan.* She scoffed at herself and moved on to another spot to clean. She moved a Hummel out of the way and stopped. Her mother gave it to her when she was young, not thinking she would keep it safe until adulthood. Yet here it was, twenty years later, smiling back at her. She picked up the figurine and stared. The sticky sweet smile of the child's face was almost mocking her misery. Evie started to dust it and then looked at it again. She felt like it was smiling at the betrayal by her mother. Thoughts overtook her mind. *Mom, you left me here with no answers, with your own crazy life to haunt me forever. Everything you said, I did, and never questioned why. Then you died without saying goodbye ... without any explanation.*

Anger surged as she stared at the pink cherub cheeks and vacant porcelain eyes. She grabbed it by its head and threw it at the iron wood-burning stove across the room, smashing it into pieces. Evie wiped bitter tears away with the back of her hand before anyone could see and left the room.

Evan met her halfway up the stairs. He took her hand, checking her over for injury. "Hey, are you okay?"

His genuine concern melted Evie. She wanted nothing more than to dive into his arms and sob. Instead, she smiled tensely and nodded, walking past him up to their room and shut the door behind her.

Evan watched her walk away with sadness in his eyes and went downstairs to find the mess of porcelain all over the living room floor. Confused, he went to gather a broom and cleaned up the pieces alone.

Chapter 4

Evan was a strong, agile man in his late thirties who had been into martial arts most of his life. He was a third degree black belt in karate who lost interest in being a Sensei at a training facility in Atlanta. He then moved his focus to a new form in the early 1990s when kickboxing became all the rage. Within the last year he realized it still didn't sate his need for what he called "therapy," and started up the first 'no holds barred' mixed martial arts studio in the little podunk town where they now lived. He came here as much as possible, just as today, to stay away from his seemingly ever-stressful home life. He trained to defend and protect at all costs, and was deadly fast. He was six and a half feet of pure trained muscle, but moved at such lightning quick speed it always surprised whomever he was fighting.

At his day job, being a Chief Financial Officer for a worldwide banking company, he carried stress on his wide shoulders every hour of the day. It was up to him to make sure the entire company's finances were straight. He was on the board of directors, and always found himself at work after hours, traveling, and sometimes just falling asleep on the couch in his fifth floor office, never making it home for the evening. Even after the incident with Ms. Smith, he found himself there almost every night since. The office was buzzing with speculation about his marriage even more now, but with a stern, but quiet grace, he was able to keep the rumor mills at bay. His CFO job provided his family with so much. "But at what cost?" he mused. "My wife threw me out. My kids don't seem to care much."

The younger man in the ring yelled at him from the opposite corner, bringing him back to focus. "Hey old man, you gonna fight me or stand there with your teeth in your head?"

In the blink of an eye, Evan closed the gap between them and slammed his hand hard into the face of his opponent. Stepping back, he kicked him square in the chest so quick; the man didn't have time to react. He fell like a tree onto the mat as his trainer rushed to his aid.

Evan wasn't even out of breath. The sound of the man hitting the mat was almost satisfying. He spit out his mouth piece and unwrapped the tape from his gloves. Out of the corner of his eye, he glanced to make sure the guy was still breathing and headed for the showers, with Jack, the co-owner and full time manager, hot on his heels. "What the hell, Evan?" the squat man demanded.

"What, Jack? He wanted to fight, I gave him what he was looking for," Evan smiled, throwing up his hands innocently.

"Man, you can't keep bashing members around. We're liable here. You have got to keep your temper in check!" Jack scowled at Evan one last time and threw him a clean towel.

"I don't know what the hell is going on, but you have been coming here every day this week for hours and beating the tar out of everyone. It's just not like you."

Evan knew he was right. Jack was the only friend he'd made while being here. They both had trained in the MMA for years and always strove for more. Moreover, Jack, of all people here would know his tendencies of violent outbursts. With their commonalities, he befriended Jack and made him a co-owner in hopes of selling him the gym when they moved to Atlanta.

"I know. I'm just stressed-out. Evie's having her family over for Halloween and it's just got me worked up. I'll watch it, I promise." Evan grabbed the towel and headed to the showers.

"See that you do, man. I need you here 100% mentally, not just physically," Jack said, walking back into the gym to check on the howling younger competitor.

∞

Evan stood in the gym's shower thinking of the party he would have to endure later in the evening. He always hated these functions, but knew they were always a necessary evil. Every Halloween he would concede to a party with Evie's side of the family, which was just a perfect stage for her mother's crazy ranting about "wee folk" and nonsense.

They all would feast on the usual Halloween fare and did all the usual seasonal fun; trick or treating in costumes, pumpkin carving, the apple bobs, spiced apple cider, roast marshmallows and the telling of ghost stories. The kids always adored it. Evie loved it all. He would smile, laugh, and endure the in-laws. Evan talked it up and rubbed elbows, promising he'd look into finding a job for some, listening to money woes for another, always being the executive. It was never the chitchat of ball games or hockey season. It was never about his MMA fighting or the trophies he'd accumulated and for which he was very proud. They never seemed to inquire about Evan's well being or his interests. They always wanted something.

He dreaded it every year and of course it always ended the same. The kids would always tuck in their beds giggling about goblins and ghosts. Then Evie's mother, Mama Killie, would drink too much Drambuie and go into a tirade about how she spent her early adult years in the mountains of Scotland in the year of 1200-something, while everyone nodded and smiled, knowing she was completely off her rocker, silently hoping for her to pass out.

Every year they'd listen to her mourn a lost lover. She'd cry about her escaping the murderous rage of someone whose name Evan forgot. After her rants, they would have to carry her, sobbing, back to her bedroom in the guesthouse and wait for her to fall asleep, in fear she would run into the woods and never been seen again.

Unfortunately, it was exactly how she had ended her life. At last year's party, after the ritual of putting Mama Killie in her room for the night, they thought she was safe and went to bed. The next morning they found she was missing, and after a daylong search, Evie had found her mother lying in a clearing, deep in the woods. The very woods where he heard the drumming, he added absentmindedly.

He remembered Evie in his arms as she wept for her loss, her body wracked with grief. She seemed so frail, so small. He held her for the entire day, whispering love into her ear. She came to him then and they made love throughout the night. Evie had returned to her stoic self almost immediately following the funeral. It was the last time they were close and it tore at his soul.

Evan stopped to think of how it might be different this year, since Mama Killie's death. Would the family sit around and discuss it? Would they fight over the farmhouse? Would they set more of his things on fire in the front yard? Would they even come at all?

"Hell, I couldn't be that lucky," he murmured. He'd finally convinced Evie to sell it all and move back to Atlanta. Though now he was staying out in the barn, he wondered if divorce was imminent. He was worried about his marriage and most importantly, his wife. Evie was haunted by this town, the house, and all the insanity surrounding the last days of Killie's life. Her mother insisted something on the farm was quite special, but he could never see what. All he saw was a farmhouse in great disrepair and a broken down barn where he now slept. The hundred acres of adjoining woods filled with hunters every year, and Evan knew it would eventually be an expensive liability when someone got drunk and shot a person instead of a deer. He previously tried to put out No Trespassing signs, but no one seemed to care. He always heard them in the woods. He had yet to see anybody, but knew people were out there. It was just a matter of time before something happened.

Toward the end, Mama Killie became maniacal in trying to show them what it was drawing her family here. Everyone thought she was just suffering from a long bout of senility over the years. No one believed her. "Crazy old Killie." He stopped to remember his recent encounter with the land's peculiarity. Perhaps there was something to say for the area.

He shook off the thoughts of his deceased mother-in-law and upcoming evening and studiously washed his short, spiky, auburn hair. The hot water covered his face, and blazed a trail down his wide shoulders. He breathed the steam in slowly and thought about Evie as he lathered his body, and recalled how she was so strong over her mother's death. Evan's mind stopped on the picture of his wife. *Oh Evie … My strong Evelyn …*

Simply mouthing her name made his cock rise with longing. Even though they hadn't been intimate in almost a year, he still ached for her. The want never stopped. Evan closed his eyes and leaned forward in the shower stall, bracing himself against the cold tiles with one hand, letting the scalding water rush over his tightly muscled back, down his taut buttocks and legs as he took himself in the other hand to release the strain. He breathed deeper as he thought of her eyes penetrating him. Thoughts of his face buried in her neck and the smell of her sandalwood scented hair whirled in his mind as he stroked his hardness with a strong grip. Evan felt his wedding ring rake across it, adding a sting of ironic pain to the experience. He thought of Evie's body pressed against the length of him, breasts crushed against his chest, her head thrown back in desire—waiting, wanting, needing. *In need of me …*

Evan's breath became ragged as he thought of her smoldering stare. His strong jaw clenched tight as his ecstasy rose to near uncontrollable. He felt as if he could break a hole in the wall with the sheer force of his bracing hand. He didn't care that anyone could walk in at any moment. In his mind Evan saw Evie arching her back and writhing underneath him as he threw his own head back, letting the hot water splash on his chest and straining not to yell as his desire spent into the water.

With the fantasy fading away, he opened his eyes. Evan cursed under his breath and turned off the shower. He grabbed his towel and headed for his locker to don clothes, steeling himself again for his next encounter with the one he wished he could have again. He thought bitterly, what little emotion he had left to give was slipping down the drain, quite literally.

Chapter 5

The Halloween party arrived like a hurricane. Everyone was on edge, waiting for the storming to start. It all started out innocently enough. Everyone was having fun and socializing. The kids were doing the monster mash with their younger cousins, only stopping long enough to scare the trick-or-treaters. It was almost a normal night, Evie decided finally with a faint smile. She was busy being the perpetual hostess, waiting for Evan to come out of the bedroom. She reluctantly admitted she was fixated on his presence even though she didn't want to be. Not tonight. It wasn't just the first attempt at making appearances for the extended family after their separation; it was most importantly the one-year anniversary of her mother's death.

Evie vowed to focus the night on her mother and her life. She wanted to talk to her family about everything she could, while she could, since this was generally the only time she would be able to get the whole clan in the same room at once. She wanted to know once and for all if they experienced the same demented storytelling she endured growing up. Mama Killie tended to treat her, the oldest by a good ten years, differently than her stepsiblings who had a different father. Evie never met her father. She didn't even know his name or if he was even dead, despite Mama Killie's insistence that he died before she was born. She was desperate to know if she was alone in her mother's insanity.

Lost in thought, she was startled to see Evan walk down the hall toward her. She caught her breath, realizing he'd been convinced to wear his family's clan kilt for the night. Watching the way the red plaid material swished around his strong calf muscles and outlined his hard thighs made her face flush. He settled on a compromise;

deciding on wearing his old combat boots—his early 1990s holdovers he bought in the UK. "Doc Martens or nothing," he'd said earlier when she braved him long enough to hand him the kilt. Evie agreed with a curt nod.

It did complete the outfit, she decided as she saw its effect now. He smiled at her, cocking an eyebrow at her outfit; a corseted number, which she found in her grandmother's room of all places. "What?" she asked him slyly. "Granny was rockin' the corsets fifty years before your beloved Docs."

He grinned slowly at her, taking in the view of the tops of her breasts, pushed up as far as humanly possible without spilling over. "I have nothing to say about old Granny right now that wouldn't give me ten more years of therapy, but I sure as hell doubt she ever looked as hot as you do in it right now," he replied, taking Evie by surprise. So much time had passed since he'd made a comment like that to her. It was out of character. It was what despondent spouses said when they were up to something, or so she thought.

Evan wrapped his arm around her waist and pulled her closer, the hardness below his kilt pressing against her. Her entire body went rigid. Where did this new Evan come from? Something was terribly wrong with this picture. Her mind raced.

"Good God, Evie, you still make me hard just being near me, can't you tell?" He dipped his head to nuzzle her neck. The very scent of him made her dizzy.

Evie closed her eyes and breathed it in, just letting go for a moment. He kissed her neck. His breath was warm on her skin, sending tingles down her spine and making the corset feel even tighter than it was. Her breasts begged to be set free, pleading for his mouth to be on them. The span of his hands trailing from the small of her back to her hips made her knees weak. She admitted to herself for a moment—she missed him. She missed this.

Nevertheless, Evie's brain wouldn't shut up long enough to enjoy it. Something was wrong. This wasn't Evan. What was he up to that would make him try and take her in the middle of the hallway after so long? It had been a whole year, almost to the day, since they were intimate. The same day her mother died. Evie stiffened and pushed Evan away at the memory. It all came rushing back to her … the sight of her mother's lifeless body in the woods. She choked back tears and looked up at Evan. "I can't do this, Evan. Not today."

Evan leaned against the wall crossing his arms over his chest. His face turned rock hard, as she normally saw it. "I'm seeing a pattern here."

"I'm not sure what you're talking about but I just can't do this today. Please understand."

Evan came at her, growling with his fists clenched at his sides. "What I understand is that you've been putting me off for a year. You won't listen to a damn word I say. You threw me out of the house and begged for a divorce. Then you invite me back in to put me in this obnoxious outfit straight out of a trash novel, shove your tits in a corset and flash them at me. You're trying to humiliate me for something I don't deserve. And it's working. "

Evie gasped at the words and railed at him, "Excuse the hell out of me for wanting to be festive! I didn't flash my tits at you, I was going with a theme here, you jackass!" She pulled herself up to her full five foot six inches and pushed him back with her chest.

Evan took a step back and spat. "Maybe I should find another who will flash them at me. At least with them I'll know what the hell is going on instead of wondering if the Ice Queen has melted." He regretted the words as soon as he said them and clamped his mouth shut.

Evie stood in silence and then staggered backward a few steps as if physically hit. "I see now." She turned around and walked off into the living room to the sea of family, who stood stunned, having heard the entire thing.

"Evie, come back. I didn't mean to say that," he fumbled, trying to save the moment. She grabbed the manila envelope off the bar and thrust it at him.

"Here are the papers, Evan. Sign them and let's be done."

He felt like she'd hit him with a truck. Evan looked down at the envelope and opened it with the slide of a finger. He glanced at the papers inside and crumpled them in his fist.

"Fine. If this is what you want …" He was lost for anything coherent.

"Now you can go on to whomever it is who is flashing tits at you and have a good time. I'm sorry I've wasted your evening, or worse yet, your life," Evie said numbly, not even realizing her family was surrounding her.

"Evie you're twisting my words. You never let me explain that girl. I never said … ” Her stepbrother Alec slammed the living room door in Evan's face as her daughters whisked her away to sit down. She fought the urge to run back to him and let him finish his sentence, but she knew it was just lies.

∞

Evan watched as the door to the living room shut in his face, at a loss for words. Standing there listening to the rest of the family take her side burned him and the shock was eaten away by anger. Shaking his head in renewed disbelief, he stormed for the back door, slamming it as he left the house. He always hated when they fought, never managing to say the right words. His heart tore with the thought of Evie's accusations. He'd only existed for her, and she still thought he'd betrayed her.

Everything was always for her. Evan loved her more than his own life. He woke up at before dawn every day, to work long hours selling his soul to lifeless bastards at his company so he could give her the life she wanted; the life he knew she deserved. Evie never seemed to notice or care and if she did, she'd call him uptight. Evan held to the belief, if he unwound, his whole life would come undone. Now he realized it never mattered. Even though he had held together for so long for her, it came undone anyway. He looked down at the wad of paper in his hand. So this is how it would end, he thought. He fumbled through the sporran hanging between his hips and retrieved an ink pen, and scrawled his signature across the bottom of the page.

Rage overflowing, Evan punched the side of the house until it shook. Paint chips fell from the back porch onto his head, and he stepped away, cursing under his breath. “This damn house will be the death of me.”

He meandered down the walkway leading to the barn. Taking a deep breath of the cold night air, he tried to numb the events of the evening. Looking to the sky and fighting back tears, a light flashed out of the corner of his eye. He wiped his eyes, blaming stress and anger—and again, a flash came from the woods, making the hairs on Evan's arms stand on end.

He stopped to listen to the world around him and caught his breath, for there was nothing but silence. No cicadas chirped. No birds' wings flitting, or frogs croaking. Evan would always remark to Evie that even though he came from the city where everything was so noisy, it paled in comparison to all the critters in the country. However at this very moment, the silence was so profound, all he heard was the blood pounding in his ears.

For a full minute he stood completely still, ready to attack anything, until a thought crossed his mind and he breathed easily again. "Some drunken hunter has wandered off on our land and has his gun sight on me. This will be fun to explain in an obit," he grumbled, sighing in brief relief, but still heading into the woods. He was fully expecting to find someone who wandered too far. At least if he found someone out there, he could take his anger out on trespassers.

He walked deep into the forest, almost losing sight of the faint glow of house lights. Then the drumming started; as rhythmic as if it were in time with his erratic heart. He spun around to face its direction, but it faded away as abruptly as it started. "Damn that noise!"

Annoyed and startled, he stopped to wait for the flicker again and followed the general direction. The farther he got into the woods, the more Evan was convinced some drunken hunter had lost his way from their camp. Trying to charge his anxiety back into anger, he continued walking, determined to find out who was out there. Finally seeing a great deal of light, he stomped around some bushes where he thought he saw a campfire. He turned past a rather large bunch of trees, drew a breath to start yelling at someone, and stopped in his tracks.

Evan stepped farther into the clearing to find a small fire that seemed to dance in mid air. His heart beat wildly and his head felt light. He heard a faint hum in the air. Thinking stress of the evening finally overtook him, he stepped closer to the flames to investigate. His heart beat even louder. Frightened that he was going to pass out and catch on fire he tried to step away.

"This isn't the way to go, you idiot," he grumbled as he collapsed to the ground, never quite making the connection.

The sound of his heart pounding morphed into the maddening drumbeat as his eyes started to close. It was tribal, wanton. It grew louder and Evan moaned at the discomfort it seemed to cause. He put his hands to his ears in a feeble attempt to block it out and tried to roll over onto his side but his body kept rotating as if doing turns underwater. He growled through his teeth in pain and confusion as the faint hum grew louder too, turning into something else. *Something sounds like a cat being tortured. Or is that ... bagpipes? Bagpipes at midnight in Virginia at Halloween? What. The. Hell?*

His chest tightened and he roared in pain as he closed his eyes to hide from the dancing flames and succumbed to unconsciousness.

∞

Evie stood in the middle of the now empty living room. It was official, Evie decided, staring vacantly. She was alone. Her family took the hint and left after the fight. She hated it when she and Evan fought, and this time it involved an audience. Groaning in continued embarrassment, she picked up a bottle of wine from the bar and flopped unceremoniously on the couch, taking a long drink as she did.

The entire evening had turned into a nightmare. The anniversary of her mother's death and her husband practically admits he's been cheating and then leaves. Could it be more obnoxious? She scoffed at the thought and stared out the windows into the woods. He was out there, she knew it ... stomping around punching things. *Punching them wearing that hysterical skirt even.* She grinned at the thought.

Evan had all but owned up to the indiscretion with his assistant, she mused. He'd surely grant her the divorce now. She would be raising three kids alone. Alone. Evie put her head in her hands and cried. She let the waves of depression wash over her until she was certain she was crying dust. She sat back in the couch staring out the window toward the woods again, taking a long drink from the merlot. "I should get a glass," she muttered, then retaliated against herself. "Shut up, brain. You've got me into enough trouble tonight." She said aloud, standing back up and walking over to the window. Evie looked off into the distance, her eyes unfocused, thinking of what she was going to do. Evan would surely leave her here to rot in this town. Now it didn't sound like a bad idea. He would at least go back to Atlanta and leave her alone. The kids would be able to visit back and forth regularly, and Mason was about to graduate. He'd most definitely want to move there with him. They were so much alike. So strong, so sure, so in control ...

As she shut the blinds, she attempted to shut any more intruding thoughts with it. She pulled the blind cord and stopped cold. She saw fire in the woods blazing so brightly it almost hurt to look. She grabbed her cell phone off the bar and ran outside, frantically dialing 911.

Tripping over kudzu vines, Evie ran straight into the woods, totally ignoring the pathway. Panting with exertion, she screamed to the 911 operator what she was afraid to admit. Evan was out here. Her husband was in the woods. Seeing the blaze top the trees, she screamed and dropped the phone, running toward it as fast as she could. She must save her husband.

Panic stricken, Evie reached the same clearing where she found her mother. Her anxiety from the realization doubled with the fear of fire engulfing the area. However, what she thought was an uncontrolled fire was quite the opposite. She stood in total shock at the sight before her. It was a cyclone of flames shooting straight into the sky, cresting the trees. Not a single limb burned. She rushed around the fire looking for Evan, but didn't find him. Instead, she saw something glinting in the light toward the center of the clearing. Afraid of the tornado-like fire taking her, she carefully moved around it to investigate. The only thing left behind was his wedding ring. She sobbed, grabbing it and clutching it to her chest. *Please don't let him be dead. Give me another chance. I'll listen.*

Evie took her head into her hands and started to sway. She felt faint … *The heat of this thing is getting to me. Gotta move. Gotta find Evan. He'll know what to do; he'll make it all right again. I have to find him…Maybe … Maybe I should just lay down a minute. Remember what Mama always said. If you're lost, stay put. They'll find you …*

With the thought of her mother, she fell to the ground and closed her eyes.

Chapter 6

The drums were pounding so loud, Evan thought his head would burst. He cracked one eye open to see what appeared to be a movie scene. There were a dozen men, standing over a half dozen drums, naked to the waist, the rest of them donned in kilts. With their heads down and sweat dripping down their muscular bodies, they drummed harder and faster, causing Evan to pinch his eyes shut to the pain throbbing in his temples. The humming noises he thought were tortured cats were the screaming songs of two bagpipers. Women were dancing in the bonfire light, chanting, and singing in some vaguely familiar language.

He felt something sharp in his back and rolled to one side to relieve the pain. Evan felt someone's hand push him back down and forged out of instinct from a lifetime of training, he grabbed the hand, and in one swift motion, flipped its owner onto its back, pushing his forearm into a man's throat. The young man screamed in terror, but strained by the sheer force of Evan's arm and an odd accent, he couldn't understand the words.

The drumming stopped and chaos erupted. Men grabbed Evan from both sides, pulling him off the man he held. Half a dozen men jumped on him, trying to restrain him by force or by weapon. Evan had been convinced the weapons were movie props but changed his mind as he took one nick to the face from a sgian dubh to make him realize they weren't acting. It was time to defend himself.

One by one, Evan disarmed them with his bare hands and threw them off his towering form, leaving bodies of men strewn throughout the clearing in various states of unconsciousness. Women screamed and ran. The men yelled what sounded like Ruadh Donas had come to kill them. Evan wasn't sure what Ruadh

Donas was, but he wasn't keen on stopping to ask for clarification. People scattered in all directions while Evan stood there amidst the unconscious bodies, wondering when he'd hear the familiar "cut" come from a director … It never came.

Evan was now alone. Everyone had fled the area and those who were left weren't saying anything. He cautiously walked toward one of the unconscious and knelt down. He took the knife that had cut him from the man's hand, and stuck it into the top of his own boot.

"Dammit, I made it so far without a scar on my face," he grumbled, wiping the blood from his cheek. He sifted through the man's sporran to find a few coins and stared in confusion, for they were little bits of metal that looked like someone pounded them with a hammer. They were like the ones he'd seen back at the house, on Evie's small wrist. "There's no way."

Everyone in his family knew that when Evie was a child, Mama Killie kept coins like these in a little worn leather pouch, making the sweetest little jingle. Evie always wanted to play with them growing up, but wasn't allowed her because "they are too special," her mama said. Killie had never explained where they came from and claimed no one would believe if she did. Evie had felt blessed when Mama Killie made them into a bracelet for her to wear on her wedding day as her "something old" gift. Evie never took them off and they could hear her on any given day through the house wearing them like a cat with a bell around its neck. That is, Evan recalled, until her mother's death. She took them off after the funeral and hid them. With growing concern, he frowned, tucking the coins into the other side of his boot.

Evan stood to look for the camera operators, waiting impatiently to see if someone would come to make sure the cast and crew was unharmed. When no one showed, he figured he'd head back up to the house to call the police. They were on his land without permission and needed to get the hell off it. Something nagged at him though. Something just wasn't right … *And they cut my face!* The light dwindled from the dying bonfire. He could barely see the woodsy trail leading in the direction of the farmhouse, but started to walk back anyway. He needed to call the police … *These jerks will hear from me. They will all owe me a chunk of money for trespassing.*

Stomping through the vines, he wondered if it had been this overgrown when he wandered down this way. Evan hiked up to the top of the hill where he started his journey and stopped cold. The farmhouse wasn't there. He rubbed his eyes in disbelief, his mouth agape. There in its place stood a stone castle, several stories high with torchlight illuminating the figures of people who inhabited it. Everyone was dressed in the same garb he had seen at the bonfire.

There were no cars, no trucks, and no camera operators. No lampposts lit up the sky. There were only people and fire light, and this massive stone structure where the old farmhouse should be standing. His stomach sank in realization of what might be going on and he dropped to his knees.

How could I have been so blind? That old woman was trying to tell us all along. No, no, this is crazy. This can't be happening.

He rubbed his face with both hands and stared at the scene again. He desperately searched for anything that would make sense. Cameras, booms, spotlights? Nevertheless, there was nothing.

He sat down in the dirt and pulled the coins out of the side of his boot to examine them again. They looked exactly like the ones on Evie's bracelet. Cursing under his breath, he pulled the knife from the other boot and examined it too. Crudely made, it only had a wooden hilt and the blade's shine was dull from age. Burned into the handle were the initials T. M. "Dear, God. This isn't a prop."

He clutched them to his chest and closed his eyes, trying not to hyperventilate. At that moment, Evan knew exactly where he was, and this time Crazy Mama Killie didn't sound so crazy anymore. He wouldn't be finding the barn or farmhouse tonight at all, nor would he find a Hollywood set built for a major motion picture on their land. He would only find this very familiar castle, built and maintained in the thirteenth century; Scotland, to be exact.

Gathering up his courage, Evan slowly rose to his feet and returned to the spot where he woke up to see if there was any logical way to figure out what was happening. Frustrated at not being able to see much in the dark, he cursed, kicking at the dirt. His boot made contact with something and sent it flying.

Evan went to the base of the dying bonfire where the object landed and knelt. He sifted through the dirt and was surprised to find his wedding band lying there, the fire light gleaming off the gold.

Closing his eyes and with his hand tight around the metal, he pressed it to his heart. Evan sighed, and wished for home.

Chapter 7

The days seemed to run together. Evan was so very out of sorts he just maintained as well as possible, given the circumstances. He tried to keep thoughts of home at bay; fearful it would cause him to go insane. Camping outside the keep in the woods nearby, Evan observed the inhabitants, trying to decide what he should do. He hoped they would repeat the same ritual they performed the night he arrived. Unfortunately, it seemed they had moved on. For weeks, he sat and watched the people work, play, talk, and fight. He would steal discarded, half-eaten food they dropped on the trail. Begrudgingly, he would catch and kill small animals to cook over a small fire. Even though he was without toiletries and a beloved razor, he'd wash in the stream nearby at night, away from everyone. He wasn't quite sure how to approach them, or if he should try to move on to a different place. Unable to make a decision, he remained hidden in the woods.

He heard the villagers speak of his, or the Ruadh Donas' arrival. It was soon found out the name meant "Red Devil" in Gaelic; and the tales included his now legendary ability to kill or maim scores of people with his bare hands. The retelling of Samhain night turned into a fairy tale in record time, and hearing new exaggerated bits always brought a smile to his face. He was 8 feet tall. He had hands quick as lightning. He had fire shooting from his eyes. He emerged from the Fairy Glen or Hell. With every new story, he was more outlandish than the last.

Day after day, he watched men of all ages travel to a clearing close to his hiding spot and would watch them train for battle. Sometimes with fists and sometimes with weaponry, the men would fight from dawn to dusk, only stopping for a bit of food, water or occasional whistle at a passing maid. Evan loved this part of the day, longing to get back to the gym. His muscles ached with inactivity. Evan was conditioned to sparring twice a day; before and after his high-stress day job, for most of his adult life. Here he would sit in awe, trying to decipher the Highlanders' sword play technique. He committed their dance to memory, in case he ever had to join them or fight them himself.

Evan woke to hear the sounds of struggle. Usually waking as the dawn broke, he found himself squinting at the sun high above him. He heard the noises again, and rolled over to face the sound. Again the men were training, just a few hundred yards away in a clearing. Yearning to join the lists and train with them, he watched avidly as two men wrestled each other to the ground. Grunting and cursing at each other, they wrestled for what seemed to be the better part of an hour. Obviously equally matched, neither man gave any hint of being defeated. He shook his head. *No form. Neither one of them is going to win at this rate. They'll likely just fall asleep from exertion. Och, what a mess. Wait, did I just say 'och' in my head? Dear God, I'm going mad.* Evan rolled his eyes and sighed.

Without thinking of consequences, Evan stood from his hidden space in the woods and walked into the middle of the grappling men, determined to teach them. One by one, the men stopped and stared at Evan. He immediately stopped and gauged the situation, his heart frantic with anticipation. With a quick glance, he realized he was still wearing the red tartan from Halloween night. Scanning the others, he saw that they were similar. He hoped it was a good thing. The Docs look a little weird, he thought, but hopefully not enough to get him killed.

He cleared his throat and spoke in the best Scottish accent he could muster. "I wish to help with your technique. I, uh, come in peace?" He stood in the eerie silence for what seemed like an eternity, waiting for the assault from any side.

The men circled him, speaking to each other in Gaelic. Evan stood silently with his fists clenched at his sides. He was a good head taller than the majority of them, definitely more muscular, and still felt as if he could be hacked to bits at any moment.

A younger man jogged in their direction, smiling at Evan. "Och, there's our Red Devil! I was wondering when ye were going to show your face at the castle instead of sleeping in the bushes with the bugs." The man walked directly to him and clapped him on the back with such familiarity it knocked Evan forward a step. He had an infectious smile, Evan noticed. He relaxed and smiled despite himself.

"After I rendered a dozen men unconscious that night, I assumed I wasn't welcome," Evan said, almost in a question, trying to feel out the situation. He offered a hand to the younger man. "Evan MacDonald," he said, and the man took it to shake enthusiastically, his eyes lighting up at the name.

"Liam MacDonald. Laird of the MacDonald's of Dunscaith. Why have we not seen the likes of ye around here, cousin? We could use yer strength and battle wisdom these days." He nudged Evan in the ribs, he quipped jokingly, "That is, if the legend is true."

Evan couldn't believe it. Of all the places in time to be, he had gone back in time to his ancestor's home. He thought briefly and answered in a fractured mumble. "Uh, I left home early in my childhood and went to live with monks far, far over the ocean. They taught me how to fight. My parents died and I found my way back home. I only recently returned." He scratched his head, hoping the lie was fathomable.

Apparently, Liam didn't care that Evan was a terrible liar and took his word without a single question, smiling genuinely and clapping him on the back again.

"Of course you did. In any case, we are glad ye have found your way to us, Roy. With all the talk in the last few weeks, you have managed to drum up quite a name for yourself."

Evan started to correct him on his name and stopped, remembering an anecdote Mama Killie had rambled on about; how in Gaelic, the term for the color red was actually ruadh, which was pronounced more like roy. Turning that piece of information over in his mind, he ran his hand through his wild mess of red hair, wishing he had a mirror just to see how crazy he looked. Over a month had gone by without a haircut or good razor. Armed only with the sgian dubh he had allocated his first night, his attempts at shaving were minimal. Evan gave up on keeping it cut close and settled for a short goatee.

As Liam prattled on, Evan tuned him out and remembered how much Evie had complained of his stubble when they had first started dating. Her face came to Evan's mind, her lips raw, well kissed, her eyes heavy lidded with passion. He felt bad for the way it seemed to bother her so he shaved it. It felt like a lifetime ago. Now it might as well have been. He was now somewhere, hundreds of years in the past, and she was home in their time, assuming the worst. Evan decided it was time to be someone else for a little while. Roy would do fine.

He took a deep breath and tuned back in to find Liam staring at him, concern in his blue eyes. "Och, man, are ye all right?"

"Aye, just stuck in my own thoughts, is all. It's been a long, interesting journey, to say the least," Evan said, dismissively, casting aside his thoughts of Evie for now.

Liam nodded and added, "I probably understand more than ye know." He began walking in the direction of the castle's doors without looking back. Evan followed closely behind.

Evan followed Liam and sighed as he walked past the bystanders who were gathering. He squared his shoulders and stood up straight, giving his full height attention. He towered over them, and in waves, the men would grumble and scowl or reach for a weapon. The women held their children closer, and the babies started to cry. Evan scoffed in disbelief, and Liam chuckled. "See what I mean about the name you've acquired, Roy?" he asked, smiling infectiously. Evan nodded his head in acknowledgment.

"I suppose if I'm going to have a reputation, at least it's one that will keep me out of trouble, aye?" Evan responded.

"Oh, I agree. However, the young men are going to start trying to test ye, so be aware. They're all cocky bastards wanting a turn to battle Ruadh Donas."

Evan grunted noncommittally as he took in the castles' interior. Not knowing what to expect, he was surprised to find freshly scrubbed dark stone and walls covered in ornate tapestries of what he assumed was family. This family was apparently very proud of its heritage and very wealthy for the times.

Liam's wife greeted them after entering the great hall. A veritable wisp of a woman, she moved gracefully to the men. "I am Rosemary, Liam's wife, and I am honored that ye have finally worked yer way up to our home. I have been pestering Liam to retrieve you from the woods for days now." Rosemary took Evan's hand in hers, a pretend scowl on her face. Liam winked at her and grinned while she directed them toward the giant stone stairs leading to their quarters.

"I saw ye coming with my husband and took it upon myself to order up a fitting meal, after ye have rested." Rosemary's eyes glinted with a smile.

"Rosie, love, the man is a warrior, he knows how to take care of himself," Liam jokingly reassured his wife, removing her hands from a dumbstruck Evan.

"How long have you known I was out there?" Evan asked. "I thought I was hidden."

"Oh, we've known since Samhain. A man yer size is easily tracked," Liam chuckled. "The kitchen help had been under strict orders to keep dropping food near ye, because for a warrior, yer gathering skills are lacking."

Evan's face blushed and he ran his hands through his hair. "That makes me feel like a giant oaf. I thought I was just lucky." He sighed heavily and continued. "I do appreciate your indirect hospitality. Had I not feared being slaughtered, I would have been a bit more direct with my visit."

"No worries at all, cousin. Please accept our welcome and do make yourself home at our castle. If ye were clear of engagements, it would be an honor for a man of yer unique skill to help train our men. Of course we would compensate and feed ye; at the table this time," Liam ended, laughing.

Evan couldn't believe his luck. Employment, housing, and he got to keep his skills honed ... *What about home? What about Mason and the girls? Evie must be furious. Would she care at all? She is probably still reeling about the party, or assumed I shacked up with that damn assistant. I should have fired that girl ages ago.*

Steering his thoughts from Evie, he knew his children still needed him regardless of his wife's thoughts. He had to get back. "I, I don't know what to say. I need to find my way home before the winter sets in," he managed, still shocked at all the changes whirling before him.

Rosemary again took his hands and replied warmly with hopeful green eyes. "Just say 'yes.' Stay with us for a time. Let us take care of ye, cousin."

Unable to speak, Evan nodded in agreement and was lead upstairs to his room by a chattering Liam.

Chapter 8

"There is no way a simple-minded girl could achieve this delicacy," Chieftain MacLeod said, pushing away from the table satisfied, for the third week in a row. "There is something odd about her, but she isna daft. That girl is hiding something huge," he concluded, looking at his wife.

"Dear, I dinna ken what to say other than what ye refuse to hear," his wife, Lily, answered shaking her head. "She was found wandering in the pasture below the castle, laughing hysterically at the cows, dressed in what appeared to be either a harlot's clothing or gypsy clothing – not that there's much difference between the two," she added, lowering her voice. "She had babbled to our young Malcolm in some strange accent that he was on her land and needed to make a call to nine one and one before she kicked his arse."

Lily shrugged as her husband choked on laughter continuing over his guffaws. "And of course Malcolm, being nothing but prideful, became so enraged that she would dare think these islands belonged to anyone but the MacLeod's, tossed her over his shoulder and brought her here kicking and screaming. She has since said naught anything to anyone since his berating her and refuses to claim even a surname. She is just Evie, and she's been a blessing in the kitchens. Even the cook, who has been with us for near thirty summers and dismisses everyone who holds the spoon incorrectly, has said she is a breath of fresh air." Lily MacLeod looked at her husband with warmth in her eyes. "Spy or no, ye cannae deny she's made gatherings more pleasant. Now, I ken she's been sleeping on the stone hearth in the kitchen. That's no place for a blessing to live."

Creighton MacLeod looked at his wife, his face hard as a stone. Lily picked up his battle-worn hand and held it tenderly, rubbing the center of his palm with her thumb.

"If she were our daughter, would ye want to know she was to sleep on some stranger's stone kitchen floor?" Lily asked softly, holding his gaze.

Creighton's face hardened more, then as he looked down at his weathered hand, held by her delicate, pale one his features relaxed and he sighed.

"No, and ye ken that, lass. If she were my daughter, she wouldn't be traipsing along the countryside in naught but a scrap, yelling at the cows. Ye have won this battle Lily MacLeod. She may have a room here. But if she turns out to be a spy or a thief, ye both are going out on yer ears."

Lily hugged her husband's neck, smiling. "Thank ye, Creighton. I'll tell her immediately. I'll make all the arrangements. Ye willna have a thing to worry about."

"Something tells me otherwise, woman," Creighton scowled.

Lily jumped up to leave as he caught her by the waist and pulled her to his lap. "Immediately can wait for another few minutes, milady," he said, with a devilish look in his eye. "The girl will have a home. Ye verra well ken there's about nothing I would deny you," he purred, pulling Lily down to kiss him.

∞

"I'm too old for this crap," Evie grumbled, rearranging a pile of rags under her head into a makeshift pillow. The cook took pity on her, thinking she was simple minded and allowed her to sleep in front of the fireplace for the last few weeks. Like a damn dog, she thought.

Evie was just so shocked when she woke up from her toss through time; it seemed absurd she would be face to face with a shaggy red cow. Evie had thought some trespassers were trying to intrude when she regained consciousness, but changed her mind when the chieftain's son, Malcolm, approached her as she laughed hysterically in the poor animal's face. Evie had cursed at the young man, and in turn, he threw her over his shoulder and took her to his mother, Lily. She grinned while she thought of that moment. What a sight that must have been. *Mama would have been so proud, seeing my butt in the air, kicking that poor kid in the gut for a half mile while blood rushed to my head.*

Evie had quit talking in fear they would question her heavy Virginian accent. Unlike Evan, whose parents were originally from London, she couldn't fake an accent to literally save her life. She always had explained her accent came in either simply southern, hillbilly, or redneck depending on her alcohol content. So she decided to remain mute with little effort.

The last few weeks were a blur. Not speaking had allowed Evie to learn so much, for everyone assumed she was simple. Yes, it came with its own set of mean people out to degrade her, but the majority of the clansmen assumed she was too stupid to understand what they said, much less use it against them. Little did they know she understood them clearly in English, Gaelic was second nature to her, thanks to Mama Killie. So Evie listened and retained information, and she managed to work her way into the kitchens.

The day she arrived at Castle Dunvegan, she was left sitting on a stool in the kitchen with the help while Lily went to find her suitable clothing. In mere minutes, Evie had taken over Cook's pot of unknown gruel and turned it into a fresh stew. The entire castle talked about it for days.

Beginning that day, she stood in the kitchen and took inventory of what herbs were available and what spices and meats were accessible. Cook began to watch what Evie did, just guiding her to the right places of the buttery, and eventually enveloped her into the castle staff. She only once said her name to anyone, which was while she sat on that stool. They interrogated for hours in the Chieftain's quarters in attempt to find any information about her, including her surname. However, the plan backfired and only reduced her to tears. She didn't even think to give her maiden name of MacLeod, and now that she did think about it, she wouldn't know how to explain her name being the same as theirs, and yet being unknown to the rest of the clan. Evie did remember enough of her Mama's ramblings to know MacLeods and MacDonalds did not get along. Years of feuds had occurred between the clans over lands, titles, and the fabled Fairy Flag.

Now there was a thought, she pondered… *The Fairy Flag?*

Legends told about the MacLeods, who the Fae themselves gave the token, in return for a favor. They promised three wishes with each wave of the Flag. Bloody battles were fought and many a clansmen died trying to steal it away from them. Evie had paid that much attention. She had grown up hearing the tales of its power. With that knowledge, Evie knew that keeping her mouth shut about her last name would probably be the safest option. She surmised she could find out where the Flag was, wave it, and ask the Fae to send her home, for she was certain it was how she got here. Now thinking harder on it, there was no other plausible explanation. Could it be the way home?

Evie's thoughts wandered to home. She worried about the kids. She suspected Evan had taken over the day-to-day activities. The worries clouded her mind. *Would he have a search party for me? Are the girls freaking out that I'm gone? What if they sold the house without me and moved away where I couldn't find them? Did he move in with that girl?* Evie threw her hands over her face and pushed away the thought, trying not to cry. She tried not to ever cry at home. It wasn't strong. It wasn't in control.

Evan's face crept back into her mind. His lopsided smile warmed her, with his clean cut face. Evan kept his hair cut close in a military fashion. She always knew him to have short hair, but as the years and stress went by, he became a little more fanatical about it; which, in her eyes, was a shame, for he had hair women would kill for. It was the perfect shade of auburn, and perfect wave. Her thoughts wandered to the rest of him. He was ever conscientious of his body, and kept himself in the fittest condition possible, and boy did it pay off. Evan swept her off her feet and kept her there.

She thought back to Halloween night in the hallway when he'd pushed her against the wall. What had she been thinking not to give him a chance? He had been hard beneath his kilt, ready and willing. He'd wanted to love her, and she'd fled. He wanted to offer her explanation and she refused. Now he was lost in time forever. He'd surely filed those papers by now. Their twenty-year love affair dissolved with a single pen stroke. Evie clenched her eyes shut, pushing the feelings away and banged her head on the floor grumbling, "Stupid, stupid, stupid, Evie!"

She heard a voice behind her call out. "Evie, darling! I have wonderful news!" and a flushed Lily rushed into the kitchen toward her beaming.

Evie rolled over, muttering through clenched teeth. "What? Did you happen to find a De'lorean and a case of plutonium for its flux capacitor?"

As Lady Lily neared her, she forced her face back to docile and mute.

Chapter 9

Getting used to being without electricity was the worst. No flick of the switch would make the world light up. No hairdryer, no electric shaver could clean his face. No coffee pot perked to start the day. Evan found the urge to walk over to a laptop and check his email overwhelming. It hurt to know his in-box was filling up at lightning speed. It was all a fleeting thought as he groaned, laying in his new four poster bed, about to get up for his first real morning at the castle. He stretched his long legs, enjoying one last moment of solitude before he joined the ranks downstairs. Last night he drank way too much after having not slept on anything but the cold ground for so long, and didn't quite remember making it to his chamber. There had been an entire bottle of whisky left in his room, which lasted approximately forty-five minutes, he thought, groaning.

Evan pulled back the long burgundy velvet drapes that encased the bed and all but hissed at the sunlight streaming into the room. The maids had apparently brought a copper tub while he slept, filled with steaming hot water. Thankfully, Evan thought, someone had the foresight to build up a fire so he wouldn't freeze to death when he finished. He looked down, noticing it was very drafty and realized why. Chuckling to himself and his morning salute from his manhood, he hoped those drapes had stayed closed when the servants arrived, or else the Ruadh Donas legends would be even … bigger.

∞

Evan walked outside in the cold drizzle to the lists to find what appeared to be every able-bodied man waiting for him. Evan approached slowly, brows furrowed in suspicion as Liam joined him with his usual jovial self. Liam seemed a little too happy for this time of the morning, especially with Evan's kind of hangover.

"Good Morning, Roy. Nice audience ye have. Once the word got out that you would be joining us in today training, everyone wished to be privy to yer technique."

Evan stared out at the crowd of what had to be seventy-five people and he shook his head in disbelief. He took a deep breath and strode to the front of the crowd, leaving Liam on the sideline. "This is definitely more interesting than sleeping in the woods," he said under his breath, wading into the throng of people. He realized he was at least a foot taller than the majority of the men.

"You're not joining us, Liam?" He turned around to face the Chieftain.

"Och, no, Roy. I intend to stand this one out and watch the Legend work," he crossed his arms across his chest, face beaming at Evan's exasperated expression. Evan shook his head at the man as he continued on to the front of the crowd, swearing he could hear Liam laugh behind him.

For the majority of the day, Evan worked with the large group, reveling in the exertion for the first time in over a month. With every punch thrown, with every wrestling match ending in success, Evan realized he was finally content. This was the very thing he had needed back home. He sank into a comfortable leadership role with ease and had very little time to think of his predicament. He taught the men until dusk, when the last group of men finally ran out of what seemed to be boundless energy to learn the mix of martial arts he had perfected over the majority of his life. They were all like sponges, and so very open to his advice, criticisms, and a lot of out-of-place laughter.

Evan dismissed the last of the crowd to go find their dinner as he decided to take a moment to walk the grounds before the sun completely set. He wandered in the direction of some cliffs, following the sound of the sea. The scenery reminded Evan of every movie, documentary, and postcard of Scotland he'd ever seen—which was quite often in his life. Evie and her mother had always been very submerged in their ancestry. With her maiden name being MacLeod, there was always a considerable amount of information to weed through, both fact and fiction. They would spend days upon days gathering even the tiniest bit of information they would ever need to know about their clan's history, as Mama Killie had always said with a smile, "Just because. You never know when you need to know your stuff." Evan wondered if she had always known something like this was bound to happen. Nothing seemed unlikely anymore, given the circumstances.

Now Evan stood before the castle of the MacDonald and knew every stone brick in the walls. Evie probably had them numbered somewhere, he thought. It was eerie to think of how much decay had changed the castle in seven hundred years. He wondered what Evie would say about him being right here in this spot. He smiled as he thought of how she would react to the sight. He took a deep breath of misty air and turned back to face the castle doors. "I wish you were here to see this with me," he whispered.

He stretched his currently overused muscles in one great reach over his head, and trudged back toward the castle to eat a well-deserved dinner in the great hall, wishing it was Evie's great southern cuisine. *What wouldn't I do for some sweet tea.*

∞

Evan's time at the castle slowly shaped into a routine, and days slipped into weeks. He would wake at dawn to train all day until he met Liam, Rosemary and the rest of the clan for dinner. Afterward he'd sleep like the dead. He had no time to think of his situation and preferred it that way. His constant activity helped push away the painful memories of home.

The men were slowly taking all his teachings to heart and accepting his ways of training. They listened with rapt attention and followed every command willingly, and most of the time, cheerfully. They were shaping up into a strong ground force, not reliant upon weapons or horses to keep them safe in time of battle. Evan's chest swelled with pride that his army was progressing along, but there was a nagging feeling that some other proverbial shoe was about to fall.

During meals, Evan could always be found to the right of Liam at the High Table, with his wife Rosemary on the left, discussing the day's mock battles. These winter nights had turned long, so he found himself spending more and more time with the Chieftain and his wife, in order to gain any and all information he could pertaining his station in this time.

Evan found himself staring into his tankard, looking at a different person staring back at him while Liam discussed the day's events. As his voice droned on beside him, Evan paused, barely recognizing the reflection. The face who stared back was wearing a half smile, guarded by a goatee of red, blond and brownish whiskers. The lines in between his brows from years of work-related stress were gone and replaced with laugh lines around his eyes. Though the sun had all but receded for the duration of winter, he was still out in it long enough to have developed a bronze tan. All these things were so foreign to Evan. In just a short time, he was no longer a "stuffed suit." Now he sat in full Highland regalia. His shirt was a hand-me-down, slightly too small for his defined chest, but gave just enough to not rip across the front. He had begrudgingly hidden his Docs in his chamber in order to wear more common boots of the time. He tried to remain as inconspicuous as possible. *Not that a mutant, huge guy who drops out of the sky on Halloween and beats up a bunch of folk is conspicuous, or anything ...*

Though he had much on his broad shoulders here, he noticed that he was nowhere near as stressed as he was as the CFO. Other than the occasional mistake a trainee would make, causing him little to no injury, he thought there was naught better. Other than finding home, he was at peace here. He paused in momentary thought, and drank the reflection away.

Pushing the painfully bitter possibilities back, the crease between his eyes returned as he downed the remaining contents of his tankard. He stood to dismiss himself for the evening, but Liam caught his arm, having noticed his abrupt change in mood. "Something bothering ye?"

Evan breathed deeply, running a hand through his now longer hair, and smiled sardonically, "Nothing another round of drinks couldn't fix. Just thinking about things I cannae change." Evan suddenly realized his brogue had adjusted to theirs almost naturally, as if it were always there. He attempted to pull away from the Chieftain and Rosemary, yet Liam stood.

"Dinna drain the reserves of my whisky just yet. We have business to discuss before ye take leave." He ordered the serving maid over to refill Evan's drink before they both dismissed themselves to Liam's study.

As they walked down the corridor, through a few turns and up winding stairs. Evan noticed that it was secluded away from the loud and rowdy great hall. He followed Liam into the room, the heat from the fireplace an immediate relief from the larger, draftier dining room.

Taking a seat, Evan watched Liam as he poured yet another two whiskeys from a cabinet behind his desk and handed one to Evan. He then unceremoniously flopped into a nearby chair and propped his feet up on the desk. Evan sat uncomfortably with the two drinks then decided to down one without flinching. Something told him he would need the mental buffer tonight.

"So what brings us here?" Evan asked first, breaking the awkward silence. He had never been in the study with Liam before and the serious tone was amplified by their location.

"Eh, just the MacLeods, they're holding something that … I want. I need—something beyond normal understanding." Liam stared into the fire unfocused as he took a sip. "They have had it for generations and now it should be mine. It will be mine."

Evan inhaled sharply, knowing already what the man wanted before he uttered the words. He knew by heart. It was in the tales his wife had told their children at bedtime. He had always listened as Evie had rocked the girls to sleep; the tales woven from her memory, passed down from her mother; tales of damsels in distress to the girls; tales of warriors and battles to young Mason.

"The Fairy Flag," Evan whispered under his breath.

As the story went, it was the cause of and solution to most problems on the Isle, and had been for hundreds of years. The Flag contained unknown limits of possibilities for its owner, yet only three waves of the Flag would grant the owner whatever the heart's desire. One wave would equal one request to the Fae.

Evan blinked back as he flashed back to the thoughts of hovering in the doorway while Evie spoke of the Flag, and the mighty warriors who had fought and died to save it from the hands of thieves. They had twisted it into a fanciful tale for children … his children. He tried to pull his mind back from the drunken numbness he tried to obtain earlier so he could focus on Liam's words.

"Aye, the Flag." Liam confirmed. "I want it for my own and with your help I'm just that much closer to gaining it. I feel the Fae themselves sent ye home to your clan so that ye could help me get it back." Liam's gaze, once settled on the fire was now fire itself, staring Evan down.

There it was, hanging out in the air. The other shoe Evan had expected to drop. Evan heard it like an echo in his mind. Liam wanted him to be the juggernaut to overthrow the MacLeods in order to steal the Fairy Flag. He could assuredly kill them all with his bare hands, as legend had it. Liam had been sucking up to Evan, twisting him into his right hand man and his warriors' trainer, just to throw him into the fray. This would mean the ultimate war of clans. It could mean death of innocents for one man's greed.

It was now obvious Liam had known all along that Evan wasn't from this time. All the pieces fell into place. It all made sense now why Liam accepted Evan's terrible lies and his quick welcome into the fold of the clan without question. Liam actually thought he was a gift from the Fae to take back what he thought was theirs. Liam could rule the world with the Flag, or so it he predicted. Evan could only gather two words to answer. "I see."

"Then what say ye, Ruadh Donas?" Liam asked, without a trace of the friendly smiling cousin who had always been so welcoming. He stood before Evan as a desperate man, willing to kill for what he believed was something for him to posses.

Evan was silent; new thoughts rushing feverishly through his mind. Could this be the way home? Could the Flag be his answer? Did the 'wee folk' Mama Killie talked about exist?

And Evie, he thought. I could make things right. With the face of Evie in his mind, it solidified his resolve. He leaned forward, putting his elbows on his knees and stared directly into Liam's eyes, matching the intensity.

"Aye, MacDonald. I'll join yer force to take the Flag for the Clan. But I have one demand before you claim it." The fireplace light was behind Evan, providing a devilish glow around his massive form. His eyes smoldered with his own desire … the desire to go home and find his wife.

"You'll give me the first wave of the Flag, no questions asked. In return, I'll train the men as I have, but now it shall be in earnest. No other army will match our strength."

Liam swallowed hard and his face blanched as he looked away from Evan. He knew there were only two waves left to the Flag. It was a great price to pay. He got up and paced over the cold stone floor, rubbing his face with his hands. After a long silence, he turned to face Evan.

Evan, always aware of when his size was surefire intimidation, took what seemed to be several painful seconds to stand up to his full towering six feet, six inches in height. He crossed his powerful arms across his chest and slowly cocked his head to the side. He looked at Liam squarely in the eye, waiting for his answer. "What say you, Chieftain? Make a deal with the Red Devil to save your pathetic soul?"

∞

That night he dreamed of Evie. He envisioned her long legs wrapped around his hips. He heard her imp-like giggle and smelled her sandalwood hair. Evan felt the heat from her breath on his neck as she whispered unintelligible things to him. Evan could never quite get his hands on her as the pleasant reminders floated off into the darkness of his mind, replaced with the feeling of despair. Frantically, he searched for her. As her laughter drifted off into the blackness, Evan struggled to call out, but his voice was gone. There was no sound. Panicked, he tried to follow the sound of her laughter but could never quite move. Then clear as a bell, he heard her sweet southern voice. "Honey, I'm here. I have never left your side."

Evan woke in the dark covered in a cold sweat. He noticed the velvet drapes pulled back, letting the cold winter wind into his confined bed space. Taking a moment to remember where he was, he stood up and stared out the window into the moonlit sky. "I'm coming to get ye, hon. I'll find my way back home."

Chapter 10

$\mathfrak{E}$vie stared out her new chamber window clutching a wool MacLeod tartan around her shoulders watching it snow. It was too beautiful. She couldn't stand to watch it any longer. She turned to look at her quaint room that Creighton allowed her to have and walked toward her large bed to lie down. She sank down into the heavy wool blankets and curled up with her knees almost to her chin. The Chieftain and his wife were so welcoming. She would do just about anything to repay their kindness. For them to take in a possibly insane stranger and find her work in the kitchens doing exactly what she loved, she was very blessed.

Although she had everything she should need, Evie wasn't happy. She missed her children. Her family would at least be frantic at her disappearance. The kids were old enough to manage, and she hoped Evan wouldn't be that much of a schmuck to leave them at the house alone. However, he'd be working like a dog as usual. She wondered if he would even bother coming home from the gym to face them. Her business would be in shambles, if not shut down entirely. No one could replace her. She was the only one who knew how to run the show. She anxiously thought of all the weddings and parties ruined because of her. With a heavy heart, Evie realized it didn't matter anymore. She sighed and succumbed to resignation. She needed to face the stark reality of being in the here and now and make the most of it.

Evie closed her eyes and pulled tighter into a ball on the bed. In her mind, Evan's face returned. Her whole adult life had revolved around that man. They had not spent a day apart for 10 years, and here she was without him. Alone.

She blinked back the stinging tears as she tried to focus on something mundane to take it away. She thought about the newfound herbs in the garden outside the kitchen and a discarded pestle she retrieved from a pantry ... parsley, sage, rosemary, and thyme. She had hummed the tune to herself earlier that day while making dinner to receive some strange looks from Cook ... *I should figure out his name, the crotchety old bastard. He probably thinks I am a witch and wants to burn me anyway, seeing how the chieftain keeps saying my food is magical. I just don't boil it beyond recognition. How hard is that? At least Evan had liked my food ... Dammit ... Evan.*

Evie opened her eyes to stare at the fireplace. He was always on her mind. There was no escaping him. Her heart pained at the memory of the way he used to do a little happy dance, as he called it, around the kitchen when she cooked. "My little Kitchen Wench," he'd say. He contained so much happiness it practically overflowed. She smiled, remembering how he had practically bullied her into starting her own catering service. He always pushed her to do what she loved ... *Where did it all go wrong? What did I do to make him stray?*

Questions swirled around her head as she closed her eyes again, attempting to shut them out. It was useless. She let the vision of her husband float back to the top again, this time in his tuxedo for their wedding. Neither one of them wanted the big church wedding but Mama Killie insisted on the biggest Catholic service known to man. To her knowledge, Mama Killie had never married Evie's father, so she was hell bent and determined her daughter would have everything she did not, whether she wanted it or not. No daughter of hers would live in sin ... "Not over my dead body. You get married and have fat 'n' happy grand babies. That's what southern women do," she had said.

Evan's hair was a little longer then, his face was softer and free of lines. She focused on his crooked grin smiling back at her as she saw him through her veil. He towered over everyone in such stark contrast. He always made everyone uncomfortable. Nevertheless, there was no other person who could make her feel the way Evan did. She recalled walking toward him as if she were reaching out to a lifeboat in the middle of the ocean. In slow motion, she had reached the altar and automatically her fears had drained away as soon as she could focus on the dimple in his cheek ... It was safety.

Home.

She took his hand and perfectly recited everything in Latin as the Priest said, and then in a fit of rebellion, ended it with her own personal vow, "Forever and ever, amen." It gave her the giggles. Evan did the same at the end of his vows, much to the dismay of the scowling, ancient man who married them. More Latin was recited as they tried their hardest not to fall over laughing at their inside joke. They exchanged rings with little excitement. Then at last, Evan was told to kiss his bride. He swept Evie off her feet with one arm and kissed her until the priest cleared his throat in agitation. Again, the giggles had returned and they felt the need to run down the aisle in order to escape the priest's wrath. Since that moment, all notes, emails, and phone calls had ended in "Forever and ever." Until recently, anyway. All the familiarities vanished. They were doing good to have a conversation that didn't end in a door slam, or more recently—someone's clothes burned in the yard … or, well, someone being sucked back into time.

Evie felt felt a pang of pain at the memory. Her wedding was one of the happiest days of her life. She was complete. The best days afterward always revolved around Evan. The birth of all three of their children and every milestone thereafter, her business thriving, his martial arts studio opening; they were all momentous occasions surrounded by love and happiness. His strength, his security, and his unending love made her thrive.

They had been in their own world. Nothing else mattered. Their love was the focus of their lives … *Where did my Evan go, forever and ever?*

∞

In the morning, Evie woke up cold with the covers scattered in the floor. It was the result of a restless night. She picked up a heavy blanket from the floor and with chattering teeth, walked to sit near the fireplace. It was still dark outside, but knew she'd have to make way to the kitchens to help Cook start breakfast. She got dressed and ran downstairs to join her crew in the kitchens.

As she ran, Evie noticed the quiet was back. There had been a strange difference to the noise the last few days at the castle. It had become eerily quiet. She thought of the noise contrast between here and home. She had always loved the train tracks near the farm to let her know she wasn't the only soul there; that life did lay outside her house. Here it seemed she was alone, in a castle full of people. She hadn't uttered a word to anyone for so long it was emotionally draining. Evie just wanted to find someone, anyone, to talk to, if it wouldn't get her killed. There was an upside to being unable to speak. Her eavesdropping skills were in top form.

Evie arrived to her station in time to overhear Malcolm and a friend in the hallway. They didn't see Evie behind the doorway scouring bowls as they talked about the latest political gossip and someone else whose name she didn't recognize.

"They say he's taller than a horse," Malcolm said, taking a bite of an apple he stole from the kitchen earlier and continued while still chewing, "and he's killed a hundred people with his bare hands."

Evie repositioned herself closer to the doorframe to hear easier.

The friend scoffed at the news. "I doona believe it. Do ye think he'll try and attack here?"

"I'm no sure. Da said he wouldn't put it past the people of that castle to do anything these days. They probably conjured the man from the Devil himself. They call him Ruadh Donas. Their Chieftain has gone insane since his father died last year. I'll never ken why that clan put him at the head. He's off his heid. I can only assume that we'll be hearing from them sooner than later. My Da has a feeling."

"What do ye think the MacLeod will do? Will we go to war with them again?" the friend asked, a little more concerned.

Evie heard Malcolm pause to crunch loudly on his apple. She fought the urge to reach around the wall and smack his rude mouth.

"Da will try what he can to keep peaceful but he's not above starting war. It's been nice without all the fighting, though. God knows I dinna want to fight anymore. I'm sure they'll all try to work it out, if ye can with a crazy man." He belched almost in punctuation to his statement, threw the apple core on the ground, and watched it roll around the doorway to stop at Evie's feet. She stopped what she was doing, scowled at the boy, and picked it off the floor.

"What is it, ye daft cow?" he spat. "Get back to work before I tell me Ma you're no good. I've the right mind to toss ye into the field where I found ye." He swaggered off while his friend laughed after him down the hallway.

Evie resisted the urge to box his ears and threw the core into the trash pile. She returned to her kitchen duties and mused on what she heard.

Later that morning, Evie found out that news traveled faster than a forwarded email around this group. She wasn't the only one who had heard the rumors of the Ruadh Donas. The kitchen staff had also caught wind of the story. She had to stifle laughter as the stories became more and more out of hand. The man was not only killing people scores at a time with his bare hands, his hair was made of fire, he stripped women naked with a mere look; he was taller than a horse and hung like one too!

So far, Evie's favorite was a story she overheard in a conversation by a kitchen maid to Cook. She explained how a groundskeeper told her he overheard a priest absolving the sins of a peasant girl for gossiping about the stranger's manservant fighting with his lover because the lover had brought in hot water for Ruadh Donas' bath, saw him in all his naked glory … and fainted. The guards carried her out. In addition to that, the stranger had slept through the whole thing! He even snored. Evie coughed so hard trying to hide laughter she thought she'd choke, and with a wave of a hand, silently excused herself. The day progressed and the tales got taller. Evie didn't know how she was going to cope with playing stupid all day with the racket. She wanted to tell them all to shut up, but the stories were downright amusing and she didn't have anything else to do. It was the best story she'd heard since she'd been in the thirteenth century.

The rest of the week went by with a new story every day. Every new myth was a little more farfetched and disjointed. She couldn't believe these people would believe something about a stranger but she figured it was a sign of the times. Though she'd done so much research about the area and the families that existed in this time and beyond, she didn't know much about how they reacted to one another. It was definitely an interesting lesson she was learning. She smiled as she suddenly thought of her mother. Mama would fit right in. She'd tell them all they were damned fools for believing such nonsense. Evie smiled at the image of her mother bossing everyone around and somehow it felt like it had already happened.

∞

By the weekend, the scarier stories began. At the weeks' end dinner, a young man abruptly entered the great hall. He was drenched with sweat and pale as the moon. He ran straight to Creighton and Lily's side and fell to his knees. He explained there had been an attack on the path that left two clansmen dead. There were no stab wounds or cut marks on the bodies. One had a clean break to the neck. The culprit stole their valuables, their horses slaughtered on the road as their blood stained the freshly fallen snow. The young man choked on tears as he recalled the scene and explained of a note stuffed in one of the bodies' mouths. With trembling hands, he pulled the parchment from his jerkin and gave it to Creighton, who read it aloud.

"Be prepared. Ruadh Donas comes."

There were audible gasps. Evie watched in silent horror as Lily grasped Creighton's hand. The Chieftain's brows furrowed and he closed his eyes as he crumpled the bloodied note in his fist and threw it to the floor.

Distraught and unable to continue, the young man covered his face with his hands and sank down to the floor, weeping like a child. The MacLeod's face softened as he patted him on the head while he grieved for his clansmen.

"There, son, rest ye head. There was naught you could do. It's nae yer fault. We'll see what bowel of Hell this Ruadh Donas comes from, and send him back there."

The horrific encounter threw the household into turmoil. The wives of the deceased gathered in the castle and were told. Evie's heart broke for them. *They're so young—younger than Evan and I when we met. Their babies aren't old enough to remember their fathers…* She held back tears as she thought, trying to remain calm and keep her docile façade as she hurried to finish her duties and escape to her room. She couldn't bear the pain on the women's faces. She couldn't imagine being without Evan in such a way. She was suddenly so angry with someone whom she'd never laid eyes on; someone who had been the brunt of her laughter up to now. *What kind of animal would do that to a person?*

∞

The attacks became more frequent over the next few weeks. They cut short the upcoming Hogmanay and Ne'erday celebrations because of the safety concerns. The entire clan kept close to home, having small, quiet celebrations instead of the usual large events in which they were accustomed. What once used to be an entire week worth of parties, feasts and hunts for game; became hunts for the people responsible for their nightmare.

Over a short time, the attacks became more bizarre and more brutal. The women never left the keep and the men stayed armed to the teeth and traveled in packs of no less than five people. The quietness that had once plagued Evie before was now gone, replaced with a constant hum of tension and fear. The MacLeod promised he would avenge their deaths, yet when Evie would see him alone in his quarters; he looked scared out of his mind.

One evening, while clearing a late dinner from his chamber, Evie overheard the Chieftain and his wife discussing the current state.

"Creighton, has there been any clue as to who has been doing this? This, this … monster cannae be real, can it? There's no reasoning to it. I ken Liam's been stressed to the point of break, but do ye honestly believe that he's called upon some demon to slaughter our family?"

Creighton took Lily's hand in his and rubbed the top of it with his thumb. He looked as if the weight of the world was crushing him. His eyes were dark and heavy with lack of sleep. He had been talking with his advisors nonstop since the attacks began, and they still had no answers. They increased general safety precautions and put posts out in every possible place. Yet like a ghost, Ruadh Donas hid from them, only leaving behind horrific reminders of his existence. "Lily, I do not know what to do. I have sent word to Liam to meet. He has agreed to see me in a fortnight." He looked up at his wife, his aging eyes full of exhaustion. "I can only hope we can find out what the man wants without causing all of our demise."

His wife smoothed his graying hair away from his face and kissed him on the forehead. "I have no doubt ye will find a way to keep us safe. If we have to call upon the Fae Army for help, we shall." Creighton shifted away from her and sat up straight, not looking her in the eye. "What is it, love?" she asked. "We still have two waves of the Flag left. If we need this to keep our family safe and alive there should be no question."

"That is just the problem. There are only two waves in the Flag.

This cannae be used every time the wind changes. It has to be thought through." Creighton stood up to pace the floor, running his hands through his hair. "There have been wars fought without even the mere mention of bringing the Flag out in the open. We have to exhaust all options before resorting to that."

Lily rose to meet him, taking his face into her hands. "Creighton, we have to accept that this may be someone who can break our entire clan. If we have the Fairy Flag, who's to say he hasna summoned some evil creature to do battle with us? We cannae dismiss this."

The Chieftain took her hands from his face and kissed both palms. "I know, lass. I know. I just doona want to use it just yet. We'll find a way, peaceably if possible. I cannot stand the idea of losing any more people. We'll see the MacDonald in a fortnight and figure out a way. I promise ye that, my lady."

Evie heard the name of the clan and her heart stuttered. She tried her best not to drop all the dishes she had cleared from their small table and made her way out the door as quickly and silently as possible. Thoughts raced through her mind. *MacDonald!? Of course, it's the MacDonald clan! They've been feuding for freaking ever! But who is this crazy freak who's after everyone? I don't remember reading anything about a psychopath, though. Maybe the MacDonald has conjured some crazy thing out of thin air. It just doesn't make any sense. Then again, what does make sense around this godforsaken place?*

The next two weeks went by painfully slow. Lily and Creighton had been fighting more often about how they should handle things. The loving couple had turned on each other; Lily, still begging to use the Fairy Flag to wish the situation away, while Creighton was dead set and determined to fight it out on his own. Watching them be so cold to each other broke Evie's heart, for it looked all too familiar. Their loving relationship strained over misunderstanding after misunderstanding. His advisors had split down the middle with their allegiance to their Chieftain and their Lady and most of the clan had. There were many fights around the castle and surrounding village about what the Chieftain should do and it was taking its toll.

Evie had wished the bickering between clansmen and women would stop, for it was only damaging the entire family. She was certain that's what this evil Ruadh Donas was counting on … divide and conquer.

Chapter 11

Evan breathed the cold January night air into his lungs, feeling the burn as it entered his chest. He didn't care how much it hurt as long as it made him feel something other than the anger that seethed inside. He'd recently heard of the brutal beatings near the MacLeod castle and was sick by them. Someone had taken his teachings and used them against the MacLeod's people, leaving half a dozen clansmen now dead ... dead in a way only he could have instructed.

He sat atop his large black horse in the dark, waiting for Liam to meet him at the castle gate. He and another MacDonald soldier had been searching for the rogue clansmen for days now with no luck. It seemed every time they would get close to a trail, the attacks would get farther away. Tired, cold, and frustrated, Evan had returned to the castle with empty hands. He'd hoped to catch the person responsible and show them some discipline on his own. He despised the idea that innocent people were dying because of him. Evan had agreed to catch the Fairy Flag with Liam, yet he didn't know that someone would be underhandedly paving the way to Hell for them all. Evan wanted the Flag desperately. The way home was so close he could taste it ... *Well, taste hot chocolate with whipped cream ... Last time I remember having whipped cream; Evie covered herself in it and tied a bow around her neck on Christmas morning ...* His stomach growled and he chuckled at himself for frivolous thoughts of his wife and her food instead of his surroundings.

His riding companion looked at him out of the corner of his eye, not sure how to take him laughing at nothing. Evan caught his confused glance and sobered his expression.

"What?" Evan challenged, wanting a fight from anyone, not caring from whom. He squared his shoulders and put on his best scowl, which had gotten even more menacing as his time here went on. That, combined with his scruffy hair, definitely fit the bill for his nickname of The Red Devil. The man just shook his head and refused to respond to Evan's taunt. He knew better to tempt the rumored, most brutal murderer in all of Scotland … and hungriest. Don't forget hungriest.

Evan sighed in resignation that he wasn't going to get his sparring match and turned his horse around, searching into the woods for any sign of Liam.

He had noticed over the last couple of weeks that Liam had become a little more serious and a lot less friendly. Everyone had noticed a difference when he arrived one morning and lined up with the men, instead of his usual sidelined position. It honored Evan to think the Chieftain found his martial arts abilities worthy of learning, yet left him suspicious.

Even Rosemary had mentioned Liam had become a little obsessive and she was concerned that he was putting too much energy into this quest for the Flag. Evan had assured her that everything was all right and Liam would be back to normal when they brought the Flag home, but Rosemary wasn't convinced. She appeared frightened by it, actually, and feared it would cause more evil than good. She knew in her heart it was far too much power for any one person to control and would only cause pain and destruction to those who held it in possession. She felt it should be destroyed.

Evan noticed Liam became a man possessed with the Flag. He barely slept, rarely ate, drank too much and only wanted to talk about the relic. Evan was personally downright sick of hearing about it. If it weren't for the fact that Liam was the only one who knew where it was, he would have punched Liam in the face one good time and left on his own. The only thing left to do was get inside, take over, capture it, make his wish to whomever, and get the hell out of here. Evan gave up waiting for Liam and decided to go hunting without him. He dismissed his companion to return to the castle as he turned his horse toward the woods. Evan was determined to find answers.

The ride down to the seaside was uneventful. He took the long way around to see if there were any signs of camps made by strangers. He traveled alongside the path instead of on it, attempting to stay hidden. The trees became fewer and farther between as he began to hear the crashing of waves from the sea. He kept leading his horse toward the rocks, steadily climbing down the craggy cliff to the almost nonexistent beach.

The sand was still white from the moon and the air here was thicker and colder. Evan drew in a long breath, letting all the worries of the day fade away into the ocean's waves. He dismounted his horse, tied the reins to a close by rock, and walked the beach for a moment, looking out at the waters to the castle on the island before him … Dunvegan.

He could barely make out the lights in the castle from the moon's reflection on the water. The Flag was so close. Yet something unexplainable was drawing him toward this particular castle. The pull was so strong he almost jumped into the freezing waters and swam across. There was something calling his name from the castle, now lit up with torches from the inside and out. Evan planned on finding out what it was.

He stared out and let his thoughts wander. He saw Evie in his mind, working hard over her first real catering job. She had landed a huge wedding for one of the local debutantes in their hometown. With a four-tier cake, chocolate fountain, three course meal and hors d'oeuvres for three hundred people; she was stressed to the point of madness. Mason had warned Evan that day on the way out the door that Evie was freaking out, throwing eggs across the kitchen like cannon fire, and shot out the door for football practice. Evan took a deep breath, put his briefcase down, and strode through the house, hearing her rant from three rooms away at the front door. Scowling after Mason's disappearing frame, he checked to see if the girls were home. Upstairs there had been no sign of them, and he made a mental check of the social calendar. They wouldn't be home for hours. He took off his suit jacket, laid it down on the arm of the chair, and made his way into the kitchen.

There she was, covered in egg and flour, and all Evan could do was snicker. She stopped ranting and glared at him. Evie was completely undone at his smugness and hurled an egg at his head. He ducked and swiftly jumped over the island counter to catch her hands.

"Crazy bridezilla witch has changed her plans again! Three days before her wedding! She has decided she wants a vegan menu and I have to throw all this food away! I have three hundred peoples' worth of steak or chicken! That woman better pay me double or I'm gonna piss in her sweet tea!"

Evan stood there smiling and let her rail at him with her hands still held over her head. Her ranting eventually turned into just a random string of curse words as Evan silently backed her up to the edge of the island and deftly picked her up to set her down on its granite top.

"You aren't helping me! I have so damn much food to cook! And who the hell knows where I can get a fountain's worth of vegan chocolate!"

Evan moved in on her mouth and kissed her hard. She uttered a curse between breaths as Evan pulled her closer to him with one hand; the other still enclosed on her wrists. Evie made a feeble attempt to pull away. He pushed his hips between her thighs, her cursing slowly turning into ragged breathing. He kissed a trail of fire down her throat, pulling her flour and egg soaked shirt out of her skirt and over her head in one fluid motion. In a flash, her bra was off and she sat exposed in the middle of the kitchen. Evan stood back to admire her. Evie took that opportunity to regain control of her hands and twisted them behind Evan's head, pulling him back to her to kiss her harder. She unbuttoned his white suit shirt and pulled it back from him expecting to see skin, cursing when she saw the white undershirt that was covered his chest. Evan ginned wickedly at her annoyance, pulled it over his head, and threw it in the floor. He returned his arms to wrap around her, their hot skin touching.

Evie moved closer to him, her thighs spread to him off the corner of the counter top. Evan thanked his stars above that she was wearing a skirt, albeit a long one, and pushed it up to her hips, exposing her secret of wearing absolutely nothing underneath. He threw his head back and groaned as he returned his face to her chest, kissing, and worshipping her breasts, while his rough hands were pulling her backside toward his now uncomfortable crotch. She leaned back on her elbows to watch him as he licked a hot trail over her stomach, down between her thighs. She rolled her head backward and forgot all about the vegan food, three hundred guests, and chocolate fountain ... fountain? *What's a fountain?*

Evan dipped a hand between her legs, feeling her wetness with his fingers, and immediately stood up to pull his belt off and toss it onto the floor. Evie was still reclined on her elbows, her knees kicked up with her feet resting on the edge of the island. She stared at him with her face flushed and eyes half-open, waiting. Evan pulled her arms to sit up and kissed her again. He ran one hand down her back while freeing his painful erection from his pants with the other. She sighed with the sight of it, eagerly wrapping her legs around his waist and pulling him inside her. The new heat made her groan his name and a new wave of curses as Evan thrust hard into her, his thighs hitting the granite counter top with a welcome pain. They took each other hard, clawing and biting each other, her cursing beginning again, but this time in the throes of passion, not anger ... *My little Kitchen Wench ...*

The scene in his mind faded away as he stared at the sea. Slowly, Evan made his way back to his horse, enjoying the last bit of silence and solitude. He saddled up uncomfortably and headed back toward the castle. There had been nothing found this night; nothing but the strengthened desire to go home. In less than a days' time, they would ride back down here to cross the sea to meet with the Chieftain of MacLeod. Then they would make their plans to get the Fairy Flag, at whatever cost. He hoped it would all end peacefully, because no matter how much he trained, he dreaded using his skill for an actual battle. However, Evan was prepared for whatever it took to get home to Evie.

He closed his eyes, taking a deep breath and whispered out loud to the starry night sky. "I will find you, Evie ... make no mistake. I will find you and make you remember—you are mine; forever and ever, amen."

∞

Across the sea, Evie woke with a start, and while still in sleepy confusion, she grabbed her wool tartan and went outside. Hyperventilating from the cold air hitting her lungs, she climbed the cold stone stairs with bare feet. She managed to avoid all contact with the guards and the roaming servants on her way. Another advantage of being invisible, she mused.

Standing on the battlements in her nightdress, Evie looked over the sea. Her heart was heavy and tears sprung into her eyes. There was nothing there but stars, the moon, and the icy water. Yet there was something unknown calling to her in the frigid night. Her skin was cold through the thin linen dress, yet she could not feel it.

Tears rolled down her cheeks as she pulled the tartan around her shoulders tightly and whispered into the wind, "Save me."

Chapter 12

The next twenty-four hours were the longest Evan ever experienced. The time had come to go meet the Chieftain of the MacLeods about the murders. Evan was under the impression the MacLeod believed it was a rogue MacDonald, and Evan and Liam needed this meeting as an "in" for Evan to explore the castle for the Flag. Evan felt he was so close to home it was palatable. Evan and Liam sat in his study, waiting.

"When do we leave?" he asked Liam, toying with the bread and cheese left on his plate. He was too nervous to eat properly, though he tried hard for it not to show.

"Within the hour," Liam sighed, pouring himself a whisky.

"What's with all the heavy drinking? Shouldn't ye be sober enough to walk down the cliff and not puke on the boat?"

"I might be better off if I fell off the boat and drowned in the sea. I doona like the MacLeod. He was responsible for killing my Da last year. I have no reason to be sober, much less cordial to that bastard." Liam's eyes grew dark and his face turned somber at a dark memory.

Taken off guard by this information, Evan sat back in his chair, letting that new fact sink in. "My condolences, Liam, I didn't know. I figured ye had been the Chieftain for quite some time now."

Liam sat down in a chair again in front of the fireplace, kicking his feet up on a stool. "No, I guess I haven't shared too much about my family other than Rosemary. There had been feuding between both clans for approximately thirty summers this time around. They claimed my father had attempted to seduce, capture, and kill some lass who had been staying with them for a time and they had been fighting since. The MacLeods had accepted her into the folds, for some reason. Then, I suppose out of loneliness or insanity, my father decided that he wanted her. She was an older one; I'm no certain of why exactly they were all after her. I suspect she had bewitched them all. Nevertheless, they were completely enamored, the two clans fought, and people died. I was not even born when it all began, so I'm not sure of all the details. Da claimed she had powers beyond all understanding. I suppose she was just better in the bed and he was smitten by her reputation." Liam chuckled, paused to drink another shot of whisky and continued. "However, she was in love with this other MacLeod and had at some point left him when they thought she was with child. She left soon after they announced the news and it tore out my Da's heart and I'm pretty sure his mind. He was never quite right afterward," Liam sighed.

"My father was offered another woman from their clan as a token of peace, and he decided that if the woman he wanted was gone, he should accept the offer. So, they were married, the feuding stopped and I was born approximately nine months later. My mother died in childbirth. My father remained bitter that he had lost the real lass he wanted, lost a wife, and had me; the child he never wanted." He shrugged, and got up to fix yet another drink.

"How did your father die?" Evan asked bluntly, watching for a reaction.

Liam sneered, sitting down again. He took a deep breath and quickly spat out the words. "He went to face Creighton MacLeod, their Chieftain, and was slain. I was there to see it happen. I rounded the corner of their Hall and heard them arguing over the damned lass again. He rushed forward to the MacLeod. My father was stabbed with his sgian dubh." He threw the remaining whisky into the fire, watching it flare. "He bled to death on their stone floor. Clansmen dragged me out screaming, threw me on a boat, and sent me home. The MacDonalds named me Chieftain the next morn before my Da's funeral. That was a year ago last Samhain."

Liam's eyes lit up and looked back at Evan, "Och, aye, and the night ye arrived. Cheers."

Evan shifted uncomfortably and nodded, shoving a piece of bread into his mouth to keep from talking. He didn't understand why the two Chieftains would be arguing again, why they had met, and why they would bring a young boy to the mix. It didn't add up. Then the whole idea that Liam thought fairies sent him here made him shiver subconsciously. The conversation ended and the silence impregnated the room. The fire became too hot, and Evan found himself feeling as if he were suffocating. Liam stared into the flames deep in thought.

Unable to sit still any longer, Evan spoke, changing the subject entirely. "Right, Liam. I need to get out of here to get ready for tonight. Is there anything else that ye need me to tend to before I take my leave?" He stood up to exit.

"No, I suppose there isna anything else," Liam said, staring at Evan confused. "I'll see ye in the great hall this evening for a meal before we depart. We'll need all the help we can get."

Evan nodded, yet not convinced that any of the cooking in this castle could ever be any help to his nervous stomach, or Liam's drunken one, and departed out the door to return to his quarters.

∞

Entering the only space he had to call his own, Evan sat down on the edge of his bed and put his head in his hands. There was too much to do tonight. This would be the first battle that he had ever been in and still felt as if he had been training his whole life for it. All the work he had been doing to ready himself for something was finally come to fruition. Who would have ever thought it would be hundreds of years before his time though? All the ancient martial arts he had carried over and so many who had morphed the art into a full contact sport had made its way back in time and to another part of the world. *To hopefully save my arse and send me home.*

Evan stood up and walked to the window. The snow had finally stopped falling, and the sky was bright with the full moon. It was the first moon he had noticed since he had arrived here, now four months past. *Has it been four months?* Evan stopped the thoughts before they became too somber, not wanting to cloud his vision for the meeting. He needed focus. It could ultimately mean his demise, if not his future here, or home.

He paced the room, stopping to don a clean white shirt, then unwrapped and wrapped his plaid almost methodically. He looked down to his soft leather boots and grinned.

"Forget this. If I'm going in, I'm going all in." He walked over to a hidden chest between the bed and wall and opened it, revealing his steel-toed boots. "We meet again, good doctor."

Evan sat on the edge of his bed, kicked off the soft leather boots, and replaced them with the tougher ones. Noticing a glinting of light he saw in the bottom of the box, he stopped lacing his boots and leaned over to see what it was. He found his wedding ring tucked in the chest and paused, caught off guard. He picked the band up and twirled it in between his fingers, as he had done a thousand times in the past. Not thinking twice, he put it on his left hand where it belonged, and clenched his fist. "All for you, Evie," he said under his breath.

Evan finished lacing his boots and strode to the door, pausing briefly as he took a deep breath of strength, and exited the room to meet his fate.

∞

The trip down to the sea was a long and arduous one. Liam was so drunk that he was using all his energy to remain atop his horse. After a few stops on the way, he had just decided to lie upon the beast to make it down the rocks. Evan had to quell his fantasies of Liam falling and cracking his skull open. By the time they all made their way down to the dock, Evan had pulled him off and all but carried him down to the boat, grumbling curses under his breath.

"Perhaps we should let you sober up a wee bit, Liam," Evan said, propping him up on a nearby rock.

"Och, no. I can still see straight if I close me eye. And dinna ask me to walk a straight line. I'd never make it," he laughed, trying not to fall over. He tried to correct himself on the rock and slid sideways with Evan catching his arm and yanking him to the ground. Evan was not amused in the slightest, and every attempt Liam made at humor made him angrier.

Scowling, Evan replied. "Liam, if I may be blunt, there's no way in hell ye are going to be able to make it across that sea and have a conversation with the MacLeod like this. We should postpone this for another day or so and come back fresh. I can send the men over to let them know what we demand."

The thought of waiting for another second infuriated Evan, but the Chieftain was obviously so drunk he knew there was no way he'd be useful in a debate or a battle if it came to it. They would need to be both at full strength in order to overtake the MacLeod castle. They were a legendary fighting clan, from all that Evan had ever heard from history from his wife and mother-in-law. It would inevitably be the fight to the death. There would be no turning back if there was bloodshed. The MacDonald's were briefed in what to expect in their conversations and needed to be at their full attention, for this would be their first battle without any ready weapons other than their hands, and here Liam was at the helm ruining the whole thing. Evan noticed earlier that night, the men were gruffer with their chieftain and had begun to give Evan more attention as his ability to lead took over. There had been no questions or disagreements within the ranks. Evan was thankful for that. The last thing he needed was discord with the men while their true leader was too inebriated to stay awake, while their lives were at stake.

Liam struggled to sit upright, looking like a dejected child. "No, I doona want to put it off any longer. I havenae the energy to keep this masquerade anymore."

Evan stared at the man, his features hardening. The one sentence made Evan narrow in on him, his temper flaring. "What's that mean, Liam? What masquerade? We're on to get the Flag, right? Take over the world, and whatnot?" He took a step closer to Liam, who folded his legs under him, and looked to the ground with his hair falling over his face to hide his expression.

"Never ye mind, Evan. It will all be right in the morning," Liam said, nodding over as if to pass out.

Evan bent over, grabbed him by the shirt with one hand, and yanked him up to eye level. Liam's feet dangled off the ground. Evan's face turned hot with anger as he shook him awake. "Ye will tell me now, Liam MacDonald. Don't even think about passing out on me. I will have answers. Just remember where ye have called me from, and what I may already know. If ye lie to me, I may already know before it passes your lips. Take a second to ponder about what I shall do to your pathetic life before ye even think to betray me! What masquerade are ye speaking of, you daft, drunken bastard?" Evan dropped him to the ground and stepped away to calm his temper. The MacDonald men who had joined them at the beach began to walk away, knowing the situation between the Red Devil and MacDonald had become too volatile. Liam rolled over to his side and then crouched on all fours, attempting to stand. Evan kicked him back down to the ground.

"Ye had best stay down, man. Until ye have explained the nonsense, it might be the safest place. It won't be so far of a fall when I kick you again."

Liam coughed from the blow to his ribs and rolled back over to a sitting position, clutching his sides, spitting dark blood into the sand. "That's a mean kick there, Evan, what the hell do you have in yer feet, steel?"

Evan's lips clamped shut, remembering his steel-toed Doc Martens. "Get on with it, Liam. No more stalling!" Evan yelled, his voice carrying over the water. He stood in the moonlight, the reflection off the sea casting an unearthly glow behind his hard body.

Liam looked up at the large man from the ground and put his head in his hands.

"Just kill me. Just run me through like my Da. I'm not fit to be a Chieftain. I've summoned ye instead of the devil himself and now I've got to pay the price."

Evan rolled his eyes at Liam's theatrics and kicked him in the leg. "There is nothing worse than a drunk feeling sorry for himself, you total and complete arsehole!" he roared. Shaking his head, he walked to the waiting men, and shouted. "Send two men to Dunvegan and let them know we'll not meet until the morrow! We have unfinished business to attend to here now. If they give ye any trouble tell them it was on the demand of the Ruadh Donas. If they cross me, then they'll all die when I get there." The men scurried around at his booming voice, getting their gear ready for sailing.

Evan turned his back on the men and strode back to where Liam was sitting; now sobbing into his hands. Grumbling under his breath, Evan grabbed him by the arm and dragged him on the ground away from the dock and up to the beach to their waiting horses. As the men passed their Chieftain being drug across rocks and sand, neither man said anything as they climbed into the boat and sailed into the dark night.

As soon as they were alone, Evan dropped Liam's arm and crouched down to eye level. His gruff voice spat into Liam's face. "Now that there is no audience, tell me the story ... Every bloody word."

Liam pitched backward trying to escape Evan's voice but only made it a few feet away. A huge rock met his back with a hard thud and he gasped for breath. He gave up, knowing he couldn't back away fast enough. He hung his head in his hands, folding his knees underneath him and wailed.

"I killed those people, Evan. I killed them all. I had been practicing your fighting on my own and managed to overtake one. I killed him accidentally. I broke his neck in one try. Then I had to kill his mate because he was witness. It happened so fast and … I… I got such a rush of power I decided to keep it going. I couldn't say it was me! Not the Chieftain! That would mean certain death for the whole clan. I couldn't make a full on war with the bloody MacLeods by myself so I blamed you. No one knows who ye are. You were nothing until I called for ye on Samhain." Liam looked up at Evan, who staggered backward in disbelief and turned to walk away toward the water, putting distance between himself and Liam's words.

Liam made it to his feet and stumbled after him. He caught up and grabbed Evan's arm, trying to get Evan to face him, but instead met with a quick fist in his nose; breaking it and knocking him out cold. Evan stood over his motionless body and growled. "Ye stupid, selfish, arsehole! We had plans! I was almost HOME!" Evan kicked Liam one more time for good measure and walked toward the water, rubbing his face in frustration and punching the air. "I should throw your body in the sea. No one would ever question it. Hell, maybe I could just claim to be the Chieftain and rule like a tyrant. Bully my way into the MacLeods' house and steal the Flag on my own."

Evan's rant trailed off as he stared off into the dark waters. He thought to himself out loud. "All the time I've spent training these fools and the leader of them goes mad. What luck." He clenched his fists and looked down, seeing his wedding ring. His temper died almost instantly as he watched the band glow in the moonlight. He still had to play this game. No matter what reputation he made along the way, he had to get back to Evie. Evan clinched his eyes shut and breathed deep.

He heard a low moan behind him. Evan turned to see Liam stirring on the ground attempting to sit up, dark blood oozing from his nose onto the sand. Evan ran his hands through his hair and walked back toward him with new resolve.

"Get up and on yer horse. We shall not say anything to the men or the MacLeod. I will take the fall for yer disaster right now." He picked Liam up again by his throat with one hand, and finished darkly. "But be aware, MacDonald. I have no fear of putting ye in the ground with yer victims if you dare think of doing this again. I am not here to make ye a god in that clan's or anyone else's eyes. I only want one thing—and that is to have my wave of the Flag, and I am gone. Ye shall clean up any mess ye make from here on out." He gripped tighter as Liam clawed at Evan's massive hand around his throat. "Do I make myself perfectly clear?" His voice was steel, his eyes dark as Liam struggled to breathe. He relished the sound for a split second longer than he should have as Liam's body started to go limp. Not waiting on an answer, Evan dropped him to the ground and took to his horse. He mounted it gracefully, not bothering to look back as he pushed the animal at a furious pace back up the rocks to the castle.

Chapter 13

He returned to the castle in the early hours of the morning alone, presumably with a drunk, barely conscious bloodied Liam following. Evan didn't care enough to find out if Liam had even made it to his horse, much less made the trip back. The men who returned earlier alerted those still awake of what scene they left at the beach, and a small crowd had gathered outside, waiting.

Evan stared straight ahead, not meeting the gaze of anyone as he passed the gates. The unintelligible conversation grew louder as he crossed through the entrance, yet no one dared to stop him. He approached the stables and dismounted. The stable hand offered to take over but Evan declined. The hard and furious ride back to the castle had given him just enough time to reignite the rage. He needed time to let the happenings of the evening wear off. Evan knew if he went to the castle before Liam made it inside out of his view, there would be more bloodshed.

He stood and brushed the horse, thinking about his next plan of action. The original date to meet the MacLeod had been a fiasco, and now they were probably on the warpath. They had patiently waited two agonizing weeks, burying their dead; mourning the loss of their fathers, brothers, and sons. Evans' heart went out for those families who would never see their men again. Hatred clouded his vision as he thought of Liam. The man he now knew was responsible.

Evan finished brushing the animal and handed the rest of the duties to the stable hand as he walked outside. He filled his lungs with the cold air and looked out into the starry night sky, trying to calm himself. With one admission, his only ally and only contact in this world had turned into the one person he most despised. Something Evan had ingrained in all his students: to use their knowledge only for defense was betrayed. All his teachings to the men and all the respect he had built up with the people of Dunscaith was gone in an instant by the reputation he was branded with by Liam. They would surely cast him out as a beast once their chieftain told them that he was the culprit. All the friendly faces and families who trusted him as a person and not a monster would go back to square one. He would be on his own.

He turned slowly to look to the castle gates. Groups of people were surrounding a horse, which Evan surmised was the return of Liam, judging by the commotion and the screams he heard. *Ah, that must be Rosemary seeing that broken nose*, he thought. *Those things bleed like stuck pigs ... and drunken bastards ...* Evan didn't feel bad for his treatment of Liam. In fact, Evan smiled as he saw all the fuss being made over him as they pulled Liam's precariously perched body off the horse and carried him into the light to assess Evan's handy work.

Figuring they would be too engrossed in tending to Liam to notice him, Evan decided this would be the best time to slip into the castle. He strode lazily across the castle grounds out of the darkness, with his wide shoulders back and head tilted upward. He focused his eyes on just making it through the great hall without notice. Making it almost to the staircase leading to his chamber, he felt a small cold hand on his arm. He turned, scowling at its owner. Rosemary stood there, her night-rail undone at the bosom purposefully. Her trembles doubled as she saw the fierceness in his eyes. Her soft curves shown in the torch light behind her, and yet she puffed her chest out instead of cowering, knowing fully Evan could see her shapely form in the shadow the torch made.

Having expected her to lash out at him, Evan was completely surprised when she threw herself at his chest. She wrapped her arms around his waist, almost knocking him off balance.

"Thank you for not killing him. Thank ye for sparing his life! I will be forever in your debt. I will do anything, anything ye want to make this right," she sobbed into his shirt. He reacted in anger, forcefully peeling her from his body and held her at arms' length; staring incredulously. She began to flail, attempting to escape his grasp so she could return to his arms. Never breaking eye contact, he pushed her more forcefully against the wall and held her by the wrists. He leaned in closer to her face with the length of his body pressed to hers. Slowly, he turned her head sideways, holding her by the chin, exposing her neck. She shuddered at the contact, struggling to turn her head back to face his. Evan leaned down to speak directly into her ear. His voice dropped low and his breath was ragged in attempt to keep control.

"I would still kill him if I weren't so tired, Rosemary. Tend to your husband. There is much to do on the morrow and he needs his wife. I require nothing from you. Nothing. Do not throw yourself wantonly at me again. It may be the last thing you do."

He dropped his hands abruptly from her and backed away, keeping his eyes fixed on hers. He turned and continued up the long winding staircase to his room, leaving her against the wall gasping for air. As he turned the last corner out of her sight, he heard her drop to the stone floor, weeping.

Evan entered his room and slammed the door. He pressed his back against it and sighed. He shook his head in disbelief and sauntered across the room. He slowly went over the events of the very long day in his mind. He needed a new plan. Liam wasn't a strong enough chieftain to lead his people into a war between clans. Evan knew he was no closer to the Fairy Flag than he was the first day he arrived in Scotland. He tried to shake the night's events from his mind as he moved closer to the bed, stripping off his shirt and unwrapping his plaid. It was way too late to call for a bath, so he settled for the washbasin on a nearby table and washed what he could. He returned to sit just on the edge of the bed and begin to unlace his boots ... *Odd order to undress, Evan. Naked but yer boots. Evie would be so proud. She always liked these boots ...* He found that was the funniest thing he'd thought of all day. Evan chuckled and fell backward to land in a pile of soft and heavy bedclothes while kicking the heavy steel-toed monsters into a corner.

He closed his eyes and dozed for a moment, relaxing for the first time in a very long days' time. His thoughts drifted into a dream about home. The queen-sized bed he shared with Evie was covered in scads of decorative pillows, something Evie had always wanted. He'd never understood the things, always claiming them to be a total waste of time and energy. Yet he encouraged her to buy them if they made any part of her happy. Evan dreamed of shoving them all in the floor as he rolled up into the covers of the bed, stretching his long legs all the way out to the end. In his dream, his feet were dangling off the edge just as they did at home. It was uncomfortable sometimes, but it was always home to him. He was snuggled under the down comforter and was almost asleep in his dream when a naked Evie pressed her warm body against his back.

He smiled and groaned, eyes still closed.

She snuggled in closer. Evan caught his breath and for a second, debating on if he was dreaming fully now, or if he were still somehow awake. He tested his mind by moving his feet closer to the edge of the bed. Stretched completely out, he was still on the bed down to the very … last … toe. That startled Evan straight into consciousness. His eyes shot open and he turned his head to face not his wife, but a very naked Rosemary.

∞

Evie woke with the sounds of fighting ripping through her slumber. She threw her dress back on and opened the door. A large crowd of people was rushing downstairs toward the commotion. Curiosity overwhelming her, she left her room to join them.

Downstairs in the great hall, two men were held down and beaten by MacLeod men. Shocked, Evie pushed her way downstairs. She could see the red in the tartans they were wearing but didn't want to admit to herself who it was.

Just then, Creighton bellowed through the room to move out of his way as he pushed through the crowd to the front of the room. She watched as he manhandled the men who held the strangers in restraint, with the force and agility of a man half his age. The two beaten men fell to the floor in a heap, gasping for air.

"Say again who sent ye," Creighton growled.

"The Ruadh Donas. He sent us to let ye know that they willna be meeting this eve," one man sputtered, his eyes beginning to swell shut from injury.

"Considering it's very little time from being full daylight, I suppose that's more than obvious. Now why is it that the Ruadh Donas and yer chieftain have decided to waste more time?" Creighton barked, waiting for one of the men to catch his breath.

"More time. They needed more time."

Creighton roared, "More time for what? More time to murder more innocents? Go back to your master, your devil from hell, and ye tell him, Creighton MacLeod has had enough. Show his face within the next three nights or all MacDonalds shall be hunted and exterminated like the vermin they are!" He spat on the two men and pushed his way out of the hall, the crowd's whispering returning to a roar.

Evie's mind was reeling ... A war. A feud between clans. MacLeod will wipe out the entire family ... Her fears raced through her heart. Her entire family—erased from the future if Creighton brought down the rain of death. All the MacDonald's up to and including her own Evan, Keiran, Mason, and Leeann.

Evie found a wall to press against and choked up. This could be the end of her life at home. She had to make better headway to learn where the Flag was so she could save her family, even if it meant never seeing them again.

If she only had someone to talk to; if she could make a confidant of someone, perhaps they could help her with getting home. She had not spoken in months, and the strain was becoming unbearable. She had to reach out. However, the only two people she was even remotely friendly with were Cook ... and Lily, who had done so much for her already. Evie wondered how Lily would react to her story and if she could just make enough sense to get help without sounding crazy. She had to escape. She had to make it right with Evan. She had to figure out how to make this Ruadh Donas bastard show up in the three days or else her whole world would be lost.

Evie fought the remaining crowd out of the great hall and took to the stairs. She stayed near the wall, trying to make her way to Creighton's study to see if Lily was there. Pressed by the oncoming crowd, she made slow headway to her destination, and hopeful sanctuary.

∞

Evan whispered into Rosemary's ear, "Get the hell out of my bed, wretch," and pushed her off the bed with determined force.

With a resounding thud, Rosemary fell to the cold ground, mouth agape. Evan rolled to his side, pushing himself up on one elbow, smiling smugly. She scurried to her feet, and slapped Evan across the face. He didn't react, which enraged her further. He sighed as if bored.

"Rosemary. Ye have lost your fool mind. Gather your clothes and go tend that crazy man you call husband. There is nothing in this bed that will satisfy you, no matter what the new legend says," he laughed.

Rosemary grabbed her linen gown and threw it over her head, screaming at him. "My husband is damnable mockery of this clan! He relied on a heathen's debauchery to conjure ye here. I ken the devil's work when I see it. Ye should have beaten him to death on that beach!" her malevolence overflowed with every word. She stared at Evan who lied there idly, bored with the performance. She wiped hot tears from her cheeks and went to him, kneeling beside the bed. She grasped at his hand and held it tightly, pleading.

"Retrieve the Flag for me, Roy. I shall dispose of Liam. No one would miss him. The clan knows he's not fit for them. They adore you. I could give ye everything. The Chieftain title, gold, the castle, the men," she paused, "heirs."

Evan pulled his hand out of her desperate grasp and sat upright, throwing his feet over the edge of the bed.

"That was a lovely drama, Rosemary, worthy of an award. However, let us clear this out of the way now. I want nothing from you. If I have to travel down to the MacLeod alone and die alone then I shall. It willna be for you, or for your husband. I shall do as I wish with the Flag and if anyone stands in my way, I shall kill them." He stood up, oblivious to his state of undress and looked her in the eyes. "Now, I will say it again if ye doona recall. Get. Out."

He took her by the shoulders and pushed her toward the door. Rosemary fought to stay with him as he shoved her out, watching her collide with the opposite wall. She quickly righted herself and attempted to claw her way back into the room, just as Evan slammed the heavy door in her face, bolting it this time.

Evan put his back against the door, listening to the screeching outside. The very idea of taking these insane people with him to see the MacLeod made him ill. He steeled his resolve. He would go to the MacLeod alone. He rubbed his face and moved away from the door, deciding to put his kilt back on. The sun would soon rise, sleep was in no way an option, and breakfast would be ready soon. The yelling outside stopped, but Evan was not ready to face the outside world just yet. He decided he would stay here for a few more minutes, in the blessed silence.

He added more wood to the fire and sat in a nearby chair, staring into the flames. This was a turning point. Evan knew he would be leaving this place soon, possibly never to return. Evan hoped that was true. Never having had the problem of a strange woman in his bed, he felt violated. Under no circumstances had he ever thought to betray his vows to Evie. Not with the assistant who made his life miserable an eternity ago, and even now with a completely unknown woman in his bed. The very thought of Rosemary's intrusion infuriated Evan. He sat back and changed the subject in his head to the task at hand.

I have to get out of here. I have to make a move. Tomorrow I shall send word to Liam that I go, with or without him or his men.

∞

Evie opened the door slowly, trying not to make any noise. The crowds rushing around in the hallway were still loud enough to drown out any sound that came from her, yet she still did not want to disturb the lady. Lily was standing with her back to her, staring at a portrait on the wall. The large canvas looked ancient to Evie. She closed the door silently behind her and pressed her back to it, unable to decide how to proceed ... *Should I just blurt out or should I just wait for her to turn around and notice?* She watched as Lily lightly touched the canvas; its rough texture rolling under her delicate fingers. Evie felt as if she were intruding on an intimate moment and thought about retreating into the hall.

She focused on the picture that Lily was caressing and wondered how she never noticed it before, given its size and intensity. It was of three men. The tallest stood. The two others in front him knelt, and the other sat in a chair. All were in the most ornate armor she had ever seen. Not that she had seen many men in armor, but even given her love for history and movies, these were far more intricate than any CGI or Hollywood creation she had personally witnessed.

Aside from the armor, the men who donned them were something out of a fantasy novel. They were herculean in size; even bigger than Evan, she judged. All three had long, straight, stark white hair and eyes without any color. Evie shivered as she tried to stare into the depths of them, wondering why the artist had chosen not to add the eye color, leaving the white canvas behind them to shine through. It made the men look more like creatures than the fierce warriors that they obviously were.

Lily touched her lips with her fingertips and placed the kiss on the cheek of the tallest man standing in the back row. Evie wondered who it was to receive such special attention from Lily. A past lover, perhaps? She didn't seem the type to sway from Creighton. Although it was a tender sentiment, Evie wasn't quite convinced it was a romantic one. Lily looked over the men with a small smile of what Evie suspected was pride.

As Lily backed away from the portrait, Evie now saw the largest man holding a piece of yellowed cloth draped across his hands. It was nothing fancy or noteworthy in its appearance; just a piece of cloth. It was the way the warrior held it with such high regard that made Evie wonder. It could have been a dishtowel and yet this man made it look like the Shroud of Turin. Then it hit her. The Flag.

Evie's pulse quickened and she became more in tune to what Lily was doing; searching for clues to where this ordinary looking cloth might be located. She scanned the other portraits to see if any of them held any signs of the Flag, and her hopes sank as she quickly realized they were more of the family she already knew or had seen. Lily paid no attention to them. None was as unambiguous as the first portrait. Evie's gaze returned to it, looking for anything else that might be telling. She recognized the room they were standing in as a chamber above hers in the tower, where the Chieftain and his Lady slept. A large fireplace matched the one in the picture, and the chair the sitting man was in looked to be the one in her chamber. She began to think to herself. Was it possible they hid the Flag away in the bedroom of the MacLeod? Could it be that simple?

Lily turned to sit down at the desk and Evie had the foresight to open and shut the door as if she had just walked into the room. Lily looked up to see Evie and smiled, her eyes shining with calmness.

"Is there something I can help ye with, lass?" Her voice was sweet and serene as if there was nothing else in the world to bother her even though the household was erupting in chaos. Evie shook her head and wrung her hands together nervously, stammering over words. *Speak now or forever hold your peace ...*

The door behind her swung open and knocked her forward, causing her to tumble into the floor. Lily gasped and went to her aid. "Creighton MacLeod! Ye done squashed the girl flat!"

Creighton stood in the doorway with his hand over his mouth. "Och! Sorry, lass. I dinna meant to! Are ye all right?" He offered as Evie tried to stand up again with two confusing sets of hands trying to grab and pull her to her feet. With her courage gone, she righted herself, curtsied quickly as she ran back out the door, and headed for her room.

Chapter 14

The next morning dragged. Evan hadn't seen hide or hair of Rosemary since the early morning escapade, for which he was thankful. Liam hadn't emerged either. He found himself alone at the head of the table for breakfast. The clansmen thought nothing out of the ordinary about it, actually being more jovial than a normal breakfast with their Chieftain. Evan discovered he didn't mind being up here alone all that much at all.

After filling up on half-decent food, he made his way to the lists to burn off some steam. He knew the men would be there, still waiting on the two who had gone ahead to Dunvegan to relay the message to the MacLeod. Evan spent most of the day there training harder than before. Liam didn't join them either, still apparently recuperating from the confrontation. Evan noticed the men were listening more intently and giving him more respect. He dared not ask why, but hoped it was because an actual leader had finally stepped up instead of the backstabbing, scheming man bestowed upon them for the last year. Evan wasn't sure he was happy to fill those shoes, but it gave him reason to think.

Evan thought of Liam's father, and wondered if he was a strong figure or if he was more like his son, killed early in his life. He wondered what happened to the former chieftain in the great hall that Liam did not see, prior to his death.

Distracted for a fraction of a second, Evan found himself knocked in the jaw by a strong right fist. Taking a few blinks and a step backward, he spit out blood and stared at his opponent—a lad of 16 years, who stared at Evan, color draining from his face.

"Damn, lad, ye got me good." Evan rubbed his jaw.

"I'm so sorry, sir. I dinna mean to. It was a mistake. I dinna think

I'd … I would … I … " the boy stammered, backing away.

Confused at the boys' reaction, Evan asked, "What do you mean, 'ye dinna mean to?' All of ye should be giving me the run through. If ye expect mercy in battle, all would be dead. I want ye to hit me like that every time ye can manage!" Evan's anger flared. "I dinna ken what's amiss here but I want to know why you would be holding back on training, up to and including to hitting me in the face?"

The lad's father stepped up and answered. "Sire, he did not mean to offend. Everything has changed a bit since the MacDonald returned from the beach. The lad's just under the impression that we, as MacDonalds, will wind up like our Chieftain did if we crossed ye. People have died at yer hands. We saw ye appear from nowhere and rendered our entire clans' men unconscious or bleeding within minutes, and now, with the murders … I cannae explain it at all, and we damn sure do not want to anger ye, who ever ye may be; friend or foe. To some ye are a hero and to some ye are a monster, if I may be so bold."

The words hit Evan harder than the fist did. These men thought he killed those people. They saw him come out of nothingness. Evan sighed and turned, his back facing the father and son. The rest of the men who gathered stood silently and stared at him, his size now a glaring reminder of how much of a monster he appeared to them. A head or so taller, shoulders wider than most, flaming red hair and devilish goatee, he stood somberly, reminded repeatedly of his strengths and weakness over this clan … this family. They feared him for what he did to them in the drum circle on Samhain, and what he did to their chieftain. He couldn't admit not doing the murders, for Liam's sake, for his own reputations' sake. Evan was stuck. He looked at all the people staring back at him. With his mood blackening, he turned to face the father and son.

"Regardless of yer feelings toward me; I want no one to hold back. If the MacDonalds are going to war, no one will be spared; even if ye have to fight me. I want ye to try and kill me. Is that understood?"

"Yes, sire" the lad spoke quietly.

Evan walked closer, casting a shadow over the boy. "Good. For your life may depend on it." He stepped backward and faced the rest of the clan.

"I shall be leaving on the morrow to Dunvegan. I shall go alone to speak with the MacLeod. Liam is in no shape to accompany me. I expect to either come back in a box, or come back with the Flag." Turning on one heel, Evan started to walk away. Behind him, he heard the son ask, "But what of us?"

"What of it?" he responded, not stopping.

"When shall we meet ye to go along?" The son said a bit more strongly.

Evan stopped and turned. The group had banded together and waited.

"Ye think I am a monster, why not go it alone? I do not want to put the whole family in peril. I'll go, and if I stand or fall, it willna be on the clans' shoulders. I'll just demand the Flag for myself and leave the Clan out of it."

The group began to murmur disapproval. The father spoke, putting his hand on his son's shoulder.

"No, sire, we won't let ye go alone. Ye are more like a chieftain than ours ever has been. Whether our feelings are that ye are a monster or a hero, we would go into the sea for ye. We need ye, bad or good. Ye have trained us more than anyone ever has. Every day, rain or snow or sun, good and bad, you have been there for us. We cannae let ye down now."

Evan was touched. He bowed his head. "Thank ye. We shall ready before sun up. Break our fast and be off."

There was a general approval of the group as he turned back around to walk toward the castle. He looked around the grounds, almost a reflex now, to make sure everything was quiet. Over the horizon, he saw two men staggering up the steep hill coming from the shoreline. Evan broke into a run, seeing them falling on themselves in attempt to remain upright. The other clansmen saw too and ran after them in a panic.

Evan got there first to see the condition of the two—battered, broken, and unable to see. Furious, Evan shouted, "Get the healer," as he helped position them to ease their pain. One of the men collapsed into his arms panting. "Ruadh Donas, the MacLeod did this. They shall try and kill us all. He wants war." The man succumbed to unconsciousness.

"Not if I can help it," Evan said darkly as he helped carry the man up to the castle.

∞

A heavy snow began to fall again as they made their way down to the craggy shoreline of Dunscaith. Evan had sent Liam his executive decision to make their way over to the MacLeods without him, stating that enough was quite enough. He wanted to go home. If Liam wanted to have his Flag, he'd retrieve it for him, if only to get his wave and leave. He was growing wary of the lack of leadership. Evan's patience was weary from lack of sleep and random drama from Rosemary.

Infuriated, exhausted, and fed up, Evan had lead the group of unarmed men to the beach and out to the sea. As the snow kept falling, his spirits sank further with every flake that hit the ground. The two beaten men weighed heavily on his mind. He was responsible for them. The families of the men were in shambles, left for Evan to take blame for, again. For another night of sleeplessness, he had consoled their sons and daughters and their wives, instead of Liam, their rightful Chieftain; the same person who had decided to take to more drink, and stay as far away from the entire clan as possible. Tired of staring at the sea, Evan hung his head, waiting for the snow to envelope him into the nothingness that he felt inside. Something had to give.

The drifting snowflakes began to slow and all together stopped by the time they had made landfall and disembarked. The sun quickly burned through the clouds, giving them new cause for concern; the melting snow would soon turn to ice. They approached with caution, unnerved there was no one to greet them at the rocky shore. They walked slowly but deftly up the icy cliffs toward the castle gates; the sun blinding as it reflected off the new sheet of ice. The trek was a slow one, but the docks were close to the trail that would lead directly to the main castle. It wouldn't take too long to reach their final destination. Evan became weary, his pace slowing with every step up the incline.

Evan flipped his long hair in front of his face to guard from the glare that was directly in his eyes. In doing so, he caught the figure of a woman standing on the battlements and turned his head slightly to look. His breath caught in his chest and he felt all the hairs on his body stand on end with electricity as he slowed his pace almost to a standstill. Time seemed to stop. Evan squinted, his face drawing into a scowl at the vision in attempt to try harder to see her. He cupped his hand over his eyes to block the sunlight as much as he could. "This cannae be real," he whispered. "Evie?"

The sunlight illuminated her, casting a heavenly glow about her figure. Her now back length brown hair flowed around her body from the wind with a mind of its own. Her woolen tartan she held tightly about her shoulders whipped against her slight frame. His hand shook as he dropped it to his side. He was certain it was Evie. Watching her, he felt his heart drop somewhere in his stomach.

Evan heard a low whistle, snapping him out of his daze. He was holding up the line of MacDonalds behind him. They too gazed at the unearthly vision of Evie on the battlements, and a chuckle emitted from someone. A couple of them ribbed each other and made cheeky comments about her. A surge of possessiveness washed over him and he turned to growl his disapproval. He glanced back in her direction just as she seemed to shiver, close her tartan about her shoulders, and turned to walk away. Evan all but ran toward the castle that held the woman he so desired, leaving the men to catch up.

∞

The stress at Dunvegan reached a fevered pitch as they all impatiently waited for Ruadh Donas to show his face. They were notified he and his clan had arrived, but no one had gone to see him as of yet. As the Legend and his men made their way up from the sea, the keep had turned into a madhouse trying to prepare for whatever may transpire; whether it would be a peaceful outcome or war. Either way, Cook had advised there would be food, and he would be showing off his new recipes so graciously put together by his mute little help, Evie, so they had been cooking all day.

She had escaped the kitchens to her favorite hiding place on the battlements for a brief moment to catch her breath. As she approached the top, she saw the Ruadh Donas and his clan working his way up the steep incline, and she stopped cold. She couldn't make out his features from the glare off the snow he stood on, but she was certain she had seen enough to know who it was. His long, damp, shaggy red hair hid his face. She was sure she could feel the two piercing eyes on her enough to make her shiver. His ragged dress and disheveled state fit someone named The Red Devil, she decided.

What she could see from her position on the battlements was his shape. He was simply huge. He stood what seemed a few feet taller than his men, who were dirty and haggard from the trip from Dunscaith. His entire body appeared taut, waiting to pounce. His arms were tight, his strong legs showing every muscle line from his boots to his kilt; and from this angle, he appeared to be staring in her direction. She saw one of the clansmen cover his mouth—maybe a cough? The red-headed monster turned sharply to address him. She saw the clansmen duck their heads low, as if he was somehow degrading them. She wondered if he required them to avert their eyes or some nonsense to show his dominance. She scowled at the thought of what idiocy this man had made the MacDonalds endure.

She wondered if he had killed their clansmen too—if their families cried themselves to sleep at night. She took notice that their Chieftain did not accompany them and remembered the rumor about what happened to him ... Ruadh Donas had beaten him and dragged him across the rocks. The Chieftain cried for it to stop. The monster showed no mercy to the one who called him to this world. He beat the helpless man half to death and left him to die ... Though she knew better to believe all she heard in the hallway, it made her think of what nightmares this man was capable of producing. Not wanting to be noticed, Evie pulled her tartan closely around her and ducked back down the stairs leading into the castle, ready to go back to work in the kitchens and be away from the monster who had just arrived.

∞

Evan crested the hill, his legs tired from the seemingly never-ending steps. Twenty men in MacLeod tartans greeted them. Ready for anything, Evan motioned for his men to stop and stepped forward to meet an older, graying man, who barely reached his shoulders.

"Roy MacDonald. The Ruadh Donas." It was a statement, not a question, or a greeting coming from Creighton. He was also looking totally unsurprised at the man's size.

"Aye. Pardon the delay," Evan said, just as gruffly as Creighton, frowning at the top of the man's' head.

"Och, ye are here now. I'm Creighton MacLeod. Let's get on with it. No need for pleasantries," he said, turning on one heel and striding into the gates. Over his shoulder he spoke. "My men will show yours to the Hall for dining. Ye can follow me."

Evan looked suspiciously after him, but ordered his men to follow Creighton's men. He had trained them all to be able to stand on their own, and now it was time to trust them to prove they could survive. He figured the MacLeod wouldn't start something without provocation, yet he remained on guard, and slowly followed him down the hallway.

"Where's MacDonald?" Creighton asked while still walking, not turning around to face him.

"Indisposed."

"He's just too much of a coward to face me. Even his father was a coward."

"I heard differently," Evan tested, wondering what the rest of Liam's story was.

"Of course ye did. Summoned from Hell to serve the idiotic drunk son of an idiotic drunk father, I hear. What did he tell ye? I stabbed the man?" Creighton stopped now, opening a large wooden door leading to a small solarium. He motioned for Evan to enter and then followed behind. He closed the heavy door behind him with a resounding slam.

"I serve no one, MacLeod. Let us get that out of the way." Evan said, a little louder than necessary. He walked into the middle of the room and turned to face Creighton, crossing his arms. "I came to Dunvegan for my own reasons. Liam MacDonald is delusional, at best. Now, what I heard is of no concern, for I doona care who killed who or why. 'Tis not the reason I am here. Ye wanted to see me, and I am here."

"Fine. Why are ye killing my clansmen?" Creighton walked over to pause at the side bar and fixed a whisky without offering anything to Evan.

"Because I wanted to. Next question?" Evan stood as still as a statue only cocking an eyebrow waiting for the next shot. He seethed on the inside that he had been set up to take the fall for Liam's lies.

Creighton slammed the whisky on the bar. "What do ye or the MacDonald want from us?"

"MacDonald wants the Flag," Evan said plainly. He saw the blood creep to Creighton's face as he measured Evan's size. He knew

Creighton was silently wondering if he could take Evan on his own. Looking back at him, Evan knew he was an older man, his knees were probably bad, and he could use them as a first shot if need be. He took quick assessment of Creighton's outfit, wondering if he had a sgian dubh in his boot or another hidden knife somewhere in his shirt or tartan. He quickly scanned the room in his peripheral vision to see any outwardly obvious swords or knives that Creighton could reach. Seeing nothing of interest that caught his attention, he focused on the MacLeod's face staring intently back at him. The high color drained from his face as quickly as it had risen.

"I see." Creighton sighed and sat down in a nearby chair, motioning for Evan to do the same. "Ye cannae have it, obviously." He had no hint of anger in his voice now, which confused Evan. "Do ye ken what MacDonald wants with it? What's the lad got in his mind this time? Fame, fortune? Is there anything else we can negotiate on that will keep us from a full on feud between Clans? If ye are unaware, we have been at peace for thirty long years. I would hate to end that because of Liam's greed, idiocy … or lunacy, as the case may be. I am too old for such nonsense."

Evan shrugged with indecision and stared at Creighton, unsure of how to continue. He had fully expected a fight, and here the older man sat, deflated of any sign of violence, wanting to offer another choice in order to keep peace. Evan was convinced there was far more to the story than was being told. He was too complacent and calm. The old man's lack of fury confused him. He knew ultimately there was more going on. Evie was here. There had to be some connection.

Remembering his wife on the battlements, Evan paused and thought of a new strategy. "I am famished. We have been traveling all day. Is there a possibility that food has been prepared?"

Creighton nodded and stood. "Aye, the kitchen staff has been preparing all day. They imagined there would be either bloodshed or hungry men. They planned for hungry men first," he laughed, stood up and clapped Evan on the back. "Come, let us dine, and then discuss what in the world we should do after we have a full stomach."

Too complacent. Too comfortable. Yes, there was something odd here.

∞

It was the best meal he had eaten in months. Evan thought he would shed a tear if it got any better. He recognized with love, all his wife's favorite meals she'd make on Christmas Day. Passed down from generation to generation, Evie had remembered every traditional Scottish recipe hammered into her head by her mother. She labored over a stove for days before any holiday, and the result was always the same; he would eat too much and pass out on the couch while football played on television. With a heavy Scotch broth stew and barley bannocks as a starter, main course dish of smoked haddock and cheese scones, and cloutie dumplings with currants for dessert, he was sure he had died and gone to heaven. He did nearly faint when a serving maid asked him if he would like coffee. *Only my Evie would find coffee in the thirteenth century.* Evan smirked and gladly accepted. He knew his wife was behind it all and he wanted to kiss her ... *Honestly, I'd do way more than that, but it's beside the point ...*

He sat at the head of the long wooden table with Creighton while his men sat nearby at a separate table from the MacLeod men. It was easy to tell they had been just recently at odds, for most of the MacDonalds were generally peaceable with their guests. Only a few family members affected by the deaths were inhospitable. Evan noticed only the clansmen dined and the women and children were not present. Even the majority of the attending servants were male, with the exception of a few women who were delivering and retrieving dishes. Evan assumed Creighton had requested those who were not able to fight to stay away, just in case violence did erupt. If so, it made Evan respect the older man for keeping his family safe away from indefinite harm. Overall, they all seemed to get along. That, coupled with Creighton's lack of concern was still very peculiar.

Evan kept his head down and his eyes up, looking everywhere for Evie. Every woman that passed was a letdown. He thought for a moment that he just imagined her on the battlements, and he was just lucky to have a good meal. Then he remembered his clansmen looking up at her and immediately dismissed the thoughts. He and Creighton mostly ate in silence, with the occasional word from Evan.

"I havena tasted the likes of this in quite some time," Evan baited, hoping for any sign of his wife in the conversation.

"We have been lucky with our new kitchen lass. She arrived a few months ago. My son found her in a field laughing wildly at a hairy cow. She's simple though. Doesna speak, but can cook like no other."

Evan didn't understand why she was not speaking, but could see her waking up from the time travel and finding humor in her situation enough to be laughing in the face of a cow. He pushed on with a few more questions. However, he was concerned that she might be hurt or otherwise impaired. "Is she daft?"

"No, not at all. I think she is brilliant. She's downright magical in the kitchen if I should say so myself, without risk of being burned for being a heretic," Creighton joked, pouring a small shot of whisky in his coffee. "I doona ken where she found these beans or how she knew to grind them up, but it's downright foul to taste without a wee dram." He offered Evan a flask, to which he declined politely. Creighton nodded and added another drop in his, and tucked it away in his sporran. "It's just another reason to say the lass is quite knowledgeable. She brings us all sorts of tasty treats we never dreamed existed."

Evan nodded as he listened to the old man talk as he drank his coffee. "She truly is an asset to the castle then, eh?"

"Aye. There is something about her that makes everyone generally happy, though she doesna say a thing."

Evan could believe that. She has made him happy for so many years. He paused to think of all the laughter and smiles they had shared since they met.

The pain in his chest returned when he realized just how much they had fallen apart. It was mostly in part from Mama Killie, he figured. Her passing had left them with no answers and little solace. His wife had pushed him away, locking herself into her work and family obligations. He had turned to his work at the office, and more rigorous training at the gym. Then the night in his office was what he feared to be the permanent wedge between them. He recalled the only time they ever breached the subject, on Halloween. Evan thought Evie had pushed him too far by teasing him. So pent up, he had wanted nothing more than to be with his wife, yet she seemed to have given up on him ... given up on their whole marriage.

Evan wondered how she would react to seeing him here. Would she be happy? Would she still be angry about the fight? He thought about how she had twisted his words around, unwilling to hear him out. The very idea was frustrating. Even with the new attempt at his morals from MacDonald's wife, the idea of him straying was sickening. Evan thought if he had been half a man, he would have ravished the damnable wench and never thought twice about Evie. However, Evan didn't. As long as there was a chance of him seeing his wife again, he would be true to his vows. There would be no other. *Forever and ever.*

Turning his attention back to the Chieftain, Evan realized he had begun to talk aimlessly about food. Glad he hadn't missed anything important; Evan requested another cup of coffee, not wanting to miss a drop while he had the chance. For in addition to it being very good, he was sure he would be awake most of the night and could use the caffeine.

"If ye are finished eating, we could take this back to the solarium and finish our previous conversation," Creighton said, waving for a maid to refill Evan's tankard. He nodded in agreement and turned his head toward the woman who approached. Evan froze as he realized whom he had called over to serve them. Evie had changed into a heavier and warmer woolen kirtle from the linen thing she had been wearing outside, and wore a MacLeod tartan sash. Her eyes lowered and not once did she look up from the small pitcher of dark brew.

"Roy, this is the lass responsible for our fine meal. Our Evie." Creighton said, proudly. "She cooks like this for us thrice a day, and nary a complaint from any MacLeod. We shall all die fat and happy if it were up to her," he added jovially. She didn't look up to meet the eyes of either man. Evie leaned over only long enough to fill Evan's cup, and with her head still bowed, she curtsied to the Chieftain and his guest, and hastily returned to the kitchens.

Dumbstruck, Evan's mouth hung open. He couldn't believe she had walked directly to him and not once looked his direction. His heart pounded in his chest as he struggled to breathe normally. Having not seen her in months, she was just as stunning to him today as she had been the first day he ever laid eyes on her. Her face was pale from the lack of Virginian sun in which she was accustomed. Her chestnut hair was much longer, pulled back haphazardly in a bun; her stray curls escaping every attempt at restraint. With having lost weight from the complete change in environment, her eyes seemed bigger pools of brown and her lips seemed fuller in contrast. Evan became uncomfortable sitting there, watching her. *What the hell is wrong with me? She's my wife ... Wait, what the hell is wrong with her? Why isn't she looking at people in the eye?*

Evan was instantly thankful for his sporran, hopeful that it hid the large uncomfortable signifier of his reaction to Evie. Slightly embarrassed, he hoped she hadn't noticed when she had bent over in front of him to pour his coffee. It had been over a year since he had any physical contact with his wife, and she was the only person on this planet who he wanted. He knew in his heart and mind there was more to his relationship than physical attraction, but at this very moment, the thought of shoving all the remaining dishes and food to the floor and ravishing her on the vast wooden table in front of everyone in the castle was the first on his imaginary "To Do" list. He shifted in his seat; silently pleading the old man would take his time in wanting to return to the solarium. "She is a lovely lass, MacLeod," Evan managed to say, staring off after where Evie had exited the hall.

Creighton looked at Evan out of the corner of his eye and grinned. "Aye, she is, Roy. Eh, if yer, uh ... up to it now, we can return to a quieter place to discuss business."

Evan felt like hiding.

"The men can rest here or they may join mine in the lists if ye think they can behave," the old man added, changing the subject.

Evan nodded, taking mental inventory of his body parts and soon decided it was safe to stand, and followed Creighton down the hall.

∞

Evie angrily slammed the coffee pitcher down on the counter as she entered the kitchen. She could still feel the man's leering eyes as she had served him without even looking at him to tell, and it made her feel dirty ... *How dare he stare at me like that? Who the hell does he think he is?* He even had a hard-on for Pete sake! *Pervert.*

She couldn't even bear to look at the creature that was responsible for such horrors in her new found home. She was sickened and confused to see Creighton so friendly with him. Evie felt she had half the mind to throw the coffee in his lap instead of serving him. She entertained the idea of poisoning his food earlier, but knew all the men would be eating, and didn't want to cause undue strain on the already tenuous peace. She remained demure and silent even though it grated against her nature. It took all her energy to keep her head down in his presence, when all she just wanted to scream at him ... *I hope I have the opportunity to inflict pain on him before he goes off to do anyone else any harm. And Roy? What the hell kind of name is that? Roy MacDonald? Ruadh Donas ... my ass.*

Evie began to start cleaning the kitchen to be ready for the next meal. She went through an arsenal of nasty things she could do to the monster in her mind, and for the first time in a while, she smiled.

Chapter 15

The solarium was noticeably warmer this time, a fire now built in the large stone fireplace. Evan and Creighton entered and sat across from each other. Still enjoying his coffee, Evan's mind wandered briefly to where Evie was right now, and what she was doing. He fought off a wave of sleepiness as the food and the warmth settled in his bones, waiting for Creighton to start this order of business.

"What's wrong with the lass?" Evan asked absentmindedly, not knowing how to approach the topic of the Flag.

"Wrong? Och, nothing, I suppose. Just not talking. Havena heard her utter a word in the time she has been with us. Why do ye ask? Ye are awfully interested in her," Creighton ribbed. "Does the Ruadh Donas have a soft side when he's not killing innocent clansmen and assaulting yer Chieftain?"

The tone shocked Evan awake and he returned all his attention to the older man. "There are reasons for everything, MacLeod. I've just not explained them to you."

"I would like to hear yer explanations. So would the wives and children of the men ye slaughtered." Creighton's voice shook as he answered Evan.

The two men stared at each other for a short time, the heat from the fire becoming overwhelming. Evan wanted to yell at Creighton that he wasn't the murderer. He wasn't responsible. He was incapable down to his soul of such an act. Instead, Evan breathed deep and exhaled slowly, trying to calm himself down enough to respond.

He steeled his jaw and spoke deliberately. "In time, I shall explain everything," he managed. "Now ... I am here on business from the MacDonald, and then I shall take my leave. If ye are not willing to hand over the Fairy Flag, or if we cannae reach a negotiation, I shall return and let the MacDonald know that yer answer is war." The last word hung in the air as if it had taken on a life of its own.

Creighton closed his eyes and bowed his head.

"I want no war, Roy. Not with you, not with that sotted lad in Chieftains' clothes, not with anyone. I doona ken ye, but you have to listen. I have to keep my clan safe. I have to keep the secrets in this castle within these walls. Liam MacDonald is drunk with power when not with whisky; and when both he's insufferable. I have known him since he was in nappies, and his Da was not much different from him. Liam thinks the Flag is a Holy Grail, and I cannae allow him to have it so long as I live."

Evan had to think fast. He knew Liam would come after the Flag on his own if he didn't bring it back with him. He knew there would be unnecessary bloodshed for the power hungry Chieftain to have his precious item. Evan still didn't know why Liam wanted it to begin, but he was more apt to believe Creighton who had experience with the Flag, than the pile of waste hiding at Dunscaith Castle. He knew that they had a long way before they reached a peaceful situation, and perhaps he should keep his perceived enemy, Creighton MacLeod, closer.

Evan also now had to consider Evie's safety. She should be with him, whether she realized it was him or not. He briefly considered that she didn't know he was here. She hadn't looked at him, so Evan could assume she didn't. *That might be better; if she was still mad at me ... I could use that as a motivator to get her to safety. Then she could be pissed off at me all she wants as long as she is close by ... but how?*

"I will to report to MacLeod. He must be involved in this discussion." Evan stalled, hoping it would give him some time to think of what he needed to do.

"Aye. Do that. If ye can keep him sober enough to make the trip. The fool is still convinced I killed his Father here last year." Creighton said, looking up at Evan and relaxing back in his chair.

Evan looked over the older man's face, noticing the hard lines that made from long years of defending his land; defending to keep the Fairy Flag in his hands and out of dangerous hands. Hands like Liam MacDonald, who had nothing but greed on them. Evan was torn. Should he return to Dunscaith and take over the clan by force as originally planned, or scrap the idea for working with MacLeod and being as close to Evie as possible? The choice was obvious to him; to stay with MacLeod and Evie, but the clansmen already despised him for the despicable things Liam had done to his name. He was a monster to these people. They had no reason to welcome him. They would attempt his life at every turn.

The two men sat in uncomfortable silence for a moment. There was a knock at the door and Creighton advised them to enter. A servant opened the door and explained that the snow had begun to fall fast, rendering the path to the shore impassable almost immediately. Given that it had snowed a great deal already that day, Evan took the news to mean he and his men would be staying at Dunvegan for a while or tossed out into the snow. He looked to Creighton and cocked an eyebrow.

The older man returned the look, shook his head in disbelief, and turned to the man at the door. "Make arrangements for the MacDonald men to sleep in available beds." Creighton dismissed the messenger and stood, pacing the floor. "I doona ken why, but I like ye. I see more than ye probably know. Moreover, I see that MacDonald has used ye as a pawn. I hope we can reach a peaceable agreement. In the meantime, since it's obvious that we'll be spending more time together here at Dunvegan, I offer ye my hospitality. I shall make sure that yer stay is as pleasant and safe as possible. To be certain, I am confused as to why ye killed my men. We still mourn for their loss. I cannae be sure that the majority of my clan will feel the same way as I do about yer presence right now, and I shall make sure they are not out to cause any harm. So until I find out otherwise, consider our castle a neutral place. I'll consider us at an impasse, given the circumstances."

Evan found himself surprised by the Chieftain's offer. Again, Creighton had responded with the peace. Evan knew that Creighton could have thrown him and his men out on his arse in the snow and that rose both confusion and suspicion to him. Evan nodded in acceptance, and stood to shake Creighton's hand. "I thank ye, Chieftain."

∞

The rest of the day centered on Evan's men in the snowy lists practicing with their sword skill, something sorely neglected since his arrival. They had only practiced hand to hand when he was around, so it was refreshing to hear the clashing of steel instead of the thudding of fists on skin. Evan stood off to the side of his men with his arms crossed against his chest, watching toward the keep and making a slow scan of the premises.

He noticed this side of the castle was a newer design from where he had been earlier. The stone was more uniform. He noticed there were also newer, gated entrances on this side, showing off the center courtyard beyond the bars. He kept looking and realized quickly that from where he was standing, he could see straight into a side portcullis, which was diagonal to the kitchen. He soon realized he had a perfect view of Evie through the slow and steady snowfall. Discreetly, he watched her, with something apparently flour-like, given the cloud of dust she was fanning away from her powder-covered face. Evan grinned crookedly as he watched her work, something he had done subconsciously for over a decade. A laughing older man came into the scene and slapped at her with a cloth, trying to rid her of the floury mess.

Evan frowned at the familiarity, wondering who this man was, and what position he was in to be able to smack his wife with a towel, even if it was to help clean her. He watched as Evie waved the man away, her laughter softly heard over the snow. She finished cleaning up and continued on to her next task out of his view. Evan scowled at the loss of sight and begrudgingly returned his attention to the clansmen, still pounding out their aggressions with one another with sword practice, murmuring to himself, "This is going to be a very long visit."

∞

Later that night across the island, a figure stood on a rocky mountaintop overlooking the castle, cloaked in black. Overnight, the snow had changed to an icy downpour of rain and sleet that was now pelting down around him, yet never touching his body. His hair was strangely dry, unkempt, and tangled, hanging in his ominous crimson and black tinted eyes. He stood there, exhaling heavily in a guttural way, staring down at Dunvegan's torchlights. The wind suddenly picked up and whipped around him, causing his cloak to billow out around him, exposing his kilted form and an incomprehensible bare chest, and matching bare feet. The frigid temperatures and blinding rain had no visible effect on the man. He smelled the air and whipped his head sideways as if the smell of the frozen rain offended him. He seemed to sense something down at the castle. With bulging ocher eyes, He snarled loudly as he drew his features into a scowl and made his agile descent down the side of the mountain toward the castle grounds.

∞

Inside the castle, down the drafty, winding hall in the solarium, sat Lily MacLeod, looking at an odd assortment of treasures. Scattered on a large intricately carved oak desk were coins, a button, an out of place Cuban cigar box, and most importantly, photographs. She fingered them delicately as she gazed at the people looking back at her from the fading Polaroid. There sat younger Killie MacLeod holding hands with a child-sized Evie, laughing by a swimming pool. Lily sadly smiled and touched Killie's face with a delicate finger. She put it in the bottom of the small wooden cigar box and pulled out one more. Another reach across time; Killie with her lover, Lily's half-brother, Lochlann MacLeod. The love radiated from the snapshot. Lily put her hand over her mouth to cover a sob. The couple held each other in a casual embrace. There stood Lochlann, a younger, bare-chested and kilted, long black haired man holding Killie around the waist, smiling broadly at a long lost joke. Killie's head tipped back on his shoulder in laughter. It was the happiest of moments caught in a single second.

Lily recalled, it was the day of their hand-fasting and the day they found out Killie was with child. She was asked to take the photo and was befuddled with the contraption she was given. A few colorful words were spoken, Killie and her young lover laughed. Lily pushed a button and a bright light flashed. Lily yelped, and a magical parchment shot out the camera's bottom. It was truly confounding, but now she cherished it.

A single tear fell and Lily caught it with the back of her hand before it dropped on the picture. The grief over the loss of Lochlann was hard to bear. Death came to him too young at the hand of a lunatic and was never able to meet his daughter. She put the picture in the bottom of the box and pulled out another; a wedding shot of Evan and Evie. The young woman in white was stunning. Lily had never seen so much resemblance to one's parents as she did in Evie. Every strand of long dark wavy hair could have been her father's. Her deep-set, chocolate eyes could be that of her mother's. She was product of a perfect love's fire extinguished too early. She also knew now, the redheaded man beside her in a strange black and white outfit was most certainly the Ruadh Donas, and the love for his wife was written clearly across his face, as obvious as the sky was blue. His eyes gleamed for no one else but his darling wife. She could tell by this single photograph that he was not a monster. He would move heaven and earth to be with her.

Creighton told Lily earlier how the stranger had been asking about Evie, and easily realized Roy was keeping up with Evie at a distance. She smirked at the thought of how Evie had so resisted his attempt at facing her. It was a finely choreographed dance, and Lily sincerely hoped it would not go too far and hurt them. There was much stress in the castle now, and Lily wished the best for the younger couple. They deserved to have the long and happy life together that Evie's parents did not have.

She pulled the picture of Evie's parents back out and laid it beside the wedding picture. The love across the ages was so apparent it hurt. She turned over the wedding picture. Written on the back was a note to Lily. She had memorized it many years ago as a testament to her dearest friend.

> *I don't know when she'll come, but she will. Please keep her safe at all costs. She is our love, our baby, our Evelyn. She is my heart.*
> *Yours,*
> *Killie*

She tucked the pictures and other bits back into the small box and placed it into a small hidden compartment in the false bottom of the desk drawer. She stood and walked to the window looking out, shuddering involuntarily. "Oh, my dear friend, Killie. If ye only ken what was going on here."

A chill up went up her spine and she began to feel faint. She staggered backward to lean back on the desk. She called for a servant to get Creighton. Within moments, he was at her side, holding her up as she fought to stay conscious.

"Lily, dear, what is it? What is wrong?" Creighton asked, half carrying her to a nearby chair. She gripped his arms and stared into his face, her eyes full of horror. "Creighton, he has returned. The Slaugh is among us." Creighton shook his head in shocked disbelief as Lily fainted in his arms.

∞

Creighton, after seeing Lily to her chambers, wordlessly escorted Evan to his quarters and left him to rest before dinner. Evan thought to question the chieftain's silence but was distracted with surprise as he opened the large door and stepped inside. The room was even bigger than the one at Dunscaith. The ceilings were at least fifteen feet tall and the bed was twice the size. Evan felt like he had walked into a five star hotel made for men just his size. The only drawback was that there were no windows, being that it was on the interior wall of the castle. He did however have a huge fireplace, already blazing its warmth. Two royal blue overstuffed chairs faced it, and a desk and high back chair was in the corner.

He instantly felt at home.

He noticed a small door off to one side. Evan went to inspect and found a garderobe, and a door on the other side of the small room. He peeked through the door to find the adjacent chamber empty. Too nosy to stop himself, he glanced around to find discarded female clothing, an unmade bed and all the general things his room contained with the exception of a window. Turning around to exit back through to his chamber, he noticed an item of clothing tucked underneath the bedclothes. Unable to stop himself, Evan went to see exactly what a medieval maid would hide underneath a mattress. Tugging on the material, it fell out into his hands, revealing a very familiar corset.

Evan whistled. "How convenient. We're neighbors."

A broad smile crept across his face as he chuckled to himself and returned the corset back where he found it.

Still smiling at his new secret, he returned to his room, locking the small garderobe door behind him. He leaned out the oversized door to the hallway and caught a servant walking by and ordered a bath to be drawn. Looking about his chamber, he found new shirts on his bed. Evan made a mental note to try them on after he bathed. The one thin hand-me-down shirt he had acquired at Dunscaith was now threadbare, and still so small it bulged at the seams and around the laces across his chest. *I guess someone doesn't agree with my fashion expertise. However, I do look like I should be on the cover of a romance novel ...* He grinned and flexed once jokingly.

He stripped off the old one off and laid it on a chair. Evan sat on the bed to unlace his boots when the door opened behind him. Assuming it was the servants to come pour his bath, he ignored the entrance and continued with his head down.

"Put it near the fire," he said, eyes still focused on his boots.

Behind him, two large men entered with his large copper bathtub, and four women followed with steaming buckets of hot water, Evie at the end. They busied themselves with pouring the water in the tub as Evie caught the sight of his naked back bent over his boots. Her jaw dropped, staring at all his tanned, sinewy muscles glowing by the firelight, his shaggy auburn hair draping over the side of his face. She took a second too long enjoying the view when she was elbowed in the ribs by her servant companion to leave. They turned and left as Evan looked up, completely unaware, and began to ready for his bath.

∞

The next morning, Evie strolled through the small courtyard garden, planning the next seasons' herbs. She fully expected to be here at the castle for longer than summer at this rate. She had made no headway on finding the Fairy Flag, and without help, she was certain she would remain here for most of her days. Well, unless someone slipped up on where it was, or she had time to search on her own. So far, she wasn't that lucky. Creighton and Lily spoke of it often, but never a hint of a location passed their lips. Evie thought of ways to approach one of them and speak, hoping perhaps they would just understand her plight and help her home. She dismissed the idea, thinking it was too unlikely. The MacLeods had been so giving to her as a stranger already, but she knew Creighton still did not trust her because of her mute status. He'd never trust her with the Flag. Evie wasn't even certain that was the way back home. She remained faithful to the idea that it was because she had found no other alternative.

Pushing away some snow with her slippered foot; she bent over and inspected the ground where they planted her last bit of herbs. She took mental note of what she would need for a successful gardening plot of ground. Evie rose to stand upright and saw the large redhead staring at her from the other side of the courtyard, beyond the castle gates. Her heart skipped a beat as she stared back at him, still unable to see his features clearly … *He looks so much like Evan from here, though there's no way Evan would ever let his hair get that long or be unshaven. He'd rather die than look like a shaggy wet Saint Bernard ...*

She thought of the last time she saw him anywhere close to being shaggy, which was a two-day growth from a camping trip when he forgot the razors. He had complained the entire time, almost resorting to picking out the whiskers with his fingers. She smiled as she recalled the trip. She was six months pregnant with Mason, yet she craved being outside the same way other pregnant woman would want ice cream or pickles. Evan agreed reluctantly to the trip, even though his idea of camping was having no room service in a five-star hotel. He bought a ton of unnecessary things, not knowing what to buy. Everything had to be high-tech for Evan. Evie knew now he was just trying to be thoughtful. He wanted her to be comfortable. She teared up, knowing she had just thought he was being difficult, not wanting to get "away from it all."

They fought about it, and Evan had taken most everything back to the store before it made it to the woods. She now saw how he just wanted her to be happy. He had bought air mattresses, portable heaters even though it was early fall in the south, three kinds of Swiss Army Knives, fancy GPS systems that had just come out in stores, and every sort of edible treat he could stuff in a cart. Evie didn't want any of that. She just wanted him, a tent, and nature. She had never been good at explaining her feelings, and this was just another blunder on her part. They fought most of the weekend.

Her teardrops fell, indenting the snow as they landed. Evie knew she would never have the opportunity to tell him thank you. She would never have a second chance to make it up to him, to appreciate him. She thought of the night she threw him out of the house—and how he vowed he'd never sign divorce papers. Evie couldn't help but wonder if it were true. Would he have stayed with her, had she not disappeared? She began to think of all the other fights they'd about his overspending, his overreacting, and his overworking. It was all over her. He had tried to tell her more about the night at his office, yet she refused to listen. She was simply too hardheaded and too proud to listen to the one man who held her whole world together.

She inhaled sharply as she realized for the first time all the things that he did for her; all that he did for the family. And there she was, acting like a spoiled brat the entire time. *How did I not*

*see? He's loved me from day one and all I've done is be a hosebeast
to him. No wonder he ran. I pushed him away. Maybe this is hell.
Maybe I'm dead, and being here without him or my family is my
hell. Perhaps purgatory since I've got a kitchen to make food in, but
still dead, and still not home with him ...*

She mourned on the inside as she wiped her face free of stray
tears, stopping as she saw the redheaded start to move toward her.
Unnerved, she picked up her skirts and dashed toward the kitchen
door. He was no one to be caught alone with. She valued her life
even if it was a purgatory. And as menial as it may seem, she was
needed at this castle and wouldn't let herself be harmed. He began
to move faster toward her. Evie picked up the pace and all but ran
into the kitchen door, slamming it as she did so, feeling as if she'd
just escaped certain danger. On the other side of the door, she
could swear she heard him laughing.

∞

The days became nights, the nights became days. They fell into
a routine with the MacDonalds, patiently waiting for the weather
to break enough for the clan to return to face Liam. Evan found he
was more comfortable here and dreaded having to leave Evie's side
for even a day now that he was used to seeing her again.

Just like every day, today he watched the men train with swords
and he helped with their hand-to-hand battle. He found himself
impatient for dinnertime so he could watch his wife. He also
knew he needed to begin looking for the Flag. He kept thinking
of ways to gain access to the rest of the castle but knew he would
fare better after everyone was asleep. There would be too many
questions asked if he were to wander around in the daylight hours.
Evan figured he would wait until after dinner when everyone was
milling around, and then make his move.

Making it through yet another day, he sat back in his chair and
watched as the serving staff entered the room. He scanned around
for the familiar face; his dark-haired mute angel among them. He
spotted Evie serving the first course of stew to the clansmen who
came from Dunscaith with him. They looked at her as if she was
nothing more than a common harlot, and made raunchy comments
about her. Evan strained to understand the Gaelic taunts they
were making but the expressions on his wife's face said it all. The
man closest to her grabbed her backside with one hand. Her face

flushed a deep red and she dumped hot stew all over his lap. With a mock look of concern and her eyes popping wide as if she didn't understand the taunts, she slapped the man's scalded crotch with a cloth while he yelled in pain.

Evan tried to hide his laughter behind coughing, but couldn't quite manage. His huge shoulders were heaving as he feigned a fit. Creighton, who had been engrossed in low conversation with his wife, looked to Evan out the corner of his eye and then over to the commotion being caused in his hall. Chuckling in amusement himself, he cleared his throat to get the attention of the MacDonald's man. Evie disappeared into the kitchens as the chieftain took notice of the situation.

Regaining composure with a few extra coughs, Evan decided enough was enough. The more he thought about the situation the angrier he became. A jealous surge overcame him and he found himself having a hard time stifling it before he made a scene. He knew Evie was woman enough to take care of herself, but this was going too far. She was his wife. This place was different from home. The men who accompanied him here from Dunscaith would treat everyone here with respect or regret it.

He pushed his chair away from the table and stood, towering over everyone. A hush overcame the room as Evan walked to the man's table where he was beginning to harass another serving maid. Evan stood behind the man's chair with his arms crossed and a huge scowl across his face. Another man at the table elbowed the offender and he turned around and looked upward.

∞

Evie stood in the doorway to the kitchen watching the scene unfold. Roy MacDonald had his back to her and though she could only see the side of his clansman's face from her angle, it was worth it. The color drained from his face as he turned to look up at the gargantuan redhead, only to say "aye" a few times and turn back around to face his table. She didn't know why, but she felt vindicated.

Evie left the great hall while everyone was enjoying the last course of the meal. Wondering if she would ever get an opportunity to look for the Flag herself, she decided this was as good a time as any. Making one last round to check on drinks and extra food, she ducked out the door back into the kitchen. Seeing that Cook had already dismissed most of the servants to eat, she felt more confident this would be perfect timing. Everyone would be finding beds or their drink very soon. Evie was glad she had taken the extra time mingling in the hall, even though it meant having to deal with the Neanderthals of the MacDonald clan. This gave her a great edge on separating herself from any kind of wandering person she may encounter during her hunt.

She took her time cleaning up the rest of the dishes, and prepared for the next morning's breakfast. She did anything to stall until everyone was on the way to sleep. She had a general idea of where the Fairy Flag might be, armed with the hints Lily had given her in the solarium the night the MacDonald's men had been roughed up. Tonight, she decided, was turning out to be the perfect night to explore.

For a moment, Evie felt guilty for taking advantage. Lily and Creighton would be distraught over her betrayal; yet Evie had to do what she could to get home. The Flag had more than one wave left, so it was possible they wouldn't be stranded without help for the Ruadh Donas and the magic would not be wasted on getting her home. They could still call upon the Fae Army to defeat him.

Evie stopped at the thought of Roy MacDonald. Something about him drew her like a moth to a flame. She despised him and the evil things he had done to her clansmen, yet she found herself thinking about him daily, almost seeking him out ever since she heard his name. There was no rational reasoning behind her feelings. She hated herself for thinking of him at all and mostly because she found herself so painfully attracted to him. The man had evaded her seeing him up close for days and with good reason—she was quickly becoming obsessed with it. She held fast to the idea that he would be so plain or just so grotesque that all this insidious fascination would drain away and she could continue on to find the Flag without distraction. Yet finding him within arm's reach had been the hardest task. Perhaps he was the curiosity that might kill the cat, she thought. She repelled the idea of him away for the hundredth time and continued with her chores.

Looking around at the now tidy kitchen, she felt the pang of guilt again as she thought of the others who had helped her so much in acclimating. Her own little home away from home had turned into something she knew could never exist in the future where she lived. They had all been so quick to take her in and teach her the ways of their life, and how to get along without even uttering a word. They knew nothing of her or her past and yet they trusted her fully as one of their own. Tears stung her cheeks as she thought of leaving this great family behind to return to the dysfunctional mess she had created in her own time. These people had no pretense. They had no ulterior motives. They were real and had been real to her. Yet Evie knew she must carry on with the plan in order to get home. They would carry on fine. Their future was not her concern; hers was.

Packing up the remnants of loose dried herbs into their rough material wrappings, she placed them on the counter as she left the kitchen for the night. She extinguished the last torch as she exited.

She noticed the corridor connecting the kitchens to the great hall in one direction, and the hallway that led to her quarters was pitch-black. The torch had burned out, she figured. She tucked her hands into her apron pockets and left the kitchen to seek out the Flag in the dark.

The hall seemed to have grown longer at night. Evie was finding it difficult to navigate her way, even by touching the wall and following by memory. She soon noticed she made a turn down a different hallway. Like the others, there was no light here either. Uneasiness sank in her stomach as she noticed there was more than one torch extinguished. It was no longer a case of the torches being just out, but someone had put them out. A chill went up her spine and she turned around quickly to run back toward the kitchen to the other exit and the great hall. She would start her search over from that side.

She made her way back to the dim area near the kitchen entrance when she heard movement behind her. Evie turned to face the direction the noise came from and stopped in renewed panic. She saw a glimpse of red hair in the remaining torch light in her peripheral vision and whipped her head around to face its owner. She wasn't fast enough. Evie already knew who the owner of the red hair was and her mind threatened to shut down in horror. She felt his arm snake around her waist from behind and his other hand closed around her mouth before she could react. He pulled her close to his body and she sucked in a breath, steeling her nerves not to scream. He shifted his position and deftly pulled her back against him into a darker corner out of the hallways' direct path. Evie glanced around and knew exactly where they were. It was one of her hiding spots to eavesdrop, and she knew no one could see them here even if they walked right past them.

Evie was acutely aware of his body as he masterfully held her. His chest felt as if it were made of granite. She could feel every curve of his abdomen, the hard thump of his heart in his chest, the rock hardness below his kilt. Her pulse quickened and she swallowed hard, her face flushing from pure adrenaline. She fought off the memory of seeing him in the great hall for the first time, bending over near him to pour his coffee, taking way too much notice of his sporran and the contents beneath.

He ran his rough cheek along the delicate skin of her neck and then to her ear, inhaling as if he were an animal smelling his prey. Evie shuddered as his hair tickled her shoulder. He leaned closer to her neck, his breath hot; the earthy smell of him intoxicating. She closed her eyes tight, fighting the urge to relax and sink into his dominating embrace; fighting not to turn around him and meet that face with an open mouth … *Wrong reaction, Evie*, she nagged herself. *This guy's gonna kill you. Fight dammit.*

Someone walked around the corner toward the hiding spot. Recognizing her opportunity to be noticed, Evie regained her senses and started to squirm away as he held her tighter, shushing in her ear quietly, forcing her to remain still. Her every instinct told her to scream if she could, yet she held silent. And just as she had suspected, the passerby kept walking, taking no notice of them whatsoever. She watched helplessly as the man rounded the corner to return into the great hall. They were alone again. Evie felt something, and didn't recognize it as fear, but more of relief they weren't seen. She inwardly damned herself for the notion.

Regaining her furor for stealing her away against her will, she stamped his foot and recoiled immediately when she struck her leather slipper-clad foot to his hard steel-toed boot. She picked up her injured foot and tried to kick backward into his knee, only to completely miss her mark and kick the wall behind them, further injuring herself. She wiggled, trying to get out from his grasp but he was too strong for her to match. She elbowed him in the stomach to receive a faint "oof" out of him. His grip tightened and she could feel him chuckle beneath her back. She growled behind his hand at his smugness. He chuckled harder.

Evie was infuriated at his ability to contain her with such little effort. However, after her noble attempts, she resigned to fight for now. From the feel of it, he was at least as tall as Evan was, if not taller. Given what she already knew about him, she figured he was double the strength of her husband. Evie succumbed to the realization that her attempts were futile. She would to have to wade through the situation to find an escape, if she wanted one, because her fighting him wasn't working. He released his hand from her mouth for a moment to see how she would react, pausing to brush the pad of his thumb over her bottom lip. Evie begged to bite it, yet somehow resisted, almost hypnotized by the contact. After a minute of just the background noise from the great hall penetrating the silence, he was confident she wasn't going to scream for help and slowly dragged his hand down the length of her body to join the other arm wrapped around her waist. He opened his mouth slightly and spoke, barely a whisper in her ear. Evie remained painfully still, unable to think rationally as she focused on the words.

"Beautiful, speechless lasses should not be wandering around in the dark alone." His voice was velvet, his Scottish brogue light, and his breath hot on her cool skin. She turned her head reflexively up toward his mouth as he spoke, her own lips falling open in response and her eyes closing. Confused at herself, Evie clamped her mouth shut immediately as she realized her own reaction to his voice. The sense of danger scared her, however she didn't want to run … yet. Something told her to stay and find out what he wanted, other than the obvious. She could tell her subtle physical response to his voice had affected him too, for she heard him suck in his breath and pull his head back away from her upturned face. Evie wished for just a flash of light; just a moment to try and look at him directly. It would break the spell and allow her to fight him. Nevertheless, that wasn't her luck.

He took a step backward to put distance between their bodies and swiftly picked her up without any strain. He threw her over his shoulder like a sack of potatoes. Hanging upside down, Evie pondered what to make of the situation. If she spoke to him, then he would most definitely tell Creighton she was not mute. Then they would berate her for not speaking sooner and cause more strife between them. The last thing she wanted was to be cast out of the castle for being a spy like Creighton always suggested. She decided to remain quiet and see where he was taking her, watching the dark kilt below her face sway back and forth as he walked. She knew her eyes were tricking her when she thought she saw a Dr. Martens' tag out the back of one of his tall boots. *You've officially lost it now, Evie ...* She tried to squint harder to get a better look, but decided it was just the blood rushing to her head and gave up; concentrating on the direction he took them.

They traveled upstairs. Evie wished for him to take her back to her quarters. Perhaps he was having a touch of moral sense and just wanted to see her safely to her room. She held her breath when she saw the door to her room pass by and then was shocked when he took her to the very next room. He opened the door to the chamber, closed, and bolted it. *Oh dammit,* she thought, realization sinking in. *Welcome to my parlor said the spider to the fly ...*

Chapter 16

In here, there were no lights and no window, unlike her room next door. Evie tried to focus on anything in the darkness, but the attempt was fruitless. He slowly took her by the waist with the span of his hands and put her down on what she suspected was his bed. Her eyes hurt while she struggled to find light and her panic started to return. She put her hands out to her sides, trying to figure out where her captor was. She found nothing but the cold air. If she called out, she risked giving herself away. Her other senses slowly adapted to the pitch black and she could finally hear him breathing somewhere far away from her. Evie dared not leave the bed, and instead clinched her eyes and tried to regain control. There was no fire in the fireplace. Her teeth began to chatter, from either fright or freezing, she couldn't tell. She curled her knees up under her chin and wrapped her long arms around them, trying to focus on not shaking. She sat there for indefinite amount of time trying to center in on his breathing and track his location. Maybe she could get across the room and out the door. She assumed he couldn't see her just as she couldn't see him.

She noticed the breathing had moved. Evie turned her face and tried to reposition him in her mind, attempting to retain some sort of control over her senses. She felt a warm hand touch her back and jumped forward off the bed in surprise. His other hand caught her before she fell into the floor. She tried to pull herself away from his grasp but he caught her waist and pulled her close to him. Frantically, she tried to get away, only to be pulled down to the bed underneath him with her hands pinned above her head.

Evie's thoughts conflicted as she lay there, stretched out on the huge bed. Her arms were high above her, pinned down with one giant hand, and straddled by the faceless beast above her. She was hot for him, undoubtedly so. All the running away she had been doing was simply just running away from the truth. She knew in her mind that he wasn't her husband. This was a cold-blooded killer, and yet she flushed with anticipation. Her body betrayed her, feeling a very lonely ache below her stomach where he was currently perched over. How could she feel this way about another man? How could she let go of so many years with her husband, for a fleeting infatuation with a man whom she'd never seen? Yet she wanted to be here, under him and letting him take control. Feeling the hot tears escape her eyes, she tried to pull her hands down and met firm resistance.

"Tsk little one, be patient," he said quietly.

It was just enough to send her panic soaring again, this time in fight mode as she began to kick wildly and pull at her arms. He changed positions and laid almost completely on her with the weight of him stilling her legs. Her arms were now free from his momentary release, and she began punching as hard as she could on whatever skin she could land a blow. He rethought his decision to let go and caught both her wrists again with one large hand, pulling them back over her head. She heard him fumble around near them and then heard the ripping of fabric. Evie's heart lurched as she felt the velvet material being tied around her wrists tightly, and then to the nearest bedpost. He made a noise that sounded almost like a self-compliment and got up, leaving her lying there.

She quickly turned over on her belly and scooted up on all fours, her elbows bracing herself on the bed as she tried to shimmy off the over large monsters' bed, pulling on the restraints in an attempt to rip them. She had to get out of here somehow, before he changed her mind completely. Before she could put her feet down on the ground behind her, she felt the two hands again behind her, circling around her hips, the hardness from under his kilt pushing up against her behind. She heard him chuckle. She cursed under her breath taking notice of just what position she put herself. The curses just made him more amused, reminding her of how Evan used to chuckle at her random strings of profanities. She kicked backward with one foot, hoping to make contact with him, but he side stepped too fast and grabbed it, swiftly flipping her onto her back with the familiar crush of his body on top again.

"Impudent little imp, aren't ye?" His words burned a hole through her skin as he whispered them somewhere above her head. Evie used all her energy trying to dispel the feeling between her legs as he straddled her, his thighs crushing hers. The cat and mouse game was too much. She didn't know how much longer she would be able to fight, and not just give in from want and need, not because of defeat. She felt only the thin fabric between them and the heat radiating from his body. He was as turned on as she was. Evie couldn't stand it any longer. She had to try and talk her way out of this.

Working up the nerve to speak, Evie choked out the only words she could manage in a tiny whisper, "Please, don't hurt me." She waited for a response.

He went completely motionless as if stunned. Then, his reaction was swift. He placed both of his hands on either side of her face and leaned down; close enough for his whiskers to touch her cheek he responded in a near growl.

"Never."

Suddenly his mouth was crushing hers in a furious kiss. She was surprised at his almost angry reaction to her plea. Was this man who she had built him up to be? Why had he been so angry?

Evie became so lost in the feeling that her mind went blank. She was possessed by her carnal self, allowing herself to feel and not think of who exactly was parting her lips and rushing his tongue beside hers. His hands fell from her face to her neck and ran down the length of her body, leaving her skin goose bumped in its wake. He freed her breasts from the ties of her bodice and kissed them almost lovingly. He pushed her dress up to her waist, causing Evie to arch her body upwards into his in attempt to get closer to his attentions. He ran his hands over her soft stomach and thighs, breathless at the discovery he found in the dark. Evie had never worn underwear, and today wasn't any different. She was certain she heard him say, 'Thank you, God' right before he kissed her stomach—and she relished the contact.

Evie let out a small whisper of disapproval, yet it had no feeling behind it. She cursed herself for allowing this to happen, for going against her vows to Evan. She knew she would regret this later if she let it continue, yet didn't know how to make it stop, or if she did want him to stop. She was obviously not getting away and half of her wanted this, wanted him ... The nagging voice returned ... But what of Evan?

Her inner argument escalated with a sudden fury as Evie remembered the shirtless girl in his office. Faces flushed and Evan's hands holding her wrists just as Evie's wrists were tonight. Her mind flashed to the fight in the hallway on Halloween, at the mere mention if his infidelity. The way he finally submitted to the divorce papers. They were no more; she had no reason to resist this man. *He did this to me. If it's good for the goose is it good for the gander?*

Evie attempted to rationalize the feelings she was having as she noticed he had stopped kissing her stomach and had moved southward with his attentions. A moan escaped her lips and the reaction caused him to keep going with more intensity. He braced his hands on her hips as he worked her center with his mouth. The last shred of her inner conflict tore. Evie felt sudden relief of being tied to the bedpost in the pitch-black darkness in a castle in the middle of Scotland. She wrapped her legs around his back, arched upward toward him as she was quickly carried away, overcome with a flood of physical and emotional release.

As the tide of momentary bliss ebbed and her body completely relaxed in afterglow, she felt him leave her side. All the stress of the night was gone and left her languid. A contended sleepiness over took her, though her mind was not relenting to the same need for rest her body craved. Now with her body suddenly exposed, her head spinning with sensations of what just transpired, Evie was confused. She felt suddenly more alone that she felt in the months she lived here. Unable to figure out why, she felt completely shattered by his actions. Not because he had abducted her in the hallway and decided to abandon her vows and submit to him with very little resistance, thought they were good reasons, but because he left her laying there, cold and alone. The man who had apparently watched her every movement since the day he arrived at Dunvegan, the only person who has heard her speak, had used, and abandoned her. Feeling dirty and violated, she fought back the overwhelming sadness and refocused on his breathing, trying to find him in the dark. Hearing him farther away, she assumed he was in a chair that matched her room near the inactive fireplace.

Evie thought of more confusion. Why had he not taken her? He had only thought to touch her, to ignite a long lost passion in her, to coax her to climax in submission and yet he did not reach his own ecstasy. He moved away, actually leaving her longing for more. Without needing to accentuate the darkness, Evie closed her eyes trying to quiet the chaos in her head, and quickly fell asleep.

∞

Evan sat in the chair facing the bed with his head in his hands, feeling defeat mixed with disgust … *Just going to look for the Flag, huh?* He berated himself. Being that close to Evie for the first time in so long overtook him and once he had his hands on her, he was lost. His struggle with what he should do and what he wanted to do had driven him over the edge. Making himself stop before he made a bigger mistake left him in pain, both physically and mentally. His bride now lay asleep tied to his bed, most likely confused, and it was his fault. His mind was uproarious with conflict. His possessiveness over his wife had overflowed from the MacDonald who tried to debase her. He stood up for her in attempt to make her seem more of a person and less of an object. Yet here he was. Evie had fought him in the hallway, fought him on the way up to the room, pleaded with him, and then suddenly gave in with a cry of pleasure.

Did she possibly figure out who he was or did she honestly want to give herself to someone who wasn't her husband? He rubbed his face and sighed into his hands. He wondered if he should tell her now who he was and take his chances on her reaction. He mulled over how he should explain it to her quickly before she attacked him. He was confident that he knew his wife enough to know she would physically assault him once she knew his identity. If the bonfire was any indication, he knew her threats were not idle.

Evan knew there remained the benefit of her not knowing his existence here. Without her knowing, he could move freely and remain the fearless monster everyone had made him out to be and find the Fairy Flag. He may need her to hate him for now, so he could keep her safe. He also didn't want her to accidentally slip in their association and cause both clans to rally against them. They would both be stuck here and their children left orphans. He had to keep Evie safe. He decided for now, the solidarity and the anonymity would be essential in order to keep them both safe until the last possible moment. *But what the hell do I do now? She's half-naked in my bed waiting for something, anything at this point. I want to just lay down with her and hold her, to smell that hair that's been driving me crazy since I got here. To wrap up in her arms and feel home again. I could just bury myself in her until I blacked out, it still wouldn't be enough. I need all of her … When did I become such a bastard?*

With a temporary resolution reached, Evan stood slowly to return to Evie. He first opened the small doors that separated their rooms and let the small shaft of light inside. He then lied down beside her, listening to her slow and even breathing. He reached above her and untied her wrists, rubbing them. She sighed in her slumber and rolled over on her side, sliding one arm over his stomach and curled her head on his chest as they used to lie so long ago. Evan propped his head up with one arm behind it so he could see her. With the other hand, he delicately tucked a stray strand of hair behind her ear. He brushed the remaining tears from her cheek and she stirred. A smile touched her lips and his heart ached. She was the epitome of beauty and strength.

Reluctantly, he slid out from under her and stood up as soundless as possible. He remained near the bed in the darkness to watch her sleep, with deep longing. Knowing he had done enough damage, he must return her to her room partially unscathed before his will was tested again. He leaned over, slipped one arm under her head, one below her knees, and slowly lifted her off the bed. She sighed and put her face to his warm chest, wrapping her arms around his neck. Evan looked down upon her barely visible face, wishing he could hold her forever. *In time, man …*

Evan slowly walked to the small door, pushed it the entire way open, and carried her through. He gently placed her into her own bed. Tucking her into the covers, he took one last look at her peaceful face, knowing tomorrow, she would hate him again. He touched her cheek, and kissed her lightly. Noticing the chill of the room, he stoked her fire and exited in the same manner he entered, bolting his door behind him.

∞

Early the next morning, Evie woke slowly in her warm bed, with a slight smile on her face. She had a wonderfully glowing fire in the fireplace and someone had left her a plate of food in her room. Sighing in contentment, she arched her back and stretched her body from some of the best sleep she had since she was here.

She felt a twinge in her wrists. A blush covered her cheeks as she remembered the night before. Evie examined her wrists to find small bruises where from the velvet restraints. The whole scene flooded back to her … the stalking, the masterful way he eventually convinced her to follow his lead without struggle. His ability to make her beg for his affection. His uncanny way of making her feel so wanted, so needed.

She quickly left the bed, feeling soreness between her thighs she hadn't felt in a long time. Evie let something that resembled a growl out of her and decided to motion outside to the servants for a hot bath. Once the maid had wandered off, she sat down on the edge of the bed and stared vacantly into the fire. "What have I done?"

She recalled the event that led up to being tied up in his bedroom and realized it was inevitable. Evie knew she had no choice in the matter, and she had fought a hard fight against him. Nevertheless, it still made her feel guilty. He had used trick after trick to break down her barriers and what lay inside was frightening. All the emotions she had tediously stacked up over the years were toppling over. It was uncanny how he was able to know her mind and body as well if not better than she did … *Well I suppose the Devil has to know his stuff in order to gain that title.*

The maid had returned with help bringing in her copper tub and water just in time. Evie's mind was slowly unraveling into a panic attack at the thought of betraying Evan. She quickly removed her clothes and sank completely into the water hoping it would absolve her from her sins. As she let the steaming water sink into her skin she made a resolution. *Today I'll find out who he is. I'll brave Lily and ask her what she knows. I'll follow that redheaded monster around the castle until I figure him out.*

Chapter 17

The lists were cold and still dark. The men seemed unaffected as they flowed through their motions like a finely choreographed dance. Evie never got tired of watching them. With such precision, they ducked and dodged every attempt at contact with the large steel weapons. The noise of the clashing metal had become the same as a car siren in her modern world; almost non-existent until she focused on it.

She could see their breath in the cold air, a billow of dragon-like smoke that swirled around their heads as they bobbed and weaved. Evie took notice that they were insatiable in this fight, for the sword training seemingly never ended. Every day they were here, in bad weather and in good. The times spent here had lengthened with the threat of war with the MacDonalds, even though they trained with them at times. It was confusing and Evie wished she could understand exactly why they were allowing the two sets of men fight with each other. Nevertheless, training was training, no matter whom with, she figured. If they were going to learn some secret tactic, they would find out eventually. They did naught else other than train, eat, sleep, and spend time with families before or after the lists.

Evie often wondered what they would do if they were suddenly rendered without their weapons. She had never seen them train disarmed—just as it was the opposite in her world. She had never seen anyone but her husband train, and only with his hands and body strength. She never saw him with a weapon. He preferred to only to use his knowledge and raw power.

Evie skirted around the edges of the woods looking for the redhead, trying to remain hidden. She knew it was far too late to be out here, given that it was almost time for breakfast and Cook expected her to participate in helping serve; but she just wanted to be closer to the man. She rationalized that she just wished to see him in action with the long sword. His exploits had caused her to be morbidly curious of just what made him so different from the rest of Scotland's warriors. She padded on in her soft leather shoes in the snow, attempting to remain silent.

Reaching the closest point to him without compromising her obscurity, she was somewhat disappointed. There was no sign of a sword near him, with seemingly no chance of him joining in the practice. The giant man stood to the side, speaking with Creighton. He was standing at an angle, with his arms crossed over his chest, legs slightly spread as if to brace for something to knock him down. Standing this way, he reminded Evie of Evan. This was his stance too. He could stand like that and overtake a room. He dealt with high profile big shots and made multimillion dollar deals; standing just this same way. The memory was a jolt to Evie. Her face flushed as she ran her gaze over the monster that stood on the other side of the trees. She braced herself with one hand against the tree she leaned against and felt the bark dig into her hand ... Are genetics that strong that they could have carried down mannerisms hundreds of years down the line?

She forgot the rest of the men all together as she focused all her attention on his features. From here, they were masked by the dark and his angle. The torches helped very little in making out his details. Evie cursed herself for not taking a longer look at him in the great hall. She was too preoccupied with staring down, being angry and feeling sorry for the women and children who he had left widowed and fatherless. Now she found herself always craving to find out how red that hair was and how tall he was in comparison to Evan. She wished to hear his deep brogue again. She longed to find out if his eyes were the same shocking blue as her husband's. She already knew his hands were as strong and his stomach as ridged with muscles ... and the rest of him ...

The flush on her skin deepened and trailed down her chest as she remembered what was under his kilt when she had served him the first night he had arrived and what it might be capable of doing to her—what he had done with his ill-gotten kisses the night before, and what he did with velvet restraints.

The flush turned to a blaze as it ran down into the pit of her stomach and below. Was this monster capable of turning his rage into passion? She gripped the tree trunk harder, the bark hurting her hand in attempt to cast away the ache that had settled beneath her skirt ... *Not only does this murderer sicken me, I'm sickened at myself for thinking that way about anyone other than my husband. I'm sick at myself for reacting at all.*

Evie closed her eyes and pressed her face against her hand, the cold erasing the heat from her cheek, but unfortunately nowhere else. Reopening them, she focused in on him again, quickly realizing he had turned slightly away from Creighton, and was now facing her direction in the darkened woods.

Her heart skipped a beat and her breath caught in her chest somewhere as she felt like he was a hunter stalking her, the deer. She stared back at him, frozen in her place. From here, he looked so much like Evan it was frightening. Evie swallowed hard as she fought the visions of her clean cut husband from her mind. There was no room to think of him right now—no need to confuse the two. The man before her was not the obsessively clean and tidy man she thought. He was not the stuffed suit she complained about, nor was he the same person who could make her limbs tremble with a single cocked eyebrow and a crooked, dimpled grin. This man was not one to pine over. He was a cold-blooded killer; a soulless villain.

She panicked, watching him as he took a few steps in her direction and stopped. He turned away from her abruptly, walking off toward the castle. Her heart regained its normal pattern as she exhaled a breath, not realizing she had been holding one. Evie felt an odd sense of disappointment watching him walk away . Boy was it nice to see him leave. Her mind rebelled. *Oh do shut up, you twit. Although there's nothing wrong with a nice ass, this ass is attached to someone you need nothing to do with, no matter how freaking hot he is in the dark ...*

Evie watched to make sure he'd left the area as she made her way back to the kitchens to prepare for her next attempt at serving him. This time, she mused, she would get a good look at his face, no matter what.

Somewhere deeper in the woods, a cloaked man watched Evie as she made her way into the castle. He turned away from the scene unfolding before him and made his way deeper into the still dark morning.

∞

Evan had stood watching the men, listening to Creighton somewhere in the back part of his brain, prattling on about the men's training. He knew they all needed to keep keen on their skills, which is precisely why he had suggested the MacDonalds take up the swords out here so early. He had to get away from the intruding thoughts from what he had done last night.

He also knew nothing of sword training and trusted Creighton enough to let them hone their skills with little direction from him. However, the constant chatter from the chieftain was downright annoying at times. Like now. Evan stood with his arms crossed, looking out into the woods, feeling something was watching. He slowly scanned the area trying to find any movement. He stopped and turned back to Creighton, answering another mundane question about training then returned his focus to the woods. He knew he saw something, or someone. A flicker of the torches had cast a small light into the trees enough for him to catch a small whisper of breath. He strained his eyes to see, and finally made out the figure standing against a tree.

He stood still, the sounds of Creighton's voice fading into the distance as he heard nothing but the throb of his heart in his ears. She was watching him. His brows furrowed as he thought of her out there alone in the woods unprotected, far away from everyone's sight. He had the right mind to go fetch her and drag her back into the light where she would be safe. *Drag her back into my room and tie her back up. At least she'd stay out of trouble there ...* He was unable to take his eyes away. She was interested in what he was doing. She came to see him, in turn, putting herself in danger.

Evan had become even angrier as he saw a figure move behind her, farther in the woods. He couldn't make out anything other than a dark cloak, but knew for a fact that there was someone else in the woods with her.

Without taking his eyes off Evie or the figure behind her, Evan spoke slowly and carefully to Creighton, interrupting his chatter. "Chieftain, there are two people in the woods watching us. One is yer mute servant, and beyond her is a cloaked individual whom I cannae make out. Perhaps we should investigate in an inconspicuous manner."

Creighton didn't flinch or make any sudden moves, but nodded in silent acknowledgment. He lazily made way to a nearby clansman, advised him to work their way nonchalantly to the woods without making a scene, while keeping his eyes on both Evie and the stranger.

Unable to contain his anger, Evan made a few steps in her direction but stopped short, hearing Creighton's low voice behind him.

"Roy, hold. Let our men investigate. Doona fash, she shall be safe. Return to the castle and break yer fast. I have a feeling I ken who our cloaked stranger is."

Creighton motioned for the remaining men to continue training. Evan fumed, knowing the chieftain was right, and remembered how important anonymity was to make his stay here at Dunvegan work. He wanted to keep her safe himself. It was his job, not theirs. However, he to stay away from her and keep their relationship veiled until he found the Flag and returned them home safely. He vowed to keep his distance no matter how much it pained or vexed him. There would be no repeat of last night. He could take no more chances with his identity. He grunted his consent to Creighton, and stomped toward the castle, fighting off the urge to drag Evie to safety with every step.

∞

Lily was waiting in the corridor as Evie entered the castle. She caught Evie as she made her way into the kitchens and with a smile on her face; she took Evie by the arm and led her away into the buttery. Confused, Evie tenuously smiled back and took her escort, frantically thinking of what she had done to warrant such a greeting.

Once secured away from prying ears, Lily let go and leaned back on a large wooden crate. "Goodness, Evie, what have ye gotten yourself into?" The older lady giggled, the lines by her eyes accenting their glint.

Evie shrugged, eyes wide, wondering what the lady knew. Nervously, she searched the room for something on which to focus. Lily took her hand, forcing her to make eye contact.

"Lass, I ken more than ye realize. He's a fine man to gaze upon, but for all I ken, he is here to slaughter us all. Please take heed." She saw Evie blush and squeezed her hand in consolation. "Creighton tells me that Roy has asked of ye a fair amount. His intentions may be noble, but we cannae risk yer life to take a stroll out in the woods without an escort while he is here. From now on we will have one of the clan take ye from place to place."

Evie felt her freedom slipping away as her chest tightened …

Why would he be asking about me? What have I done that is so worthy of my notice? Does she know about last night? The look was apparently enough for Lily to comprehend somewhat and she answered. "Evie, ye are a fair comely lass. Most men in the keep take notice of yer beauty. And we both ken the fastest way to a man's heart is through his stomach, and almost all the men here would die on their own swords in order to keep ye safe."

Lily sobered as she saw the tears well in Evie's eyes. "Evie, doona think we are here to control ye. We just want to keep ye safe while that man and his people are here, until we can figure out exactly what the fate of our clan is and how to go about either keeping ye safe here, or elsewhere." She winked and started to leave.

Evie's heart pounded in her chest. *What did she mean, here or elsewhere? Where the hell would I go? I have no other home but here.* The words swirled around in her head as Lily exited the buttery, leaving Evie there, wishing she could blurt out the questions.

Now more than ever, she wished to have a confidant. She needed someone who she could trust in finding out answers. She suddenly felt dizzy knowing that the man she considered a monster was asking about her to others, not only trying to abduct her in the hallways. Unsure if it was a good or bad feeling, she steadied herself on the wooden crates in front of her.

Then there was the subject of an escort. Who would be in charge of her safety? Would she ever be allowed steal away moments on the battlements? How could she find the Flag with an escort? Evie wanted to kick herself for daring to go out in the dark. Taking that risk, she got herself caught and now her ability to be invisible among the ranks had vanished.

She steadied her breathing and stood upright, waiting for the waves of dizziness to fade. Steeling herself as she had done over and over again throughout her years, she wiped away the welling tears, smoothed out her dress with shaking hands, took a deep breath of composure and stepped out of the room into the brightly lit kitchens to finish the next meal.

∞

Sitting in the great hall to Creighton's right, Evan searched the room for a missing man. He was determined to flesh out who was in the woods behind Evie earlier. So far, everyone looked in attendance. He nodded to Creighton, who was also scanning the audience.

"Ye said earlier ye might ken who the mystery man was?" Evan asked quietly to Creighton, attempting not to raise the suspicions of his wife Lily, who was sitting at Creighton's left. The chieftain leaned back in his chair and moved his head slightly to address him.

"Aye, I have my suspicions, but I doona have proof yet." Evan nodded to him in understanding, unwilling to believe the man was not sure.

"The lass will be under careful watch, do not worry," Creighton added, noticing Evan's tight expression. Evan noticed too and attempted to relax and feign apathy. He couldn't argue with Creighton in fear of raising Creighton's suspicion of why he might show concern for Evie. He swallowed down the urge to demand the chieftain to hunt down and beat the hell out of whomever was following his wife. If the old man knew and trusted his lack of action, he must have to follow his lead for now.

Dropping the crust of bread he had been pushing food around with, he looked into his trencher as he took a drink. He paused and noticed the stranger staring back again. He took a drink, feeling the burn of alcohol making its way to his stomach; the familiar warmth and eventual relaxation making its way to his aching mind.

He had seen nothing of Evie since earlier this morning and wondered where she was. He thought of seeing her here in general and realized she was, given the circumstances, at ease and happy. Evan hoped she would remain happy after she saw him. Alternatively, would she return to the distant, cold, detached grieving soul she had become; totally consumed with her mother's death? He wished there was just some answer in this mess that could ease her pain. It hurt him to watch her suffer through her sorrow. He knew though, Killie taught to hold her own. Killie was ruthless on the instruction of what she considered polite society. "Never show weakness." She had also been adamant about the insane ranting she bestowed on her daughter too. She wanted Evie to listen to it as gospel, but then said, "Never explain anything I've shared with you to anyone," she drilled. Though in her last days, she tried so hard to do just that—tell everyone. But what was there to be told? It didn't make sense to Evan right now, but there had to be a reason behind all the madness … now more than ever.

Maybe Evie had a clue, he thought. Maybe she knew and that was why she was so at ease here. He drained the contents of the tankard, extinguishing the stranger that stared accusingly at him, and excused himself to his chambers. He bowed to the chieftain and his wife as he left to seek out the solitude of his own windowless room.

∞

Evan's routine here was quite much like the routine at Dunscaith. He would wake up and break his fast with the chieftain and his wife at the High Table, discuss the day's training, then meet outside with the men. Usually, he had no problem with them cooperating between both clans, but some days he ended quarrels and fights by allowing the feuding men to battle it out on their own. However, Evan only allowed them to use fists, never swords. This, for the MacDonalds was fine because they had prior knowledge of Evan's technique. For the MacLeods, it was a learning experience.

The MacDonalds picked up on the moves quickly though, and within a couple of weeks, they split their training time equally with swords and hand-to-hand. Upon learning the new martial arts, the fighting between the clans became daily training and general anger management therapy for them all. It rarely ended badly. Evan was satisfied there only had been a few minor breaks of noses and one hand between them all. They only baited Evan into a fistfight once by an angry MacLeod, which ended as quickly as it started. Evan rendered the man unconscious with a quick sleeper hold and resumed teaching as if nothing was out of the ordinary. Just as he had taught the MacDonalds, he welcomed the challenge. He knew he would encounter this, given the reputation and the underlying reason he was here. Evan actually expected more. However, he found they were generally accepting, which Evan found curious. Once Creighton had offered hospitality, the clan followed suit. He was still convinced something was missing from the equation.

His crowds for training had increased in size and now he would train more than a hundred men on any given day. The current area for training was always full and they eventually had to move out into a larger area outside the castle gates in the woods. This was good two fold. He had room to teach the men without notice by Evie and he could keep an eye out for the mysterious man who Creighton stayed tight lipped about.

On the days he wasn't involved with training, he watched after Evie from a distance. She was not taking to her escort easily and as he had heard it said many times at home, "Catching Evie is like nailing jelly to a tree." She would outsmart her guards and having a newfound quietness, she would escape for hours at a time before they would realize she was gone. Evan would keep an eye on her as she moved throughout the courtyard and beyond when he could, but was having a hard time with the number of men who showed up for training. He had more fun watching her escorts bicker to their chieftain about what a pest she was. Creighton's standard response was, "She's just a wee slip of a lass, how can it be so difficult?" Oh Evan knew how difficult. He had been trying to keep up with her for eighteen years. He was equally surprised she was even going along with the charade just as much as she was escaping them all. Evan knew Evie better than anyone. She was hardheaded, strong, and refused help, no matter the reason.

Evan unfortunately noticed her taking to her chamber earlier in the evening; most times directly after the evening meal was finished. It was the same tonight. He knew she must be miserable having someone following her. Evie was fiercely independent and hated having someone on her heels at every turn. Only Creighton, Lily, and he knew it was due to the damned stranger he wanted to catch and it was a necessary evil. If Evie were only aware someone was out to cause her harm, she might understand. As soon as he finished eating, he inconspicuously retired after her and made sure she found herself safely in her room, directly beside his.

Behind the closed garderobe door, Evan heard her cry. In all of his years together, he had only heard her cry four times—at each birth of their children and the death of her mother. His heart broke to hear her wracked with sobs. He restrained himself from going next door and holding her. Instead, he finished the whisky on his side bar and rested, waiting impatiently for the day he would be able to hold her in his arms again.

∞

Evie's heart ached as she curled up on the bed in a ball, her arms tucked under her knees. Evie hated them following her like a toddler all day. She was unable to think clearly in the kitchens and was equally unable to focus on what was going on outside. She found herself obsessing over catching a minute or two away from her escorts just to get a glance of the redheaded monster who was now apparently training all the men of Dunvegan. He had scores of men who wanted to see him.

Hoping it was to create a mob big enough to destroy the man, she found that they wanted to train with him, not against him. It made her stomach turn. She found out through her loudmouthed guards that the Ruadh Donas was letting the clans fight each other when they got angry; which apparently was often considering how much hand to hand combat she saw on a daily basis. She wondered why they were all rolling over like dogs for this man to scratch their bellies. Nothing made sense here anymore, if it ever did before.

The days and weeks went by quickly if she kept herself busy. Nighttime was difficult. She wasn't able to steal away to the battlements anymore, so in order to find solace, she found herself retiring to her chambers early. Having nothing else to do and refusing to take up embroidery or other busywork, she would give up and go to bed, just like tonight.

Evie abhorred company of these men so much she had to get away to the only place she had left. She felt like she was the one punished for a crime she didn't commit. Overwhelmed at times, she found herself falling asleep as soon as her head hit the pillow. The burn of homesickness hurt. Though she missed her children terribly, she found herself missing Evan the most. All the time she spent alone since her night with the stranger had been full of vivid dreams and thoughts of only him. Waking from them was so intolerable she found herself crying as soon as her eyes opened, not wanting them to end. She just wanted to feel his arms around her, to see his lopsided smile telling her it was going to be all right; that he had it under control. She vowed before her eyes fluttered shut for the last time that she would fight her hardest to get back home and listen to every single word he had to say... if just given the chance.

Chapter 18

There were weeks that went by and no one at Dunvegan saw the stranger from the woods. After much conversation and pleading from Lily, and tiring of watching Evie silently mope, Creighton decided to allow her a little less guarded time. Evie felt as if she had a noose taken off her neck. She would go on her daily duties alone, but if she exited the building for any reason, they would follow. Though it was more likely she find herself abducted inside the castle than outside, Evie thought sarcastically, but if it gave her the opportunity to be a little freer, she would take it and run.

The day dragged on for Evie. She could think of nothing else but the sun that shone down outside. She could feel the great winter reluctantly giving in to spring. With the continuous snow and sleet finally letting up, she also knew that meant Roy MacDonald's days at Dunvegan were numbered and that left her confused. She wanted the man to leave and let her get back to finding the Flag on her own, but some part of her didn't want him to leave at all. The man had worked his way into her mind and wouldn't let go. When she wasn't pining over the wrongs she felt she had done her husband, she was trying to find him. Conflicted, she didn't know what she wanted other than to see his face up close.

Longing to be anywhere but in the kitchens, she decided after the noontime meal that enough was enough. She was taking the day off. Ignoring her orders to stay on the grounds, she decided she was getting out of the kitchens to explore. Escort be damned. She hadn't been able to do much since she had been put straight to work and she wasn't about to let anyone stop her, including that redheaded beast. Evie untied her apron and tossed it absently on the counter. She gave a quick smile and wave to Cook who grumbled his noncommittal response as she left through the side door into the warm sunlight.

Evie saw the men practicing in the courtyard. As she walked by, she forced herself to not to look at any of them, especially Roy MacDonald. She didn't want to give him any sort of power over her. Not today, she thought. It was her day off from him too. Yet instinctively, she felt his eyes on her as she left through the portcullis and she blushed. She decided to swing her hips a tad bit much, just for the hell of it. "He wants a show, he can have it," she snickered. Untying the ribbon holding her braided hair, she ran her fingers through the brown waves as she left his sight. Looking to the crystal blue sky enjoying the breeze as she strolled, she wondered what the wind would bring about next. During March in Virginia, she grew up hearing, "If you don't like the weather here, wait a minute." She wondered if the phrase rang true in the Highlands at the cusp of springtime.

Evie followed a small trail toward the sound of rushing water. Never having been good with directions, she knew the bare basics. If you listen hard enough to the world around you, it's possible to pick out a noise you recognize. Back in her time, it was more cars, trains, and sirens. Here it was nothing but nature. She followed the sound of the water and easily found a stream, with a nice large, flat, boulder beside its edge, perfectly positioned in the sun.

Evie explored around the stream examining the flora, picking up stones and skipping them across the water as she had done so a million times at home. Evan had spent half a day teaching her how and when she finally mastered it, she did a little victory dance when she hadn't just chunked it into the water for the hundredth time.

Having such little tomboys for daughters, she remembered playing with the twins in the creek behind her mother's house. They would pick up tadpoles and roly-polys and "save" them in jars. Mason was, of course, too serious even at an early age to be bothered with such nonsense. Evie smiled in the bittersweet memories. Looking around for any sign of life in the stream, she found a few little fish circling around her feet. The water was icy, but she didn't care. *Not today ... I'll warm up in the sun in a bit ...*

Wanting to see if she could find any tadpoles in the deeper end of the stream, she stepped gingerly on a mossy rock, instantly finding out grace was not on her side as she slipped and fell into the water up to her armpits. Cursing, she untangled her soaked mass of dress material, shivered with cold, and stumbled back up toward the rock in the sun. Unable to wring all the water out of her dress, she weighed her options. *Walk back to the castle and endure a ton of questions thereby ruining my day off or strip and warm up in the sun while stupid medieval dress-that-could-get-me-killed dries out?* The answer was obvious. She stripped the long dress off and threw it over a limb nearby. Feeling rather hedonistic, she wrung her hair out and stretched in the sun like a cat.

Deftly climbing up on top of the large rock, she tried not to repeat the fall into the water and laid down. The rock was warmer than she thought. She closed her eyes and sighed in momentary bliss. Even with her dip in the stream, Evie felt that this was the most relaxing moment she had since she got here. *Well except that one morning …*

Trying to shut out the memory, she began to doze in the heat of the sun while her mind betrayed her of someone else warming her body.

The face she couldn't see, but her sleepy mind replaced it with Evan's face. Even though it was all wrong, her dream didn't try to replace it with the stranger. She soon found herself reliving the moments in the dark room by replacing her husband's hands with her own in the sun. Haunted by his touch, her sleepy mind reflected on the guilt she harbored for feeling such pleasure with anyone other than her husband. The surge of emotion tied to the surge of heat that rushed to her lower extremities was overwhelming. Reaching the crescendo of her own pleasure, she woke up from her doze with a startled outcry for her husband.

She gasped and her eyes flew open. Evie looked around and wondered if someone had been there. She didn't see anyone, but felt someone's presence. Feeling an overwhelming sense of modesty, she blushed from head to toe and went to her dress. It was still damp but she put it back on as best as she could and sat back down on the rock with her head in her hands. "What a fool am I?"

She hated herself for what she let happen the other night, but hated it more that she wanted Roy MacDonald at all. She wanted to feel him inside her, pounding her full of the guilt she felt. She knew it was wrong, but she wanted him to finish what he had started. *Maybe if he did finish, I could go on with my life …* It almost angered her how she felt toward the man. She wanted him to just abuse her and give her a reason to hate him; to wash away the feeling of his almost-caring hands holding her face and caressing her skin and to wash away those almost-loving kisses that were on her lips … and hips. She wanted to erase his angry cry of "never" to her plea of not harming her, and it would replace it with the hurt. Then she could rationalize the whole man and put it to rest. Maybe then …

Evie left her rock and stared to the sun, trying to make out what time it was. Her day off was tainted by the red head after all. She figured she might as well go back to work … *At least that will keep my mind occupied. I obviously can't have a day off without thinking of the beast …*

∞

Evan saw Evie walk into the woods and excused himself out of the courtyard with a curt nod from Creighton. If no one else were going to watch her, he would have to be the one to do it. Although, he did much prefer that to the alternative of a stranger watching. He knew the man remained hidden since the first time in the dark weeks ago, but he still feared her safety. He also knew Lily hadn't given Evie the full reason she was to stay under watch; therefore, Evie would take any opportunity to escape that she could. Knowing someone watched her, Evan's heart raced as he watched her enter the woods.

Putting safe distance between them, he watched as Evie wandered the forest, stopping to examine the new buds on the trees, and picking up flat stones around the water's edge. She looked lost in thought. Evan noticed every little thing about her. So beautiful she was to him, with her hair down, blowing around her face in the breeze. The reflection of the water cast flickers of light on her, causing her eyes to shine. She smiled as she crouched down and skipped the stones across the water. He wondered if she was remembering the times they had spent as a family near the creek, doing the same exact thing. He wondered if she remembered how he had taught her how to skip rocks. She was so happy over such a simple thing. He smiled at the memory himself as he watched her stand up and cross the stream stepping on rocks; and had to stop himself from going to help her as she fell straight into the water, landing on her rear. Hearing her curse, he ducked down below the brush he stood beside and stifled his laughter. He forced down his smirk and turned to her direction to see through the brush. What he saw struck him dumb. *She's taking off her dress for God and everyone to see ...*

The humor drained from his face as he watched her strip down to nothing and threw her heavy dress over a branch. He frantically looked around the woods to make sure no one was watching but him. He crept closer to her to make sure he was in a position to attack someone if needed; and well, get a better look. Still, Evan couldn't believe she would be so brazen as to leave the castle grounds alone, traipse into the woods alone and then expose her to every element known to man.

He watched furiously as she climbed up and laid down on a nearby rock. She was so trusting and totally oblivious to everything around her. Evan watched as she lazily closed her eyes and stretched out with her face to the sun. He was close enough to hear her sigh and watched with rapt attention as she began to stroke herself in a round of self-admiration. Evan found himself not able to blink. He had to stand up hopefully out of her eyesight to make sure no one else was watching and because his crouch had become painful with the bulge in his pants.

He thought of the way she had walked out of the courtyard, flinging her hair back and swinging her butt as if she owned the place.

The more he thought about it and the more he watched her pay self-respects so wantonly in the sun, the angrier he became. Her intentions were now clear to him. Convinced she had led him into the woods on her own volition to bait him, Evan turned around without caring she could see him and stalked off back to the castle grounds.

As he exited earshot, she cried out in her rapture. "Evan ... "

∞

He paced the shadows outside her chamber door awaiting her return. He fully intended to throttle her for taking such a risk outside. Yet, Evan knew she was unaware of the dangers that lurked behind her and the man who followed her. *Other than me ...* Taking a deep breath, he opened and closed his fists in attempt to relax.

Creighton's suspicions were still unknown or untold to Evan and it infuriated him. *I'd feel so much better if I could just get rid of whoever it was and be done ...* He froze in his tracks with the thought. For in that moment, it was the first time in his life he considered ending someone's existence. He crossed his arms over his chest and mused. It made perfect sense. Evie was his only love; of course, he'd kill for her without question. If he could only find out who it was, maybe they could solve the mystery. Creighton's mood darkened when Evan mentioned it yet he still never made a move to approach the stranger—another thing to annoy Evan.

He paced a few more steps back and forth in the darkness. He hated himself for wanting to lure Evie in and hated himself for being the same kind of predator he so despised. Yet there he was, lurking, ready to take what was not his. Losing the anger, he turned around to open his chamber door and go in until he heard footsteps. Caught off guard, Evan smelled the familiar smell of Evie before he heard her approach.

Just talk, nothing physical. I'll tell her who I am. Then she can slap the fool out of me ... that's all ...

The soft smell of sandalwood made his heartbeat quicken, knowing what he really want to do with her. However, this time he had planned to reveal himself, not let his body control the situation as it did the other night.

He turned around to face the hallway still guarded by the shadows of his recessed doorway and watched her saunter by. She slowed to a stop as she reached where he stood and raised her head, not looking in his direction.

"I know you're there," Evie whispered, causing Evan's heart to miss a beat. He could tell she was nervous. Her breath shook with every word. He raised his hand to touch her, letting it roam up her arm, past her shoulder, resting his fingers on her cheek. She took a tentative step toward him and he dropped his hand in surprise ... *Is she submitting to me? The stranger?*

He reached out again to take her hand and she responded by gripping his. Evan silently opened his chamber door and pulled her into the darkness, shutting it behind them.

She stood in the middle of the room. It was so dark it could have been space. Her eyes hurt in attempt to draw in any light. The room was frigid again without the fire. Evie shivered immediately in response. Her senses swam as she recalled the first meeting in this room.

"What do you want, you murderous bastard?" Evie knew she

was pushing her luck, possibly putting herself in danger, yet she didn't care. She was in no mood for real words or sappy emotions. She wanted to feel his fury. "If you want to hide in the dark like a coward, you can show me the door. I have no time for it." *Ever heard of poking the hornet's nest with a stick?*

All Evan's good intentions fell to the wayside. All the worrying he had done over her in the last few days came down crashing. He made no sound as he circled around to face her. He grabbed her by both arms and threw her against the wall, almost knocking the breath out of her. She didn't care. Evie wanted this. She wanted a reason to despise him. Yet he didn't abuse her. No, he made her wish for more.

The darkness took away all distractions. She had nothing to focus on but his touch. He pressed the length of his body to hers, kissing her neck. She opened her mouth to hurl more insults at him, but he was kissing it before she had a chance to inhale. She became nervous, no longer sure of what she wanted, but still unwilling to fight. She wanted to scream out obscenities to him, yet she held still. Every moral fiber in her body was ripping away with every stroke of his fingers, every lick of his tongue.

He released her from the wall and knocked her knees out from under her. Evan caught her and pushed her onto the stone floor a split second before she landed. He kissed her furiously as he poised himself above her, grinding his hips into hers, scraping her backside into the cold ground. She moaned a cross between protest and coercion. Evie grabbed his hair in both hands, pulled his head back, and bit his neck. Growling, Evan pushed his hips forward again, rocking his painfully hard erection against her mound in response. She wrapped her legs around his waist, pulling his head down to hers with his hair still caught in her grasp.

"Show me what the Ruadh Donas has," Evie hissed in his ear as she nipped at it with her teeth. She reached down with one hand and grabbed his full length from under his kilt, causing him almost to climax with the abrupt contact. He grabbed her hands away and threw them over her head, holding them with one hand. Kissing her ruthlessly, he grasped her breast a little rougher than he intended with the other. She yelled out, either in pleasure or pain, and Evan pulled away, panting. Regaining his senses, Evan jumped up and stepped away from her with his mind and body arguing … *Just talk,*

*remember? But she's begging for it. She wants me back; finally …
though it's not me she wants. Dammit!*

He knew he shouldn't do this. It felt wrong, no matter how she was reacting tonight. However, seeing her acting so at ease earlier today, taunting him at the creek side, he knew for a fact that Evie was baiting him. These last few nights alone with the taste of her still in his mind had taken the patience of a saint not to go to her. She was trying her hardest to make his life hell … And it was working.

He heard a huff from the floor. Material began to rustle as she got up off its cold surface.

"God, you're a slow bastard," she spat. He heard her fumble around for the door handle.

Her accent made him melt. Yet, after spending the evening brooding, he'd had enough. Sainthood be-damned. He wandered noiselessly toward her, took her by the arm, and pulled her back into the room.

"I'll show ye slow," he snapped, tossing her to the bed with one hand. She fell on it, splayed on her stomach. Trying to turn over, Evan stopped her by putting both hands on either side of her waist. He pulled her hips up to him and pushed his rigidness against her behind.

"Ye keep ending up like this. Trying to tell me something?"

"Would, 'you're an insensitive beast' sound any better with my ass in the air?"

"Aye. It would, actually," he laughed wickedly. He pushed her skirts up above her waist and felt her smooth skin … *Thank you again for the lack of underwear that my wife finds comfortable …*

Evie bit back any noise that tried to escape her mouth, trying to remain in control … *So, how's that working for you?* She let out a sigh and pushed back toward him, wanting to feel him against her, inside her. Evan spread the span of both hands around her waist and turned her around to lay her on the bed. He then dipped his head down to her most sensitive place as she inhaled sharply.

"Still feel like insulting me, lass?" he growled as he ran his hands along her thighs and back to where his mouth was. She writhed in pleasure.

"Yep. Maybe later though."

Evan chuckled as he pleasured her agonizingly slow with his

mouth. He would pause, and she grabbed his head and pushed him back down to her. She felt so guilty for wanting this so bad. He stopped her hands and his attentions, rising to whisper in her ear.

"Am I still a slow bastard?"

"Yes," she hissed. Her heart ached as badly as her body did. He slipped a finger inside her, feeling her physical response. He struggled to control himself. Raking his cheek against her skin, her breasts tightened in reaction. She hated him for the way he made her feel. She hated her traitorous body. She was so hot, so ready for him and he knew it. She couldn't hide no matter how dark it was.

"Shall I be any other way?" he whispered into her ear, causing her face to flush with desire, followed by a surge of anger. Evie was tired of the tease. "Go to hell," she spat, and she slapped him across the mouth.

Evan's temper flared. He ran his hands along her stomach as he pulled away from her face, positioning himself between her thighs. He pulled her behind toward him with both hands.

"I'm the Devil, remember? I'm already there." He thrust himself deep into her, causing her cry out in the darkness. Evie's mind went blank with the onslaught of sensations and against her better judgment; she was damn ready to beg for more.

Evan froze. She tried to grind her hips into him but he refused to move. His hands locked tight around her waist. He knew this was wrong. He knew if he gave into motion, his desire would consume him. The lure of her long legs wrapped around his waist and being buried in her most carnal place was intoxicating. *Leave. Pull away and leave before there's more damage done ...*

"Please, don't stop." Her hoarse whisper came from the darkness so unexpectedly, his skin tingled, and all his muscles flexed in response. His manhood throbbed deep inside her, reacting to her voice. Evie reached out and touched his stomach with one hand, then joined it with the other. Wrapping herself around his waist with all her limbs, she pulled up to press her face against his chest. Evan was statuesque in his stillness, fighting to maintain any control. He supported her with both hands under her behind, their bodies still connected.

"Finish this before I go crazy. Don't make me beg ... I need this as much as you do."

It was all the convincing he required. All logic left his mind as he held her up under her arms and lay down with her, turning over to position her on top of him … *Let her make this decision. Let her control this … if she wants this stranger—let her have him …* She took initiative and rode him hard into bliss, her cries of orgasm thundering in his ears as he was assaulted with wave after wave of this forbidden moment.

This is what Adam must have felt like biting that apple …

Evie collapsed after a second round of more silent, urgent lovemaking. Exhausted. Evan savored the moment, listening to her sleep. Her hair splayed out on his chest and her fingers curled around his. He had developed a massive headache with all the thoughts swirling around, pushing his guilt to maximum capacity. He knew tonight was wrong; very wrong. He just didn't know to what extent. Tomorrow he knew he would have to answer a slew of questions.

His head pounded. He had to get away from her before he did something worse. She deserved to know the truth. Evan slid out from under her with little resistance and picked her up. He returned her to her own bed through the tiny garderobe door, pausing to cover her up. *Please forgive me, Evie …* He kissed her on the cheek and left her side, with a strange hope that it wasn't for the last time.

He stoked her fire on his way out and locked the small door behind him. He lit a candle in his chamber and put on his kilt again. He had to get out of this castle before he went crazy.

Chapter 19

The rain chilled her to the bone. She had been wandering aimlessly on the castle grounds, trying to find him in the dark, filled with near madness. Evie had no idea why she felt compelled to leave the warmth and dryness of her room, but she couldn't bare the thoughts anymore of what had happened to her the night before. Her mind tortured her soul and heart. She could still feel his hands on her body; his smoldering kisses that burned her skin. The lust for this man she had never seen and the lust she had earlier in that afternoon for her husband—the one she couldn't have. She fought to push the thoughts away as she drifted farther into the thicket of trees that surrounded the castle.

Something, somewhere in the recesses of her mind told her it was a bad idea to go seeking him at an unknown time of morning, but she ignored her better judgment. She had to find him. She had taken enough in the last day. The Ruadh Donas had taken from her the clarity she had always maintained for her husband. He made her doubt herself and her vows. Yet she was so incredibly fascinated with this stranger it was overtaking her entire life. She had cast him in a light of such a monster for so long it was difficult to wrap her mind around this different person with whom she had come in contact. He was a vile creature in her mind, yet she craved his touch, and that made it even more despicable. Evie didn't understand how he could be so passionate about her; and yet take lives without a second glance. It didn't make any sense. Evie thought to be taken in a violent rage would have been far more acceptable than what he had done instead. He made her want him, to writhe beneath him. He made her beg, out loud no less, to take her. And she was furious, right before he did take her. *Why am I so different? Why would he murder so many and not want to harm me?* Yet he had harmed her in the worst way possible. She felt herself drowning in guilt for her desire. He had manipulated her beyond reasoning. She had vowed to see his face, even if it was just to slap it again. She had to see his eyes to make sense of it all.

She woke in her room, feeling confused and battered, yet … sated? He left her in mental pieces. She'd sprung from her warm bed and left her room seeking him, with no other reason than just to see his face. She pounded on the door to his room. It swung open, revealing an empty bed. The visions of the moments she'd stolen in that bed sealed from all light sent heat to her face. Her hands began to shake. She entered in a fury, ripped off the bedclothes, and threw them in the floor. A small wood handled knife fell out from them and clattered on the stones. She picked it up and stared at it, wondering why he'd sleep with a knife … *Was he trying to kill me? Did he have another plan?*

Renewed rage seared through her as she shoved the sgian dubh into her stocking, and turned around to scan the room. She knocked over his side table and water basin, splashing water all over herself and the floor. The water pitcher rolled to her feet and she picked it up to smash it against the stone wall. She picked up a discarded shirt from the night before and threw it in the fire. He had made her betray herself. Her family. Her husband. The realizations had made her stagger. Tears started to fall, causing her to lose control; the control she had built up over years of practice and need. The control her mother had always told her to have because, "Southern ladies never make a scene. They smile, push the pain down, and walk it off." Her mental stitching had come unraveled. She had stood in the middle of the mess, a hysterical laugh coming from her lips.

"He would have been better off killing me," she hissed, staring at the mess she made. Contemplating setting the entire room on fire, she left quickly, slamming the door behind her. She had to find him. Right now. It had to be settled.

She searched for him further in the maze of halls. Still disoriented about the time, Evie had wondered if it were early, or late enough in the morning for practice. Flashes of lightning were the only glimpses of the halls she walked. *Damn spring weather!* Thunder began to echo through the halls. She had decided to sneak out of the building to find him in the lists, if it were possible that no one heard her temper tantrum upstairs. So Evie made her way to the castle gates and left the confines into the coming thunderstorm.

Unfortunately, it was earlier than she originally perceived. She hadn't slept as long as she had thought, and it was still so very dark, even darker with the rain. She could not find the men anywhere. The storm had taken her by surprise. Instead of retreating into the castle, she forced herself toward the woods where she thought they would be. *Worst idea yet.*

Now she found herself outside as the wind whipped through the trees causing branches to swipe at her face. One too many wrong turns and no moon in the sky to guide her now turned her around. The cold rain poured down as the lightning briefly lit her way through the nightmare of trees. She assumed she was headed in the right direction, however couldn't find the usual break in the woods that was used for fight training. She kept going, running into the woods headlong.

The cold rain was overwhelming her. She wrapped her tartan tighter and closed her arms around her shoulders, but it wasn't enough. Cursing under her breath at her own stupidity, she heard the snapping of branches behind her. She jumped at the suddenly different noise from the rain on the leaves. She heard the snapping again, making her believe she was closer to the lists than she thought. *The men are close. Just got turned around in this nasty weather. Breathe. Just breathe. It's okay.*

With a brief sense of relief, she turned and began to run in the direction of the noise. Evie pushed through the uncut path, hoping it was the right way. The rain soaked her to the core, leaving her trembling in the cold.

She stopped suddenly, surprised, finding herself in the middle of a clearing she'd never seen before. She turned around quickly, trying to figure out where she was. Nothing looked familiar. And now she was very lost. Who was in the woods?

The sharp pain was so sudden she had no time to panic. She turned slowly to face where the strike had come from and saw nothing but the trees she was desperately trying to escape. She picked up her skirts and tried to run back the way she came but the pain was too overwhelming. Evie reached around to feel what had struck her. A short arrow was lodged in her side. She pulled back a bloody hand and stared at it, the rain washing it away almost immediately. Anger flared in Evie's eyes as the burning sensation in her lower back spread down through her leg. She started to run against the pain, knowing it was for her life.

With the pain overtaking her senses, she tripped and fell to her knees. She braced herself against a mossy tree, unable to go anymore. She reached behind her again with an shaking hand and broke off the arrow, screaming at the searing sensation it caused. She tried to stand again, hoping the broken arrow would lessen the pain, and shrieked, falling back to the ground. Sudden warmth washed over her as she rolled over to look at the sky, her pale upturned face wet with rain and tears. Her vision blurred, and the rain seemed to fall in slow motion as she looked up into the trees. She struggled to remember breathing techniques from a discarded yoga class and slowed her heart rate.

Save the energy for the big fight. *If whoever it is shows his face, maybe I can jump up and defend myself…* She began to retrace the few things Evan had taught her for self-defense. *Aim for the eyes and the windpipe. If they can't see or breathe, they can't do much.* Evie remembered the sgian dubh in her stocking and winced as she bent in half to retrieve it from her clothing. Clutching it in her shaking hands, she tried to concentrate on the movements of what she had been taught, yet her mind kept slipping to Evan's face, looking upon her in adoration. She choked on a sob.

So this is how I'll die; in the woods with a broken arrow in my back. I had high hopes of dying old and crazy like my mother or rocking on the front porch in Virginia drinking tea with Evan. So much for hope. With any luck, I'll die out here. Then Evan won't ever have to know about my failing him. He'll never know that I had betrayed his vows. He'll still love me, if he does at all anymore. My soul will be free. Not so bad … Come on, death. I don't fear you anymore.

Evie laid there, with little feeling in her legs. She was waiting for the pain to subside in her back; waiting for the blackness to overtake her. She wished her assailant would come back to finish the job. She was so cold now she was numb. She was no longer shaking and the occasional stab of pain was the only thing keeping her awake. The thunderstorm faded away but the rain had only slowed to a light shower as Evie wished to drown by it. She was unaware of how long she laid there. She noticed the clouds beginning to lighten with the rising sun and said a prayer to be let go soon.

If there is a God, please be nice to my kids. Make Mason smile more. Tell the girls to go to college. Be nice to Evan. Tell him I'm sorry. He deserves so much more than a sham of a wife I've turned out to be. Let the person who replaces me be more caring, more in tune to him, full of love and openness and less of a failure at being emotionally attached. He deserves the sun and the moon, not the blackness of night that I have become to him ...

Evie turned her head to the side and watched the rainfall as if the sky were crying, and began to close her eyes. She heard branches snapping in the distance, and very low voices talking, as they grew nearer. She heard someone call her name, but she knew she couldn't speak. Even if she wanted to find her voice, it was gone. She knew she should at least reach out, but she didn't. Evie had already made up her mind. She wanted to leave this world behind, to abandon this wretched place without the love she had failed. She wanted to leave the monster that had made her betray herself by making her want him. She briefly thought of trying to take her own life with the knife she clutched, but couldn't bring herself to do it. *I'll die soon enough ...* She tucked it back into the folds of her skirt and laid her hands out beside her, palms opening to catch the rain.

She heard footsteps approach her as she stared off to the side, hoping they'd pass her off as dead and leave her to the animals. Evie heard the low velvet voice of Roy MacDonald and she sighed, turning her head to face the sound. *So he came to find me ...* She saw him ordering people around. He appeared to be leading a large group of men and Creighton right beside him. After everyone dispersed, he took a few steps closer to her and stopped. She tried to focus on his face but he was too far. He acted as if he wanted to go to her, but couldn't. He was rooted to the ground. Creighton, however, ran to her side and began to speak softly to her. She couldn't understand a word the man was saying. She was trying too hard to focus on the large redheaded beast that stood too far away.

Of course I can't see his damn face. This is just par for the course. I'll die and never see his eyes ... Emotion overtook her. She let out a hoarse cry and reached out for her mystery man with the last ounce of strength she had left. He began to run toward her in what seemed like slow motion. Evie sighed in relief and everything seemed to shimmer right before the world went black.

"There now, love. Rest ye head. All is well, I am here, " the velvet voice said.

∞

She was having the loveliest dream. Evan was beside her. His sweet voice whispered in her ear. She was playing with his hair. She was so hot though. She tried to kick the covers off but couldn't get her feet to cooperate. Evie struggled to roll over but something held her down.

"Lay still, honey. You don't want to hurt yourself," Evan said. She wanted to do right by him, so she lay still, not knowing exactly what he meant. But if there was anything she wanted to do was be a good wife. She'd already screwed so much up she didn't want to miss a chance to make it better, even if it was just to lie still a while.

She felt something cool on her forehead. It was nice. Evan was whispering a song in her ear, a song he had always sang to the kids when they were little. "However far away, I will always love you … However long I stay, I will always love you."

She tried to smile and open her eyes but they wouldn't budge. She felt his chest so close, she nuzzled her face into it. Evie decided to let the dream wander and rest. She was so very tired. Though she was curious as to why Evan sounded like he was crying. That worried her, but decided to think on it later. Right now she wanted sleep. *Forever and ever, Evan …*

∞

Evan sat beside her, having sneaked into her room from the shared garderobe door. He had made sure it was unlocked the last time he had visited her, just in case he wanted to see her again while she slept. He bolted her outside door, allowing him to have privacy. She looked so pale, having endured several hours of excruciating pain as the physician had dug out the remainder of the arrow lodged in her side. They had cleaned the wound as best as possible for the thirteenth century; however, Evan couldn't bare the idea of it getting an infection, so he had come to re-clean it to his satisfaction. Now she lay there, peaceful and still, her breath barely raising her chest. Evan stood silently beside her bed, unknowing what to do now. He recalled the events of the night.

∞

The servants had gone to get him when they heard the commotion Evie was making in his room late that night. After their last tryst, he had sought out his own mental release of frustration in the woods, as he only knew how. He had found the thickest oak tree around and abused it. Since there was no gym to find a punching bag, he had to make do with what was available. He had stood in the pouring rain and screamed into the thunder. His knuckles bloodied. Evan didn't care. The physical pain was a far cry from what his mind was doing to him. He welcomed it.

His wife had finally given into his advances; yet it tore him apart that she had done it under false pretenses. In her mind, he was a stranger. Evan was elated that she was so receptive to his touch, but it meant the worst betrayal to their marriage. He felt as if he had dug a hole so deep, he felt like jumping in and burying himself. When the servants approached him, he had made the decision to come clean. He had to end the charade for his sake, and for her sake. He was tearing her apart.

He had returned to the castle to find her, and couldn't. In addition to the frustration, they advised him they also knew someone had seen the unknown figure in the woods again earlier that evening. Evan immediately knew Evie was in danger. Fear overtook him. He rushed down the hallway to Creighton and Lily's chamber, pounding on the door. Creighton woke from his slumber with a start.

"Creighton, I need ye and yer men," he said, throwing his kilt and long sword at the still half sleeping man.

Creighton jumped up from the bed without pause and began dressing.

"What is it, Roy? What's happened?"

"Yer mute lass has gone missing. The servants found and advised me that she was gone." He sighed and added, "and our cloaked stranger is also about." Evan heard Lily gasp under the bedclothes. Creighton finished dressing and looked at Evan squarely in the eye, "When was the last time she was seen?"

He tried not to focus on the details. He didn't want to let them know what had transpired between them. Evan swallowed hard. "A little after midnight. She had been seen in my chamber, destroying it." He didn't want to explain anything he did not have to. He tried to will Creighton not to ask anything else. They stood for a long silent moment while Creighton eyed him. Evan pulled up to his full height and stared down at Creighton menacingly, daring him to ask why.

Instead, he had clenched his jaw and responded. "Fine. I'll meet ye outside with the men," and he was out the door. Evan exhaled and his shoulders dropped, relieved that the older man didn't pry. He just wanted Evie safe.

Lily jumped up and sent servants into a flurry of action, preparing them for anything. Evan turned to leave, and she stopped him with her hand on his and spoke softly. "Evan, darling, I feel in my heart she will be all right. Open yer mind and ye shall find her."

Evan turned to look at her with wide shocked eyes, unable to grasp completely what she just said. *Evan, she said …* She squeezed his hand and smiled tenderly as he stood there in shock, unable to move. "Go find her. She's waiting." She pushed him gently out the chamber door. He stared back at her, dumbstruck and speechless. He blinked the confusion away as he steeled himself for the task and ran back down the hallway to join Creighton and the men.

Panic washed over him as they scoured the mountainside. They looked in the nearby woods and the castle grounds, inside and out, but were unable to find her. His heart sank lower with every turn and with every failed attempt. She had been gone now for hours. Though the search party was thorough, he felt as if they weren't doing enough. His temper flared, and his men couldn't figure out why he was so concerned. Creighton had tried to keep him calm, but his attempts were lost.

They came to the lists clearing and saw nothing. Evan cursed. "We'll find her, man. Keep yer mind clear. There's no reason to be this concerned yet," the chieftain had said. Evan fought the urge to hit him. He was way too calm. Evan was sure the façade was broken now with his reaction to Evie being lost. He would have to come clean to the whole castle now. His entire body shook with fear and rage. He looked to Creighton's solemn face and took what calmness he could muster from it. He recalled what Lily had said in her chamber; not just his name, his real name being used, but the advice she had given. *Open your mind and ye will find her …* They had to find her, he thought. His life depended on it. He closed his eyes and took a deep breath. His heartbeat slowed. He focused on the sound of the rain, and tuned out the talking men around him. He saw her face near a clearing. She was holding her hand out to him. After a few breaths, his nerves calmed. He opened his eyes again and began to walk directly into a thicket of trees.

There they found her, laying near death at the edge of the woods in the rain, like a fallen angel upon which God cried down. Blood surrounded her. His heart stopped, as he was certain she was lost to him. Unable to make himself move, he sent Creighton's men to search the woods for the culprit. Evan had wanted to go with them, to string up the bastard who had done this to his Evie and gut him. Yet he couldn't budge. He couldn't make himself verify what he knew to be true. They didn't get there in time. He stared at her motionless body. He couldn't tell if she was breathing. All he could see was her pale face, blue lips, and blood.

Everything was happening so quickly around him, he didn't feel like it was real. The men began to run into the woods in groups. He stood, rooted to the ground.

Creighton ran to her side, crouched down and whispered into her hear. She didn't move. Creighton checked her heartbeat, and looked up at Evan with his face devoid of expression. Evan's facade cracked and his knees began to give way. He watched as Creighton again put his face close to Evie's ear and spoke. This time, her eyes fluttered and opened, and she reached out and called for him … or for who she thought he was.

"Evie, I'm coming," he whispered, not realizing he was now sprinting across the clearing to reach her.

All the men stopped in wonder as they watched the Ruadh Donas run to the aid of this woman. A woman who everyone thought was a stranger to him. Evan picked her up gently and carried her the entire way to the castle. She had clung to him, her arms wrapped around his neck with what little strength she had left. A few men had brought a makeshift wagon in case they needed to wheel a body back to the castle, but Evan would hear none of it. He carried her across the open field before the castle alone, the men trailing behind him. Creighton walked between Evan and the men, creating more room between the two groups so Evan wouldn't hear the rumors beginning to spread. But he did hear, and yet didn't care what anyone thought anymore. Evie was his wife and he was tired of treating her any differently.

Lily, who gasped at Evie's condition, greeted him at the castle gates. She yelled for people to get the healer and led Evan to a room off the main hall of the castle. Evan gingerly laid her down on a small bed and hovered over her now sleeping body defensively. The healer came, and shooed everyone out of the room. Evan resisted, but Lily was there coaxing him to leave.

"Let him work, son. She'll be fine. He's a good man."

"If he causes her any more harm, I'll kill him myself," Evan said a little loudly, making sure the man heard. Lily put her hand on his arm, nodding consent.

"That sounds like a fine plan. I'll hold him down for ye, but we must let him work," she said quietly, looking at the red-faced healer. She pushed a reluctant Evan out of the room, with her exiting right behind him. He wanted to talk to her about what she had said in the chamber earlier, but he couldn't bring himself to speak now. He had no energy to spend. However, he was aware that Lily knew his real name, and that confused and almost frightened him. *What else does she know?*

The hours passed painfully. He heard Evie screaming from the tiny room. Creighton and his men had to restrain him in order to keep him from breaking the door down. Time passed by, the screaming stopped. Evan dozed and the physician had left quickly and quietly, not wanting to disturb him further.

∞

Evan finished reliving the night, still kneeling on the stone floor beside her bed. He put his head in his hands and sobbed, his voice was barely a hoarse whisper.

"I sent ye over the edge, Evie. It's all my fault. I took what wasn't mine and I'm so sorry. I lied, and it almost killed ye. I lost ye in our time and I'm fighting for ye now. Losing ye twice in this lifetime is too much, Evie, I cannae bear it. I love ye too much."

He heard her move around. He felt her hand on his head, toying absentmindedly with a stray red lock of hair. Looking up, he saw that she was trying to roll over to face him. A small grimace appeared on her still sleeping face.

He put his hand on her arm and pushed her off her wounded side. "Lay still, love. Ye dinna want to hurt yourself," he said, pushing up on his feet to be beside her. He brushed her hair away from her face and kissed her forehead, his lips lingering. He was close, but it wasn't enough. He crawled carefully into the huge bed beside her and whispered his favorite song for her into her ear. She turned her head to face him and nuzzled into his chest.

"Forever and ever, Evan … " she whispered, catching him off guard. It left Evan undone and he let himself go again, holding her close, tears streaming down his face.

Chapter 20

$\mathcal{f}$or the next few days, Evan growled at every person who entered her room and doubly so at those who attempted to kick him out. The healer who he had threatened to kill barely bothered acknowledging him anymore. Lily still tried to pry him out a couple of times every few hours to no avail. He sat on Evie's bed with her, where he had been since they had brought her in from the woods. She lay cuddled in the crook of his now asleep arm. He was afraid to move. He was afraid that any motion would compromise her state of well being. So he took the pins-and-needles sensation as a way of staying awake, though his eyelids rebelled. He had been up with her for over a day now ... Guarding her.

She had lots to say to him or about him in her sleep, and though it was rather embarrassing, he welcomed the verbal abuse from his slumbering spouse. Apparently, she had more pent up emotion than he had ever realized. Evie mumbled her fears about Evan leaving or cheating and for the love of her mother and family; and oddly enough, her new love for this strange time and Scotland. Evan continually shushed her in attempt to ease her mind, but she went on in her subconscious confessional. She shifted her focus from him to the mysterious stranger who filled her thoughts.

"I'm sorry for the Devil, but I have to see him. I'm like a fly drawn to honey." Though her speech was barely a whisper, Evan could hear every syllable that fell from her sleeping lips. He smiled and brushed her face gently, attempting to still her anxiety.

"Isna problem, lass. The Devil will do ye no harm."

She became restless and he tried to keep her from reopening her barely healed wound. He shifted his position to adjust to her movement and without opening her eyes, she ran her hand over his chest and clutched him closer. Her eyes fluttered open and Evan's heart stuttered as he came eye to eye with Evie.

"I miss you, Evan. I need you. I'm so sorry for what I've done and what I haven't done. I never meant to betray you." Her eyes fluttered shut again as if she'd never opened them, yet she stayed where she was, clinging to his chest.

The words hit him like a brick. She felt guilty for being with him—or who she thought he was. She wasn't trying to betray him as her husband. *She was sorry ... and so am I for making her believe I'm someone else ...*

Evie sighed and quit talking for a little while, falling into a deeper sleep. Evan was left to think about who exactly she had to worry about doing her harm. Now was the time he had to face up to Creighton to find out exactly who this stranger was. Her life was at stake and the situation had spiraled out of control. He'd surely die if something else was to happen to Evie, enough was enough. He resolved that as soon as she was out of danger of fever from infection he would go straight to the chieftain and discuss this.

Evan looked down on her upturned face in renewed admiration. She had endured so much in this time. They both had. It was near time they returned home. He longed to see her healthy and get home to their family. He knew he must own up to his presence and his deception to end the charade. Even if she hated him for it, at least she was still alive to do so. Evan thought of ways he could be able to get her under his care and watchful eye without having the rest of the castle think oddly of the situation. He had to think of the reputation he now held, and how he had to go about it in this time's rules. There was no way he could just abduct her and make a break for it, though the idea was tempting. He wavered over a few options of leaving and dismissed them as too farfetched or dangerous. He couldn't leave without having some claim to her. He knew Evie enough to know she would bolt at the first chance she got. Then it came to him ... marriage ... The idea flashed in his mind so quickly he blinked in surprise.

"Of course. I'll demand Lily and Creighton to have her marry me and we'll leave once we find the Flag." The idea seemed simple enough, but getting Evie to agree sounded about as likely as getting someone to move the ocean with a broom. Evan knew he had to try, and keep his identity as much of a secret as possible until they were wed. She would probably hate him, but her safety was paramount over the verbal and probably physical lashing he would most definitely endure. *I'll just have to take that chance ...*

He kissed her on the forehead, making sure it was still cool to the touch, and silently left her side to find the chieftain and his wife.

∞

Being this far away from Evie made him nervous. Though he knew she was safe, the last few days by her side had taken a toll on his mental stability. He felt as if a piece of him was now missing. He wandered slowly around the castle, pausing in each room to see if Creighton and Lily were anywhere nearby. He paused at his chamber and peered inside. It had been days since he had been down here. All the servants had been bringing him baths, food, and fresh clothing to Evie's room so he would not have to leave her side per Lily's request. No one had questioned the lady. He looked around the room. He had yet to clean it from Evie's tantrums that lead her down the path she was facing now. The servants had left it alone. Evan said it was his mess to take care of. He felt a pang of guilt as he remembered why it was in such disarray. By mangling his wife's emotions, he'd pushed her over the edge. Which caused her to almost be killed. *All because of me ...* He closed the door and shut out the memories, and walked down the hallway toward the kitchens.

Evan found them in the great hall. The chieftain was sitting in a chair facing the fireplace, drinking a large goblet of ale with his lady sitting on his lap. He paused to watch the couple in their comfortable position, longing to have that closeness with Evie. Lily leaned to kiss him on the cheek, and he leaned his head on her shoulder. It was second nature to them. They were so in love they didn't give any of the servants any notice as they milled around them, cleaning up from the last meal. Evan walked slowly up to the couple, almost resenting having to intrude on their moment.

"Ah, Roy. Ye have come to join the living," Creighton said, whistling for a servant to fill Evan a goblet of his own. Evan looked down at his shoes, feeling a bit embarrassed and nervous; as if he was about to ask Evie's hand from her father.

"Aye. I have a proposal to ask of ye," Evan said, looking up at them with only his eyes, his head still tilted to the floor. Lily smiled and winked at him.

"Go on," Creighton said, seeming intrigued.

Evan took a deep breath and raised his head, steeling his expression, remembering why exactly he had to do this.

"I think it would be best if I were to marry the mute girl to make her my legal ward and wife. I feel it is my duty to keep her safe from harm. To keep her safe from whoever is after her. And to that, I need to ken exactly who this person is so that I can dispose of him promptly. She has been tortured enough."

"That sounds like a fine idea. We'll arrange it on the morrow. Cheers." He turned up his goblet and drained the contents. Evan was confused. The answer came so quickly and finitely from Creighton, it startled him. Evan expected to have to fight and come up with an obnoxious lie to make the marriage request believable enough for Creighton to agree. Yet there was no resistance, and even a smile from the couple.

"Chieftain, are ye drunk?" Evan asked, his eyes narrowing.

"Eh, no? Should I be?"

"The Ruadh Donas, the man who has killed yer clansmen just asked to marry a mute servant who has been under your care for some time now? Did that memo get through?" Evan was completely baffled at the passiveness. Creighton laughed. "Aye. And?"

Evan blinked in confusion. *Is this a joke?* Lily giggled and moved off her husband's lap to join in the conversation. She walked to him and held his hands in her dainty small ones. She looked up at him and smiled warmly.

"Evan, we understand you, and only you, need to keep her safe. There is no reason to doubt. She obviously means a lot to ye, since ye have not left her side. No matter what yer past may be, we of all people understand the oddities of love. We'll no hold ye from her if that's what ye want or need to do." She squeezed his hands and let go, returning to sit in a chair beside her husband. *There it is again. She called me by my name. I need to know how she knows that ...*

"Aye, all right. So ... What of the man who did this to her?"

"In due time, we'll tell ye that." Creighton quipped.

"Why?"

"Dammit, man. It's late. We have to make plans now for a priest to come. I shall tell ye when the time is right. It's not right. It's a long story. Just ken she is safe in this castle."

Evan wanted to blow up against the answer, but knew better than to test him. The older man looked at his wife, who now looked very uncomfortable and close to tears. The last thing he wanted to do was to upset her. Lily had been there for him when he had most needed it. She didn't deserve any undue stress. He looked at Creighton and waited.

"Lily will inform Evie she is to be wed when she is on the mend," he concluded as Lily nodded consent.

"All right. Thank ye for your consideration."

Evan nodded and bowed slightly as he exited the room, still unable to ask Lily how she knew his name, but he knew now wasn't the time. He needed to send for help to clean his chambers now. Evie was safe and she would be his wife again ... Though the idea of forcing her into a marriage she may not want burned at him, but he knew it was for the best. He would explain everything to her, just as Creighton said, when the time was right. *I just hope she doesn't hate me for what I've done ...*

Evan decided from then on that he would give Evie the chance to heal on her own. He knew she was far from being in the clear but he kept tabs on her, making sure she was free of fever. He didn't want to disclose his identity to her just yet, as he had to remain anonymous for the clans' sake, so the farther he stayed away, the easier it was to keep secret. Evan would visit her at night in the dark, and spend the nights watching her sleep, holding her close, yet leaving before daybreak. His stolen moments became fewer between. He knew he had to talk to the lady, and soon.

∞

After weeks of near comatose state, Evie awoke. She barely remembered why she was there, but remembered the dreams of Evan. She remembered being loved and cared for. She assumed it was the round the clock nursing she was getting, but something else was missing from the puzzle. Evie felt as if someone had been with her the entire time. Laying there in the bed, she hoarsely called for someone to help her sit. The servant tentatively walked in and Evie could swear she looked nervous about doing so.

"What's wrong?" She blurted out before she remembered her mute role. The servant gasped and put her hand to her mouth. She ran to Evie and hugged her neck.

"Oh, Evie, we were all so worried. And now, look at ye, so frail, so weak, but able to talk! It's a miracle!" the girl sobbed over Evie, as she cursed herself internally for the slip. She quietly asked for some water just to get the girl to release her momentarily. The girl scurried off down the hall and left Evie there for some time alone with her thoughts.

And think she did. She thought of the feeling she had when she woke, the feelings of security and love. She realized she missed Evan so greatly now it hurt. The pain without him was unbearable. She almost died in the woods and was unable to tell him how much she cared. Evie felt now more than ever, she had to get home. Her heart ached over what she had done with the Ruadh Donas that night. She felt traitorous. No matter how many times she tried to put Evan's face on Roy MacDonald's body, it never quite fit. She had to get home before she went crazy. Evie had to find someone to talk to now. She had to confide in, speak to, anyone other than Roy MacDonald. She knew the news of her voice returning would be around the castle in mere minutes. Evie wondered if her accent could be chalked up to just being new at talking. It would have to do. She would make due and talk to Lily. Perhaps the lady could help her, somehow, some way.

The girl returned with water and a train of fellow servants behind her with a copper tub and hot water for a bath. Evie was grateful and smiled at everyone as they doted on her. As soon as she was able, she made her way down to the solarium.

∞

Lily turned around to see Evie shut the door behind her. She smiled warmly and returned to her position at the window, looking out at the battlements that were aglow with torchlight. Evie silently moved toward Lily, shaking with nervousness, working up the strength to speak to anyone other than Roy MacDonald for the first time in months. Lily noticed her trembling and motioned her to a seat near the fire, assuming she was cold. Not knowing how to proceed, Evie obeyed and sat down with a thump, and stared at her Lady in awe. Lily was a regal woman. Her beauty and wisdom of her years suit her perfectly. She was a perfect match for her husband Creighton. Both of them exerted such power and confidence. They were both so wise beyond their years. They weren't like other couples of this time that were only married for political gain, but were married because they matched each other stride for stride.

They were perfectly mated. *Just as Evan and I were ...* Evie felt a surge of confidence that she had chosen the right person to confide in and opened her mouth to speak. However Lily had a different plan and spoke first.

"I think ye would be safer if we found ye a new home. Creighton and I have already discussed the matter before ye came to me this evening and we figured out the most reasonable solution. I think ye would be suited for matrimony, even given the circumstances. For whatever reason, this person on the castle grounds seems to be targeting only you. After he's been following ye in the woods, and now this last attempt, it's time to be safe elsewhere. We've arranged with the priest and shall see ye wed immediately. The man who is interested in yer hand wishes to be wed as soon as possible. It is a great fortune for us all. It would be in the best interest of ye and our clan, Evie. If it doesn't keep us from war with the MacDonalds, at least ye would be out of harms' reach."

Confused, Evie shook her head in disagreement and opened her mouth to speak, but the words escaped her. She stared at Lily, eyes wide and body shaking. She couldn't tell if she were hearing things or if Lily was serious. She dropped Lily's hand and stood, pacing around the room aimlessly. She stopped in front of her again and spoke, her voice trembling.

"Lily, I'm not daft nor am I mute. I need you to believe all the words coming out of my mouth. I am not of this land, and I do not belong to anyone here. I can't marry a stranger. I am already married! Please listen to me! Do not marry me to a stranger! I don't understand how you could keep me safe by sending me away! I should be here with you." Evie frantically thought of a rational explanation as to why she should stay. "Who's going to make your clan food!? Cook can't do it anymore! He hasn't done it in 30 years!" She dropped to her knees in front of Lily, who strangely had a smile on her face. "Please don't send me away. I know I haven't done much in ways to thank you for your graciousness. Please, my lady, I beg you, don't send me away." Evie was petrified. The idea of Lily sending her away to some stranger so far away from this small life made her sick. It hurt to think she would be away from the only thing that could take her home to Evan.

Lily smoothed Evie's hair and smiled, her eyes twinkling. "I ken, Evie. I ken ye aren't daft. I ken more than ye give me credit for. Ye havena given us the benefit of the doubt. Look around, lass. Look at what our house holds. See the things we cherish, things that cannae be explained rule this house." She waved her arm about the room, looking at the room itself as it were full of magic. "Child, we hold the Fairy Flag. That very thing given to us by the Fae themselves. We are very aware there are things afoot that we cannae explain. We are solid in our beliefs that this is the best way to right our world. And if sending ye to be with Roy MacDonald is what Creighton believes will keep us all in peace and keep you safe, then that is what we shall do."

The name rang in Evie's ears like gunshot. "Wait a minute. You expect me to marry that ... that ... monster? The man who ravages men by the scores and kills your own clansmen? The one who ran me off into the woods and almost got me killed? You think he will keep me safe? He is the key to peace?" Her mind reeled. She paced the room again, wanting to scream. She clenched her eyes shut and tried to breathe normally. Then the next question that popped out of her mouth even surprised herself. "When?" she demanded, stopping to glare at Lily.

"As soon as the Priest arrives and gives ye direction in Gaelic, since there will be no English spoken during the ceremony. A few weeks time, I suppose." Lily watched Evie's mouth drop. "It isna that hard. Ye'll be fine."

"I'm not concerned about another language. I'm familiar with it. I'm concerned about the timing! Why so soon? Why now? Doesn't there have to be an announcement? A trial period? Anything?" Evie shouted, pacing again, rubbing her temples.

Lily closed her eyes, bowing her head, stifling laughter as she nodded slowly. "Aye, lass. I ken he will. Again, Creighton and I think this would be the best thing for ye and for us. Have a little faith." She looked up at a pacing Evie and sighed.

"I have to show ye something. Come. Stop walking a hole in my floors." She held out a hand to Evie, who reluctantly took it. Lily walked her to the large desk and pointed at the chair.

"Sit."

Evie almost ignored the request like a rebellious teen, but the smiling eyes boring into her told her she'd better not. She slowly sat down at the desk and folded her hands in her lap. Lily pulled the large drawer open, popped the latch to the false bottom, and pulled out the Cuban Cigar box that hid underneath. Evie's eyes grew huge as Lily flipped through the pictures. She pulled out the ones of her and her mother, and the picture of Lochlann and Killie, and placed them side by side on the desk in front of Evie. She replaced the top of the box and returned it to the drawer.

"Now, lass. Take a verra long look at those pictures."

Evie's hand trembled as she picked up the snapshot of her and her mother. "I ... I was ten years old. We had taken our first and only trip to the beach. She said the ocean made her sad, so we never went back." Her eyes filled with tears, remembering her mother's words. She found herself unable to focus anymore and was having trouble breathing. She knew she was hyperventilating but she couldn't help it. Her mother had been here ... in Scotland. *Mom ... Mama. She was here ... All the crazy stuff was true.* Lily called for a servant to fetch the healer as she fainted on the lady's desk.

∞

Evan gave Evie two weeks after she had been up and about before he scoured the castle looking for Lily. He had been attempting to find her and ask exactly how she knew his name for days now with little success. She had put herself into motion quickly after the announcement of the impending nuptials. As Evie was on the mend and he was unable to spend the stolen time with her, he needed answers.

On the third week of her avoiding Evan, he found Lily discussing the reception dinner with Cook. Evan placed himself directly behind the small lady waiting for her to finish the details of her conversation, casting a shadow over her. Noticing the change of light and the slight scowl on Cook's face, she turned around to find Evan behind her, flashing her a huge toothy grin with his hands clasped behind his back. Lily narrowed her eyes at him in speculation, and finished final discussion with Cook.

"Can I help ye, son?" Lily said, turning to face Evan, arms crossed across her chest and smiled sweetly.

"We need to talk."

"I see that. Casting a shadow over all of Scotland isna way to get attention of people," she joked and pinched his upper arm, unable to resist the display of muscles through his barely fitting shirt. Evan rubbed the spot with a grimace as she snickered. He held out his elbow to escort her to a more private place.

"Solarium," she said, taking the offered arm and pointing down the hall.

"Yes milady."

They walked slowly down through the great hall, and through the winding hallways of the castle, speaking with servants and clansmen who begged her attention. Evan was so impatient. The more people would stop them to talk, the more glowering he became. Lily noticed and laughed, which annoyed him even more to know he was so transparent.

Upon entering the solarium, Lily walked behind the large desk and sat down behind it. Evan closed the door and joined her, standing up in front of the desk.

"Please sit. I need the sunlight to exist and you're blocking it," she teased. Evan rolled his eyes and sat down facing her.

"Now, what is it that is so pressing that ye have been following me like a lost puppy for days?"

"Oh, so ye noticed that? Why didn't ye speak to me sooner?"

"I figured when the time was right, we'd have no distractions. Now, what's on yer mind?" She leaned back, relaxed and waited.

Evan took a deep breath. "See, ye have called me by my first name twice now. I never corrected Creighton when I was introduced, and all the rumors I hear of myself I'm Roy, or the Red Devil nonsense. How did ye know?"

Lily smiled, twirling a lock of her hair around a finger nervously. "Ah. Well ... I'm a bit more privy to information that gets lost on Creighton. Like yer name. Like yer wife's name."

"I'm sorry, who?" The color rushed to his face at the acknowledgement of Evie.

"Your wife, Evan ... Evelyn? See, how do I explain this without ye passing out before I get to the end like she did," she chuckled as Evan looked even more confused. She put both hands on the desk and took a deep breath.

"Evan, I had a moment when I was younger, about yer age, when I wished for someone to accept me as normal. I had a twin sister named Ivy, but she was very different from me. We had a very tumultuous relationship. I was on the straight and narrow, and she got into all the trouble she could find. I grew up, fell in love, and married Creighton as my parents had wished, for he was the MacLeod heir. Ivy was left to find whatever she could, as my parents had given up on her long before. Yet we both carried with us an entire family's worth of information that was heavy to hold. I kept it to myself, as I still do. Ivy was the opposite. She wished to tell the entire village. The stories we held weren't that believable for most people, so she was labeled insane—and that made her angrier. She felt that our family history should be known and be used to gain power and influence other clans. I simply did not. Are ye following me at all?"

"Trying to, aye." Evan sat back in the chair and crossed his arms over his chest.

"I'll tell ye. We come from a long line of not-quite-so-godly creatures; creatures that were cast out of society as heathenish, old worldly. These things are not to be discussed or believed. My family is Fae, Evan. We're magical beings attempting to hide in the human world." She paused, waiting on his reaction.

He didn't move or change his expression. "Go on," he said, skeptically.

"My family was put in the human realm to guard the Fairy Flag when it came to Dunvegan, dating back to the first MacLeod, so very long ago. We lived, loved, and carried on the line. I am a direct descendant, as was or will be … Killie. We made the connection in The Veil on Samhain a verra long time ago. She was lost and unsure of herself, having made bad decisions in her lifetime with her mother. Incidentally, she was also a descendant from us. Ye see where I'm going?"

"Not entirely, but don't stop."

"Killie came to us for help. She was lost in her own time with her own family. She came to find out her heritage as a Fae and was confused. She had believed herself and her family crazed. So, on Samhain almost thirty-five years ago, as your time table states, she came back into time to find the Flag herself. She wanted to either prove to herself that it existed or that her family was indeed insane. We became fast friends, because she understood my plight of remaining normal while she knew of what our family was. She fell in love with and married Lochlann MacLeod, Evie's father."

"Tell me about Lochlann." He asked, trying to keep the story straight in his head.

Lily smiled as she thought back. "Lochlann was a dream.

He was a Fae warrior who came directly from the realm when a command had been asked the first time the Flag was waved. He fought alongside my family's men. When the fighting had subsided, he was so curious of the ways of humans he pleaded with the Fae Queen to remain so that he could see the world through human eyes. She reluctantly agreed, unsure of how he would react to all the minuscule distractions humans focused on for the Fae are verra easily distracted. But he was a fine man; he took it all in stride.

"He was so tall, like yourself, so, so verra strong. He was beauty and strength personified. Everyone loved him. Faces of strangers would light up to see him arrive in their village. It is no wonder Killie fell for him the first time she laid eyes upon him. He was a joy to everyone he came in contact with." Her face grew sad as she thought back of her brethren.

"Unfortunately when he had pleaded to remain, he gave up his Fae power of immortality, as we all have … He … " She couldn't finish the thought, and finished only barely in a whisper. "He is missed every day. He adored Killie enough to perish for her and their child to be safe." Lily pulled a small handkerchief from the desk drawer to wipe her eyes with. She pulled out the small box that she had shown to Evie and set it on the desk before Evan, who eyed it cautiously.

"See for yerself how I ken ye, Evan."

He leaned forward, touching the cigar box lid, almost afraid to open it. The label was torn and faded, but still obviously a noticeable oddity in this time. He took a deep breath and flipped open the lid to find the small stack of photographs. Evan became more curious and picked them up, examining them. His mother-in-law and Lochlann, Evie and her … his wedding with Evie.

"Oh God," he sighed, lifting the last picture closer to see. He dragged a finger along Evie's face, remembering that day. His heart ached. *So this is how she knew.*

Chapter 21

Evie occupied her time in the kitchens as much as possible while the flurry of wedding activity went on around her. She refused to acknowledge any well wishes or wedding gift offers and shooed them away at all costs. She didn't want to recognize this man as her husband no matter who it was ... Didn't they realize he was the one who slaughtered their people? How could they just let it go? Where is the fury? It made no sense to Evie, and she wasn't going to celebrate anything.

She kept to herself as much as possible and hid in her quarters when anything was planned out of the ordinary. She refused to see her wedding dress, and refused to learn her vows. *I already know Gaelic; I don't need this stupid cram course ... Mom made sure I knew all there was to know about the language before I could spell my own name ...*

Cook had relieved her of her duties early every night, claiming she needed to ready herself for her upcoming wedding. She usually responded with a rude hand gesture and ignored his commands. She wasn't about to let that bastard take away everything she had worked for. There was no reason in her mind she needed to ready. Evie had vowed she would be either dead or drunk as hell to meet Ruadh Donas at the altar.

Evie also noticed for that week that the bridegroom was strangely absent from the great hall and from the lists. The times she did glance out the window in order to glare in his direction, he wasn't there. *Am I lucky enough that the great oaf jumped off the cliffs and died? They would have told me, surely ...* Yet for some unknown reason she kept looking out the window, searching for his red head towering over everyone else. He never showed.

∞

The night before her wedding she stole two bottles of whisky and a tankard from the buttery and hid herself away in her room without notice to anyone. Feeling nothing more than pity for herself, she decided she would have her bachelorette party, even if it meant she would have it alone.

Stoking the fire, she poured herself a large drink. *This stuff can't be that bad. I see men drinking it all day long like its water ...* Evie stuck her nose into the tankard and sniffed, the smell almost knocking her flat. "All right, Evie, you can do this." She eyed it cautiously as if it would attack her, closed one eye and drank, and spat the contents into the floor with her mouth burning. She heard a low chuckle from the direction of her garderobe. Scowling, she went to the small door and bolted it from her side ... *So the bastard decides to show back up, huh?*

"Shut. Up." She took another draw from the tankard, this time choking the contents down without making a noise. She stamped her foot on the ground and grimaced, but refused to make any sound that would cause the man next door to know she couldn't drink her whisky. Numbing her senses, she took another drink. *Hey, this ain't so bad ... It reminds me of moonshine from back home.*

She continued to drink until the first bottle was gone. Evie flopped down in her armchair near the fire, already feeling the effects of the alcohol. Her face was warm, her eyes blurry, and she was completely relaxed. Evie undid the plaits in her hair and stared off into nothing. She kicked off her leather shoes and threw her leg over the arm of the chair. Brushing her hair out with her fingers, she looked toward the little garderobe door latch, got up and stumbled over to it to unlock it. *If he wants me now, he can have me. It's not as if I won't be married to him tomorrow ...*

She leaned against the little door, suddenly feeling drunker than she had intended. Too much alcohol and not enough food. *Great. Maybe I'll get lucky and puke on his boots ...* That thought made her laugh. And laughing made her lose her balance and fall over onto the cold stone floor. "Oh dammit."

She heard the chuckle from beyond the door again. "I thought I said to shut up!" she yelled in its direction. Unable to stand, Evie rolled over to her stomach, putting her cheek against the cold floor.

I guess if I puke, I won't choke on it and die ... The little door opened and out came the redheaded monster who had been avoiding her the whole week. "Where have you been?" she said, unable to roll over to face him.

"Watching ye act a fool," he said. She laughed and smiled up at him, unable to focus. "Just my luck. I spend all this time trying to get a good look at your mug and the one time you come to me within a few feet not trying to tie me up, blindfold me or screw me, I'm drunk off my ass and can't see." As if it was the funniest thing she'd ever heard, she threw her head back and laughed. Evan rolled his eyes, picked her up off the ground, and put her on the bed, throwing the covers over her.

"Sleep, lass. Ye'll be miserable tomorrow. Ye never could hold yer liquor."

"What, you don't find me attractive tonight? No need to corner me in the hallway or drag me away?"

"Er, no. Goodnight, Evie." Evan turned around and exited through the door. Evie was sure she heard his latch lock on the other side. It was something she'd never heard before. Her dignity stung. For once, she felt hurt that he left.

∞

Evie resisted opening her eyes and stuck her toes out from her coverlet, gauging the temperature of the room. Discovering the chill, she retracted her foot and covered her head with the heavy blankets, refusing to emerge. The serving maids came and went without knocking, laying out her blue wedding gown, and straightening out her new MacDonald tartan sash. They poured her bath, and readied the various pins and jewelry she would be wearing. Once there was nothing else for them to prepare, one of the lasses came and tugged on her foot. "Up, Evie. It's time to face the day. Ye'll need all that ye can to be ready for that man."

Evie groaned inwardly. This was simply a nightmare. She felt as if she was being sold off to the devil himself ... Not just a Red one. The time had slowly ticked away for opportunities to escape. She thought briefly of jumping off the battlements to her death, but decided it would be too good for him, and too far away from her chamber. She would endure, and if given the chance to stay at Dunvegan, she would, to keep searching for the Flag.

She wasn't certain of what exactly would become of her after the ceremony, for she had not even been formally introduced. Her head swam with different scenarios of how this day would unfold. She stopped and thought about that coming evening, and if she would have to consummate the marriage. After the last few weeks of mental turmoil and heartbreak, it was the last thing she wanted to think about. *So wait, I get to be married and experience that man for however long until I find the Flag? There could be worse things.* The thought of their nights together drifted around in her head. Her big brown eyes popped open in panic. *That's it, I'm jumping.*

She threw the blankets back and sat up quickly, dangling her legs over the edge of the large bed. Just then, the effects of all the whisky she drank the night before caught up with her and she fell backward. The room was spinning. Her head was pounding. Her mouth began to water and her stomach churned. *Oh this is going to suck. Hung-over on my wedding day. Just great ...* She barely made it to the garderobe before she relieved the contents of her stomach. The maids frantically came to her aid. Evie slapped at them to get them to leave her alone ... *Did I just hear a man chuckle?*

She took a minute to compose herself and returned to her main chamber. Evie took a few sips out of a nearby cup and spat out the contents. *How much whisky did I drink last night?* She finally found a fresh pitcher of water and took a few tentative sips, hoping to settle her stomach. Still queasy, she returned the pitcher to the side table and decided on bathing before the water got too cold. With a wave of her hand, her busy little helpers filed out of the room to give her privacy.

Evie stripped her nightdress off, dropping it to the floor, as she stepped into the tub. Finding its heat welcoming, she sank down and tried to free her mind of all thoughts. Unfortunately, for her, it didn't happen. The small glimpses and stories of the man she was about to marry crept into her mind and made her heart ache. She was about to embark on the scariest part of her life. She felt as if she were being sold to the highest bidder to an evil man, to face certain death. Evie hadn't given much thought as to why Lily and Creighton were so set on making this marriage. She figured if Roy MacDonald had wanted her for his own to do as he wished, then they must be bound to oblige, especially if it gave them promise that there would be no war between the two clans.

After all that happened in their stolen time together, she wasn't sure what to think anymore. The day she had been assaulted in the woods and left for dead, her whole life had changed. Servants told her that Roy MacDonald was the one who carried her back to the castle. She heard rumors of him arguing with the healer and visiting her often. She vaguely remembered him running to her in the field. *Maybe there is something different about him. I guess I have no choice but to give it a chance. Or I could just be a living hell to him.* She smiled at the thought.

The arrangement still made Evie's stomach turn. She felt she was just a pawn in the plot to keep the peace. She wondered what made her so special to the Ruadh Donas that he would pick her out of the entire clan full of women. Why not one of the widows? Why not a younger lass that could bear children? Nothing added up to Evie. It as a political ploy and she was saddened to be involved. Evie sank down deeper in the water, now at neck level. Part of her wanted to just run as far as she could away from here, to save herself from uncertain disaster. But she owed so much to Lily and Creighton and their clan. She was sure if she disappeared, the MacDonald's would invade them by sundown. Closing her eyes against the image, Evie breathed deeply trying to ease the stress. She had only a moments' peace before she heard a knock at her door. It opened, and Lily entered, looking as warm as a summer day in her pale yellow gown with matching MacLeod tartan sash.

"Good Morning to ye, lass. I hope ye slept well. I came to help." Her voice was calm and quiet as she entered. Lily made sure there was no one behind her as she closed the door. Evie sat up just enough in the bath where she could listen to what Lily had to say. "I ken it is a stressful day, but know that ye are doing the best for the clan. Roy MacDonald is more of a man than I could explain right now. Please ken that ye will be taken care of, and we willna allow anything bad happen. Ye have been a bright spot in our lives here at Dunvegan and if we did not expect the absolute best from this outcome we would not have agreed to its terms." She stopped and smiled at Evie for a moment, then continued. "In the grand scheme of the world, there are far worse people ye could end up with, so please dinna fash yerself. It will be over before ye realize." Lily sat on the edge of the tub and put her hand on Evie's head in a motherly gesture.

Evie was having a hard time figuring out who could be worse

than a murdering, seducing, demon from hell. *I guess the men are slim pickings around here. Take what you can, whether he be a murdering beast or not …*

"There could be worse looking lads to be wed to, aye?" she said slyly and smiled. Evie frowned and dunked under the water to avoid confrontation and thought to herself. How would she know? She'd never laid eyes on him within fifty feet. She'd felt every inch of his body, pulled on his hair, kissed his hard mouth, grabbed his hardness and felt him inside her, but never seen him. She groaned bubbles into the water and reemerged, hearing the lilt of Lily's delicate laugh. "Ye cannae stay under there all day, lass. It's now or never."

"I'll take 'never' for a thousand, Alex," Evie muttered. Lily looked confused but rolled her eyes at the bride.

Evie sighed. "I suppose I can't stay all day. I hope I can just do this without mucking it all up. There's a ton of Gaelic in the service that I haven't practiced in years." She stood up and stepped out of the tub.

"Ye'll be fine. We've practiced a fair amount. It will be over in no time at all. Oh, and when it's all over; tomorrow morning tell me all about it," Lily laughed loudly, watching Evie blush from head to toe while handing her a drying sheet. She was thankful the ill effects of the whisky were finally wearing off. Now her hangover stomach had turned into full-on nerves. She snatched the material from Lily and went to hover near the fireplace, debating on if she should jump in it or not.

She dried slowly as Lily began to plait her hair, leaving out tendrils to curl around her face. Evie on put her pale gray stockings and matching ribbon garters, not bothering with the undergarments they had brought along. As they handed them to her, she put her hands up and said, "I've always gone commando. I'm not starting wearing your drawers today." Confusion struck the ladies faces in her terminology, but they did not question it as they helped her into her sapphire blue wedding gown. They adorned her head with a matching sheer veil to go in her dainty silver headpiece that the blacksmith had fashioned for her as a gift. Unfortunately, the veil made it nearly impossible to see what she was doing. "Why do I have to wear this?"

"Just do as I say for once, Evie. I ken it goes against everything in yer soul, but bear with us for the ceremony." Lily said, still smiling.

Evie searched the recesses of her brain to retract any information about having a wedding gown in the thirteenth century that had a veil. She couldn't remember anything. They wound the plaits in a bun on the back of her neck, adding to the dramatic effect. The neckline seemed cut a tad too low to be comfortable. They embroidered it with hundreds of small chains of silvery knot work, with a finishing touch of a small crystal thistle that rested in the center of her cleavage. *So much for modesty ...* They added a silver belt and then at last, the red and white dress MacDonald tartan sash over her shoulder. She felt as if the weight of the world was resting on her. *If I didn't know better, I'd think my skin was burning under this material ...*

Lily walked Evie to a mirror. Lily was smiling, and Evie was close to tears. Lily put her hand on her shoulder and squeezed. "Ye will be fine. Ye'll see." With a quick pat, she turned and walked away. Evie stood still in front of the mirror for a moment longer. She pulled her left hand up to her chest, holding it with her right, the wedding band she still wore glittering in the sunlight that poured into her one lead glass window. She knew it would be safe, for she was certain they put rings on the right hands here. *Bound by both sides like restraints. My heart tied up in one, and uncertainty of my life tied up in the other.*

She faintly heard Cook and another one of the kitchen staff bickering in the hall about her reception feast. She vaguely heard them as they entered her quarters, looking for Lily. Everything seemed to pick up speed as she stood in front of the mirror and stared at her reflection. She felt as if she were looking at a woman she did not know. Moments later, Lily returned to gather Evie from her quarters. She closed her eyes and finally turned away from the mirror, ready to face her uncertain future. *Forever and Ever, Evan. Today doesn't count, okay?*

Chapter 22

In a small chapel outside the gates of the castle, Evan stood and stared out the window, hoping to catch a glimpse of his bride-to-be. He fumbled absentmindedly with the contents of his sporran. It contained the small coins he had picked up on the first day here still with him, and his new wedding ring he had a traveling jewel crafter create for him. He rubbed the ring between his fingers, feeling its engraving. Evan had specially requested the MacDonald motto of *Per Mare Per Terras* (by sea and land) to be on it, and added Ad *Finem Temporis* (to the end of time.) The jeweler was reluctant to mar the true motto, but with a little less-than-appropriate bullying, Evan was pretty much able to convince him to write, *I am the walrus, coo coo cachoob* on it and have it done happily if he had asked.

The doors of the chapel opened and Evan's heart stopped. Evie and her entourage entered and quickly shut the doors behind them. He had never seen her look so beautiful. The gown, sewn just for her, matched her skin and body perfectly. It held fast on her curves like a glove. She moved as if she were hovering above the ground. Creighton nodded to the priest, who motioned for everyone to take their places for the ceremony to commence.

Evie's face, though covered with the long sheer veil, was still visible enough for Evan to see the shimmering tears that fell on her cheeks as she walked slowly up the aisle. He frowned at the notion that she was crying on their wedding day. Evan's heart was heavy to know she thought he was a murderous fiend. He despised what he had put her through in his chambers, even though he had wanted her to be with him so badly. He hated Liam more than ever, knowing that she was crying in fear for her life. And most of all, he was also nervous that she would slap him at the altar when she realized exactly who he was. He fully expected then she would despise him more for the lies he had to weave in order to get this far; this close to her. At this point, all he could do was hope that she would one day understand and listen to the explanation.

Evie walked at a snail's pace up the aisle with her head bowed, making precise and calculated steps toward him. It felt as if his whole life had stopped. He was so impatient to get to see her, to touch her, to hold her—he almost ran to pick her up and carry her back to the priest. He watched every move she made with such intensity. There it became a pause in time that allowed him to take all her beauty in account. *My Evie ...* He took a deep breath and waited.

Finally, she was before him. Evan fought to take her chin in his and raise it to meet his gaze. *In due time, man. She'll know in due time. Hang on a few more minutes ...*

The priest began reciting the ceremony in Gaelic. Evan was quickly thankful for small miracles that he had managed to figure out what little Gaelic he could in order to understand the man. He waited on bated breath for Evie to say the vows. He inhaled sharply and was greeted with the scent of his Evie; the scent he had grown to know as home. Everything was coming together.

He became lost in the moment until she spoke. With a trembling voice, Evie whispered the words to Evan. She pulled out the simple silver band and placed it on his right hand, barely able to function from nervous shaking. He knew this took all her strength and he admired her for that. He squeezed her hand as a small gesture of strength, yet she stared to the middle of his chest as she finished and withdrew her hands as if he was poisonous to touch. Evan's heart sank.

Evan's turn came and he recited the vows he had so painstakingly memorized over the last few weeks. He gently picked up her hand and placed the silver ring on her tiny right ring finger with the engraving turned in a way she could read. There was a small pause as she held her hand closer to her face as she made out the Latin phrase. Evie began to look confused.

Evan continued with his vows, and his voice, though full of unfamiliar Scottish brogue, managed to strike a chord in Evie. She began to blink rapidly as if she was awakening from a trance. Her confusion escalated with every word as she struggled to focus on his face through the veil. Evan finished the vows, and was signaled by the priest that he may seal the bond with a kiss. Evan started to move slowly toward her veil just as Evie impatiently pulled the pesky material away from her face and stared at him incredulously. He smiled crookedly at her as recognition set into her face as she stared into his sky blue eyes, tears beginning to fall anew. He moved his hands gently to the sides of her face as she blinked in shock, unable to move or speak. The priest concluded his portion of the service with a sly smile as Evan leaned down to her.

"Forever and ever, Amen," he whispered, kissing her.

∞

"I didn't bust it," Evie said, sitting down on the chapel steps beside Evan, who was holding a chunk of leftover snow against his nose. She handed him a cloth rag for him to make an ice pack.

"Ye damn near crammed it in my skull," he grumbled. He wrapped the cloth around the snow and put it back to his still bleeding, swollen nose.

"I had a good teacher," she grinned at him, bumping his shoulder with hers. She heard him growl at her and she giggled. Lily and Creighton left the chapel smiling down smugly at the newlyweds. Creighton walked on as Lily stopped to talk.

"Dinna tarry, loves. Yer reception feast will be waiting for ye. Murdock will be angry if ye miss it."

"Who?" Evie asked, confused. Lily laughed.

"The cook? Murdock?"

Evie nodded her head, finally figuring out his name.

"Oh. Huh, learn something new every day," she said, looking at Evan.

"Yes. Try not to learn his temper any more than ye have to. Be quick about showing up," Lily said over her shoulder, trying to catch up with Creighton. Evie and Evan watched Lily tuck her arm around her husband's waist, his arm slipping around her shoulders naturally, kissing her on the head. Evie sighed.

"Remember when it was that easy?" Evan asked, not looking at Evie.

"Yep," she said simply, chewing on her bottom lip. She didn't trust herself to completely answer the underlying questions. There was so much to be discussed. They had a huge reception to endure before they were left to their own devices in their chambers. All the explaining would have to wait.

Evie stared at Evan, still not believing the difference in his appearance. Now with two black eyes forming, he was scarcely the man she had met so many years before. She could see how everyone had been afraid of him. They had reason to be scared. Men were dying for no reason, and the abducting of women in the hallways was nothing to dismiss. Without turning his head, he looked at her out of the corner of his eye.

"What?" he said, gruffly.

"Nothing. Just still getting over the whole new look you have going on here," she replied, not taking her eyes off him. Evan sighed, removed the ice pack, and touched his nose gingerly.

"I'm sure I look just dashing right now."

"Dashing? What the hell have they been teaching you here? Your accent has thrown me off for weeks now. I'm surprised I never caught on that it was you ... not, that your accent is a bad thing. Are you faking it?"

"Eh, no, it just seemed to appear overnight. I dinna realize I was talking that much differently until I heard yer voice in my chambers that first night. I mean, I ken it was different, but compared to ye and the southern accent, I'm a scene right out of *Braveheart*," he chuckled.

Evie stared at him without expression, nodding in agreement. She didn't want to think about that first night. She didn't want to think about any of those nights now. She looked down, unable to hold his gaze any longer.

"Lass, know this. I never meant to betray ye. I never have before. I have always been true to my vow and now I feel I can never be at ease again. I am sorry. I lead ye to believe I was another man. I felt I had to conceal myself in order to keep us both safe. I took advantage because ... " he stammered, "because I wanted ye. I have nae excuse other than that." He looked down at his hands, unable to continue. His shoulders slumped forward awaiting the verbal assault and ultimate rejection he was so used to.

Then to his astonishment, he felt her move closer to him and put her hand inside his. She slowly lifted his chin with the other and started into his blue eyes. Evie moved a lock of red hair away from his face and tucked it behind his ear, as she had been yearning to do since she saw him from afar. Stopping to caress his cheek, she smiled.

"Evan, I've done a lot of thinking in the last few months. I know we're divorced now, so you didn't mess up your vows. I wish I could say the same—yet I can, in some weird, odd, very messed up way." She laughed and smiled up at Evan, who's eyes had had welled up with tears.

"Whatever made you think you had to lure me in without letting on who you were has to be important. And, in this particular day and age, I'm not at liberty to question much. I just hate the fact it had to go to the extremes of killing people." The smile faded as she stared at him. "That, I cannot forgive. They were innocent, Evan. I know their families and their children. I held them while they mourned their fathers, and their mothers were just lost." Her voice shook in anger. "I had to relive my mother's death over and over through these children, Evan." She rubbed her face and looked at him, rage in her eyes.

Evan drew her into his embrace, and her resolve broke. She cried into his chest as he rocked her. This was the breaking point, he figured. What will be the end all and be all to their confessions. "Lass ... that is something else I need to discuss with ye. I havena been honest about that either." She stopped crying for a moment, hope shining in her eyes.

"I dinna file the divorce papers. Ye gave them to me at the party and I never filed them. I can only assume they were burned on the way here." He wiped a lock of hair away from her face and wiped tears away from her face. "Also, it wasna me who killed those people. The MacDonald did and blamed me. I'm nae a murderer."

Saying the words, even though he knew she wouldn't believe them, made him feel so much better. He felt so relieved. Her body relaxed against him and she closed her eyes, cursing under her breath. He wondered if it was from relief or from fear he was lying to her again. He shifted to look down at her face. Evie looked up to meet his confused stare, then threw her arms around his neck and kissed his face.

"Oh! I knew you couldn't be a murderer. It's made me so sick." Evan laughed as Evie crawled up into his lap, smothering him in kisses, almost knocking him over onto the ground.

"Woman! We have a reception to go to! I ken we have a lot to talk about but if we don't make it down there soon, they'll send a search party."

"Feck'm and feed'm fish heads! I'm enjoying my moment!" Evie yelled in her best Scottish accent, still wrapped around Evan's neck. Evan cackled with laughter as he fell over onto the ground, covered by his wife.

∞

Down in the castle, the party raged on into the night. The food was divine as Evie had told Cook—er, Murdoch—a thousand times. They danced until her feet ached. The pipers and drummers kept the pace up so high she could barely catch her breath. Split from her husband by the women she had become so close within the kitchens, she was whisked across the room watching him as MacDonalds and MacLeods clapped him on the back repeatedly. She still couldn't believe this was happening. After all this time, he was here. He had always been here. It had always been him. She took a silent moment to thank her lucky stars for saving her from her own monster she had built up in her mind. Evan caught Evie's eye, winked, and motioned toward the doorway. She nodded in agreement and tried to make her way to the exit. Creighton caught the couples' near escape and lead them back toward the center of the room. He banged on the table nearby and the raucous crowd hushed to listen to their chieftain.

"It appears the newly wedded wish to depart, given the sly looks they've been giving each other for a quarter hour now," Creighton laughed, as did the crowd. Evie wished she could disappear under the table as Evan smiled and raised his tankard, cursing the old man under his breath. "Before we go spend the evening in front of their door, I'd like to thank the both of them for their service to Dunvegan as they have been a treasure to us all." Creighton raised his tankard as the Hall erupted in applause. Evie was touched that they seemed to care— *Wait, what did he say about camping out in front of the door?*

"All right, on with ye!" The chieftain announced as the band started their lively songs again and the clansmen burst into dance and cheers. Evan and Evie were carried upon their shoulders and ushered up the stairs quickly. The bawdy chatter was enough to make Evan blush. He knew that this was pretty commonplace for this time, but didn't realize how serious they were about hanging out. The escorts dropped them to the ground and all but shoved them into his chambers. Evan slammed the door and bolted it shut. Evie laughed and fell into the chair near the fireplace. He smiled at her as he leaned against the door, relishing the sound. It had been years since he'd heard her laugh in earnest. She didn't have a delicate laugh. It was a bellyful of guffaws, sometimes with snorts and tears. Deemed unladylike from her mother, but so infectious Evan couldn't resist but laugh with her. He walked to where she was sitting and kneeled in front of her. She recovered from her loud laughter, settling for a brief moment of giggles. He poised himself in front of her for a little while until her face returned to being relaxed with a hint of smile.

"I've missed yer laugh," Evan said simply, putting his hands on top of hers. Her smile faded into an uncomfortable twist, and she looked away into the fire. Evan frowned at the change. He stood and offered a hand to her. Evie stared for a brief moment at the ring on his left hand. *He still wears it …*

Noticing what she was looking at he responded. "Aye, lass. I'm still married to ye. 'Forever and ever,' remember? I'm no monster, just yer husband, here and now." She took his hand and he pulled her up to him, holding her tight. His voice was barely a whisper as he moved her hair away from her neck. "Dinna worry, lass. It's all right now."

Evie melted into his arms, unable to resist the comfort and the familiarity. She was overcome with the relief that he was here, that he loved her, that he was not the strange monster she had made him out to be and that he had not killed innocent clansmen. She desperately wanted to believe he was telling the truth. There was no reason for him to lie, yet something nagged at her.

"Who shot that arrow at me, do you know?"

"Aye, I have a feeling I do. We'll have to sort out the whole sordid tale as soon as we can. We just have to bide our time. We still have to find our way home and secure it before anything."

The idea of going home with him, hand in hand, made her heart sing … It couldn't be this good, could it? Evie thought of the MacLeods and their constant generosity. Here they thought the murderer walked and stalked their hallways overseeing his men, day in and day out since the snow had turned the entire castle into an ice fortress. Evie's thoughts raced back to the murders.

"But don't the MacLeods deserve to know who did kill their clansmen? How do they not think you killed them? Why is Creighton so calm about you being here if he still thinks you are responsible?"

"That's a good question, lass. Creighton hasna said a word about my affiliations since the first night I arrived. I suspect he kens more than he's letting on. I just cannae figure it out."

Evie opened her mouth to ask another "why" question but stopped to look at her husband. He looked completely different, and seemed much more relaxed, even given the stressful circumstances. *This world fits him so much better than the life he had … we had.*

The oddity of being here had worn off. They had worked their way into this lifetime with little resistance. Yes, she missed her cell phone, convection oven, and internet connection, but it seemed they connected better to this life without the distractions of technology. What had made their lives more convenient had ultimately broken it down. She wondered how they would go back to their time. The idea of the city of Atlanta made her even more frightened than before. She shook her head, trying to expel the fears and focused on the man in front of her.

"So, what happens to us?"

Evan shifted his weight, pulling her back against him as he laid down on the bed with her, propping up on the giant wooden headboard. She wasn't sure what the motive was, but it appeared he needed the physical closeness for comfort as much as she did. He swallowed hard and spoke, still soft enough she barely heard him.

"I'm not entirely sure. My plan originally was to find the Fairy Flag, bring it to Liam, make my wish and see you at home. That plan has since changed since I found ye here." He looked at her and smiled crookedly. "This reminds me. How the hell did ye get here, anyway?"

Evie smiled sadly, remembering the night that time abducted them both. "Do you remember Halloween?"

"Aye."

"I went looking for you in the woods after I saw this great big fire in the clearing. I freaked out, called 911, the whole nine yards. I saw your whisky bottle and thought you'd jumped in. Then I got dizzy and passed out." She chuckled when she thought of how she awoke, covered in grass. "Yeah, then I woke up in the field outside the castle where they keep their cows. Oh man, it was the most absurd thing I ever encountered that I thought I had gone nuts. I woke up face-to-face with a cow; one of those great big red hairy numbers and it totally threw me for a loop. I couldn't stop laughing." She laughed, thinking back. "So then Malcolm shows up and I'm still dressed in my Halloween wench costume and his eyes were bugging outta his skull." She laughed, covering her mouth to hide the noise. "That boy couldn't keep his eyes off my chest if his life depended on it. That pissed me off so I just railed at him, still thinking we were in Virginia, somehow. Time travel wasn't my first stop for reasoning. He told me to shut my gob, and threw me over his shoulder."

"Aye, time travel wasna in mind either. I was thinking drunken hunters were in the woods. Though it is odd, the fire was more or less the size of a campfire when I saw it, but floating in the air."

"It was in the air, but I could see it from the house. I thought the woods were on fire. When I got to the clearing, it was a smallish tornado. Hot as hell, too."

"Hmm ... I suppose someone wanted us here then; wanted ye to follow with me," he smiled down at her, squeezing her arms around her shoulders.

"But why? Why are we even here?" She looked at him, searching his face.

Evan paused, and then replied. "My theory is Mama Killie sent us to do something. I mean, look at all she taught ye growing up. All the history. All the ancestry. All the cooking, all the lessons between the MacLeods and the MacDonalds. It wasna a mere fairy tale to her. She was training ye. She was here, Evie. And yer Da, too."

Evie stiffened and pushed away, standing up next to him, just out of reach. She remembered the night in the solarium with Lily when she was told she would marry Evan. She remembered the pictures she had shown her. She didn't believe it then, and she was now having a hard time believing it coming from Evan. "My Dad? How? That can't be possible, can it?"

"Love, look at where we are. Anything is obviously possible. And what do ye ken about yer Da, if anything?"

"Not much … well, nothing much that made sense, anyway. She said she met him on a European vacation, had an affair. Some guy tried to break them up and she came home because she was pregnant with me, and supposedly the doctors were better in Virginia. She found out later my Dad died, somehow. But you know she always littered the whole thing with fantasy crap." She stopped pacing and looked at the floor. Evan watched her expression as she slowly realized what he was insinuating.

"Evan, is my Dad from here? Lily showed me a picture of my Mom and I … I don't know how she got it. And she showed me another of her with another man, but I assumed it was from our time. Lily didn't have time to explain anything. She just showed them to me and we were, uh, interrupted … Is he?"

Evan sat up and threw his legs over the edge of the bed to face her, with his hands clasped and rested his elbows on his knees. He closed his eyes, sighed, and nodded confirmation. "Aye, lass, yer Da was here. I dinna ken all the details yet. But I'm sure I'll figure it out soon."

She looked as if she'd cry. She wrapped her arms around herself. Not wanting to add a sullen mood to their already confusing and tense wedding night, Evan stood up slowly. Evie watched him rise carefully and looked up at him. Her Highland warrior, carved straight out of the history books. How could she have ignored him? She wondered how she had treated him so badly for so long and how he had managed to stay with her. No, he had his faults, but as his wife, she felt as if she had failed him. Her arms began to shake. Tears started to fall. Evan watched her confusing change of mood and was at her side in two long strides. He gathered her in his strong arms and mused in her hair. "I dinna ken what makes you so sad but listen, lass. I would move the sun and moon to fix it for ye. If it is me, then I shall leave or stay here and send ye home alone if that's what ye want. I cannae bear to see ye hurt anymore by my hand."

Evie crumbled at his unselfish words. "Please don't ever leave my side again. I'm afraid I've already screwed up our whole lives just by existing. This whole mess is somehow my fault."

"Even traveling against the sands of time will not keep me from ye, Evie. I hope that's completely obvious." He turned her to face him, lifted her face to his, and kissed her gently. He took his thumbs, wiped the tears from her cheeks, and kissed the trails they left behind and grinned.

"Say, can we try to enjoy our company? I ken it's awkward and ye probably still wish to slap the bajezus out of me, again—but can we try to put it aside? Can we let go for our wedding night? I'm fair certain there's a crowd at the door waiting for some sort of sign that I havna devoured ye in a literal sense, and we have plenty of time to catch up on the plot of the century." His crooked smile lit his face up as he looked at Evie, searching her brown eyes. She smiled faintly in response and nodded.

"You think they're camping at the door?" Evie snorted, suddenly amused at the thought.

"Aye, they assume the Devil is going to set yer soul on fire, I presume. I'd even bet ye a dollar."

He took her hands and they quietly padded to the door. He unbolted it as silently as possible and cracked it open, barely able to see in the hall.

Sitting in the hallway were a handful of men and maids, drinking and playing a crude game of dice while others made use of the dark. He noticed Lily and Creighton were there, sitting in the floor facing away from the door, giggling, and carrying on with their clansmen. Evan took a step backward and accidentally stepped on Evie's foot, causing her to yelp before she could stop herself. Her hand flew to cover mouth and Evan saw Creighton look backward at the door, catching his eye. "Oh shite!" Evan yelled and slammed the door, laughing.

"Oi! Does the Ruadh Donas need help in there? Devil forgot his tricks? I think I can show him a thing or two!" The group laughed and teased as Evan bolted the door shut again. Evie fell in the floor consumed in peals of laughter. The group pounded on the door, rowdy comments abound.

Evan snatched Evie up in his arms and flipped her over his shoulders and she squeaked in mock resistance. He dumped her onto the bed and joined her.

"I guess I owe you a dollar," She laughed.

"Yep. I'll collect as soon as we see another dollar."

"Ugh, don't remind me," Evie groaned, covering her head with a pillow.

"Ye think we will? See our time again, that is? See the kids?" It was Evan's turn to ask the questions.

"I hope so. I want to see the girls. I wonder if Mason has already enrolled them into a girls school and taken over the world yet." She recalled Keiran's and Leeann's fire red hair that matched their father's temper. They would be such trouble when they were older. Mason and his overpowering control over everything. His seriousness that could make his elders call him "sir" no matter that he was but sixteen years old … Seventeen now.

"We missed Mason's birthday."

"Not much we can do about that here, can we?" Evan said, rubbing his temples. He propped up on his elbow to face Evie, putting his hand on her stomach and tracing her bellybutton with his thumb.

"We gotta get home. Maybe together we can figure out how. If Mom was capable of coming and going, there surely has to be a way to get out of here."

"That's just it lass, I had the idea, as did you, that the Flag was the key. If she came and went that would be too many commands for it. It would be out of offers and we'd be stuck. Forever."

"So you're saying we're trapped?"

"No, I'm saying I'm not positive the Flag is our exit." They sat in silence, lost for explanations. Evie started to get frustrated again but Evan took notice of the scowl on her face. "Hey, we were going to try to not cause more drama tonight, right?"

Evie sighed and looked at him. "What else do we have to do?"

Evan chuckled wryly, rolling over on top of her. "Oh, lass. I thought you'd never ask."

Chapter 23

The next three days were blissfully filled with sex, very little conversation, and medieval room service. They woke at dawn in each other's arms and silently reconnected in ways unimaginable, and ways probably illegal in forty-eight states.

Evie wasn't sure if she had ever been this content or happy. Being able to have both her husband and her mysterious Red Devil at the same time was the same as having a mental threesome. She was unable to take her eyes off Evan for more than a fraction of second. His whole demeanor had changed here. Not only were both his bruises fading from the shiners she had given him on their wedding day, his hair was unkempt and longer than she'd ever known. His goatee was rough and soft at the same time. She also noticed a new scar had appeared under his eye. She took inventory of all the noticeable changes. He was so light hearted, even when they spoke of the seriousness of their predicament. She traced the laugh lines around his eyes with a stray finger, noticing the lines of perma-scowl on his forehead had dissipated. He looked at her questioningly, cocking an auburn eyebrow at her.

"What?"

"Nothing. It's just been a while."

"It's been a half hour, ye insatiable wench," Evan said, rolling over onto his side to face her.

"Not since that. Since I've actually seen you. Up close. I can't get enough."

"Good."

"Is it possible you've gotten more arrogant since you've been here?"

"Aye, maybe a wee," he said, flashing a stunning smile. He gave her a quick peck on the nose and got up to get dressed.

Evie scoffed, laying on her back and rolling off the bed too. "Do we have a game plan?" Evie asked, putting on a nearby dress.

"For today? More naked debauchery?"

Evie slapped him on the rear as he bent over to pick up his long discarded kilt.

"Could your mind escape the confines of the gutter for 30 seconds?"

"Probably not but I'll try. Time me." He paused as Evie stuck her tongue out at him. He opened his mouth to say something but decided against it. He winked at her and began again. "My game plan is pretty short. Talk to the chieftain about the guy who shot you to see if it is the same as the person who murdered those men on the trail. If it is, find him, kill him, go home." He paused and rubbed his bare stomach, frowning. "I'll probably eat something in there somewhere also. I'm famished."

Evie rolled her eyes at him. "More room service or should we emerge from our hidey hole?"

"I think almost a week of hiding is far enough evidence to establish that our marriage is consummated."

"Three grown kids are too, but I don't know if that counts here."

"No, I dinna think it does here. Though ye did not seem to mind the company, or am I holding you hostage?" he asked jokingly, winking at her again as he put on his shirt and tied back his hair with a piece of leather string.

Evie gave a short, humorless laugh as she pulled her hair up in the beginnings of a bun. Evan took her hands away from her hair and pulled her close.

"Are we all right?" He searched her eyes.

"I don't know what we are right now, Evan. What happens to us when we get home? What about work, the gym, the catering, the house, the kids, and us? If any of it is still there after all this time, how do we go on?"

Evan smiled crookedly down at her and turned her around, beginning to braid her hair down her back. The simple gesture made Evie tear up.

"Lass, we have to get there first. We'll figure it all out, together."

"Evan, we need to figure some of this out before we get home. I'm scared we'll just fall back into our same old habits and all this closeness will be for nothing."

He turned her around, holding her by the shoulders.

"Look at me, Evie. I'm haggard; I'm hairy, scarred and not quite bathed properly, in a kilt, and most importantly, here—with you. When we return; granted I'm going to put on the first pair of button fly jeans I can find, but I'm still going to be with ye. Till the end of time. I dinna care where. Virginia, Atlanta, I doesna matter to me. The office probably has already replaced me, and Jack is more of a gym manager than I ever was. If Keiran and Leeann havena blown through all our savings I've been tediously storing away for the last fifteen years, we'll manage fine. We havena had a dime here and fared well, aye? Have faith in me, Evie. Have the faith I've always had in you, lass. Please."

She wrapped her arms around his waist and put her cheek against his chest, holding in the tears that threatened to escape.

"It's not all about money, Evan."

Evan stroked the side of her face and kissed her head. "I ken that. Ye dinna need to hold all our world's troubles on yer shoulders. Mine are plenty big to carry for it the both of us. Ye have to let me, though."

She let go and sat down on the bed. "You know, Mama's been crazy my whole life. I met you and you were the most normal, stable person I've ever had. Then the kids came and we raised them. Then work kicked in. Somewhere in there we lost each other and Mama was still crazy and unable to hold on to reality. We moved closer to her. Your work demanded more. My work actually picked up. Then Mama died without any answers. We whisked away to the farmhouse and my whole childhood flashed to me, Evan. I couldn't ever share that with you. Mama held all this bizarre information to give to me but never told me why. All the strangeness had flooded back and I dove into the catering, the kids and the house in order to block out all the feelings and insecurities. I wanted to erase all the insanity that had been my life up until I found you. I needed to hold onto my normal, stable, sane life. In the process, I pushed you—my rock, my sanity, my love—out.

"Then when I got here, I thought I had died in that fire, and was in some purgatory that was my mind's way of holding on to my soul. I could cook, but I was stuck in the delusion that Mama had pushed into me my entire life. Then in one instant in Lily's solarium, everything crashed down on me. All the crazy lies weren't crazy anymore. It was truth. I couldn't handle it and passed out. I never got the answers. I may never get them.

"But I swear on my life that I never meant to push you out. Evan, I love you and I'm so sorry I treated you so badly. I'll never forgive myself for what I have put you through in the last few years."

Evan sank to his knees in front of her and held her face in his hands. "I love ye, lass, ken that and be still, aye?" He kissed her on the forehead and lingered, smelling her hair. She wrapped her hands around his and put her forehead to his chest with a sigh.

There was a loud, frantic banging on the door. Evan stood and and unhooked the bolt, throwing the door open. One of Evie's fellow kitchen servants stood there with terror-filled eyes.

"Ye have to come to the tower now! The MacDonald has the chieftain and his Lady—he's demanding the Ruadh Donas to come immediately!" She grabbed his hand and pulled him out of the chamber. Evie finished dressing and paused quickly in her room to retrieve something hidden beneath her mattress, and slipped it into the top of her stocking, and then ran after Evan.

Neither of them had ever been to the tower before, so they followed closely behind the young maid. They passed the solarium and the chieftain's chambers up some narrow winding stairs to the tower room. The lass came to the door and pointed at it as if it would explode if she touched it, and ran back down the stairwell as fast as her slippers could take her. Evan grabbed Evie's hand and opened the door.

Inside the room, lit by torches, sat Creighton and Lily, and near the hearth stood a very disheveled and dirty Liam MacDonald. His face stained with what they hoped was dirt and his hair matted. His eyes seemed to twinkle with thinly veiled insanity as he smiled warmly to the newcomers. Evan stepped into the room, holding Evie behind him. He looked to Creighton, who nodded acknowledgment of his arrival, and then to Lily, who looked away, attempting to hide back her fear.

"Chieftain, ye sent for me?" Evan questioned, looking at Creighton.

Liam stepped forward. "Aye, I did, Roy. So nice of ye to listen to a command from yer superior."

"I dinna recall swearing fealty to ye, Liam. However, I recall beating yer arse on the beach and leaving ye for dead. Need a refresher on that?" Evan's eyes grew dark as he stepped closer to Liam, his height overwhelmingly menacing. Liam threw his head back and laughed. A rich sound that normally would have been pleasant to hear, but Evie shuddered at its hollow wickedness instead.

"Nae, I dinna think I need that tonight, Ruadh Donas. I just came to express my congratulations to the newly wedded couple, and kiss the blushing bride meself, and welcome her to the MacDonald Clan."

Evie tried her hardest not to run screaming from the scene as he walked closer to her. He took her hand with his dirty one, and kissed her upturned palm delicately. He seemed to hover over her wrist and inhaled slowly. He lifted his head to look at her, his eyes glowing a deep red. Evie stifled a scream and her whole body trembled as she took her hand from him.

"You aren't human, are you?" she whispered, despite herself. Liam's smile spread over his face and shook his head slightly. "I'll get to that, my love, have patience."

Evan stepped between the two and pushed Evie behind him once again with one hand, never taking his eyes off Liam.

"So then, ye are done. Thank you. Safe travels back to Dunscaith, Liam." He waved an arm toward the open door. Liam laughed again as he returned closer to the hearth, stopping by the side table to fix himself a drink.

"Not quite rid of me yet, Roy. I'm sure yer lass would like to get to ken me a little more, aye? Since we're family now?"

"We are not family, Liam. We share the same name but it stops there."

"Oh we share a whole lot, Roy. Ye just dinna take the time to find out more before ye left me. Come on in, sit down and I shall tell ye a wonderful story." He waved his hand toward the door and it slammed shut by itself. Evie jumped in surprise. Evan's eyes narrowed at Liam, and he motioned for Evie to sit in a chair nearby as he stood on guard, standing beside her.

Creighton kept silent as he looked at Liam with pure hatred as Lily held onto his hand, still looking anywhere but at the

MacDonald.

Liam took a long draw from his drink and began. "Now that I have yer undivided attention, let me tell ye about myself. As the lovely lady questioned before, no, I am not human. I am not a demon, nor am I a devil, nor am I a silly Fae," he chuckled, glancing at Lily. "I am Slaugh. Far superior to the list previously stated." He paused, refilled his already empty drink, and returned to face the room, still smiling.

"I was never sure of how I came to be Slaugh. Knowing only of the woman who was to be my mother, I could smell the death on her. Now, to explain, the smell that I speak of is not the putrid stench that is left behind a body after it decays. No, this is a different smell all together. I can sense when the body is about to lose its soul. The soul is what I want—what I thrive upon. Unfortunately, my being before I became the Liam that ye know was not happy nor satisfied in its existence. I wanted more. Being Slaugh is more or less a ghost-like being, for lack of a better term, yet with the constant need for souls. And see, drifting around without a body for an extended amount of mortal time makes one weary. I wished to thrive on a living, breathing creature."

He took a few steps toward Lily, who cringed away from him. He smiled slyly at her and continued, dragging a finger under her chin with a long black fingernail.

"So, how does an evil bastard like me do that? Prey upon the most magically connected person ye can find, of course. A Fae to be exact … And just my luck, the Fae in question was right here at Dunvegan, pregnant with a half breed; bragging about herself and her family." He released Lily's chin and walked around the room as if he were teaching a class, hands clasped behind his back.

"See, human and fairy blood always make the most interesting subjects. So there, I found my target. The mother was at death's door when I found her. The babe she carried would have died too had I not taken the initiative to become its partner, if ye will. This body ye see now is nothing but a host to me. I, in my Slaugh form, wanted to feel its growth; its soul always trying to escape me … Always straining and stretching—and I in return, always feeding upon it. It's quite beautiful if ye ask me." He stopped and closed his eyes, as if he were enjoying a bouquet of a fine wine. "Just lovely." Liam smiled again, opening his red eyes and walked back toward where Evie sat, near Evan.

"I, now as a growing child, lived after my my hosts' mother died. I thought me stealing her soul along with the newborn was enough to secure me in this body for eternity. I should be sated, right? Yet, I found myself restless. Not only was I incapable of being content, my human emotions grew along with me. I had these completely illogical feelings that I had not expected. I am over a thousand years old, and felt every outburst as a child, every upset of a broken heart. Even the baser needs that a young man craves from the fairer sex," he continued, staring at Evie with half closed eyes, mouth dropping slightly open. He heard Evan growl and straightened up, smiling again.

"Once I was grown, I felt my first wave of rage because my father never paid me any mind. He hated me for being the son of an insane woman he didn't want. The fool never knew of what great power I possessed. What I could do for him. Neither did I until recently." He met Evan's glare.

"Ah yes, Ruadh Donas. Though they call ye the Red Devil, it was I all along who was at Satan's right hand. I called ye forth to do my bidding, yet ye have gone on to fit your own desires. The problem is, I have what you want already. The Flag is in my possession."

"No!" Evan bellowed.

"Oh aye, dear Evan. I thought I needed yer expertise and skill to help me battle the MacLeods. But ye lead me right to their front gate. Ye gave me back my birthright. See, being in this painfully mortal body had made me weak and left my mind a sieve. I forgot the thrill and surge of capturing souls. I was given a conscience in this wretched form. I took a wife and settled down. I managed to get by with just this ever-dying soul I possessed for damn near thirty years. Yet I knew there was to be more to have. I just, couldn't, remember.

"The only thing I did recall, through training from my Da, was that the Flag would let me take over all of Scotland, and further. So I called ye forth and ye came, and watched as ye trained my weary men with your pure strength. Ye showed me again how to fight and to kill with my bare hands; how to take one's breath away so efficiently. I wandered for days when I had crossed the sea and found the MacLeod's men on the pathway." He closed his eyes in the memory.

"Oh yes, it was delicious. They screamed in agony as I ripped their heads around on their bodies—and the smell—that soulful smell I had missed all this time. It was if I were being reborn. It was pure delight. It was Heaven in my hands. I had such a rush that I finished the friend and their animals just because I could. It was that moment I recalled my whole existence, and yet that damnable conscience took over." He returned his gaze back to Evan's direction, yet remained unfocused.

"I lamented for I thought I was insane. I drank to numb my senses. Yet, how could something so beautiful as taking their souls be so wrong? It was what I was. All my memories of before I was born in this filthy suit of flesh flooded back to me.

"Ye took me down to the beach and beat me senseless. My wife threw herself at ye and after ye cast her aside she tried to kill me with poison. And as soon as ye left my castle I knew ye'd never return. The only correspondence was a stray letter from a passerby stating ye had become stuck by weather. I am an old fiend, Roy; I know betrayal when I see it. I was enraged. I slaughtered damn near all the remaining people at Dunscaith including that wretch of a wife. I watched her as she bled out on the stones of the great hall floor and I reclaimed her damnably traitorous soul. Now, the Flag is all I want. I can reclaim the souls I have missed out on in the last thirty summers. I shall start anew with a more powerful army of the strongest Fae, directly from the Realm itself." He concluded, the onlookers paralyzed in confusion, panic, and fear.

From behind him, Liam pulled out a folded piece of yellowed cloth. Evie gasped and jumped up, recognizing it from the portrait in the solarium. Evan lunged toward him, but something unknown held him back.

"Here it is. Everything ye have always wanted. I shall wave it and every soul shall be mine for the taking."

Creighton jumped forward, yelling, while Lily tried to hold him back. Evan was paralyzed, stuck in his place, while Evie screamed. Liam grabbed her by the throat and pulled her to him.

"Now, this one … She's something else. Not only descendant seven hundred years in our future, but from the direct Fae line of the MacLeods! She's going to be delectable." He licked the side of her face as she screamed and kicked in his direction. He threw his head back and laughed. "Roy, I take her with me now because I ken ye will try to fetch her back. For in order to see her alive, ye will have to come back to my side. I cannae stand betrayal."

"You let her go now, you evil fiend!" Evan screamed.

Liam laughed, jumping up into the windowsill, still holding Evie by the throat. He shattered the glass with his elbow, causing it to rain down on them all. Evie tried to escape his grasp by clawing at his hands without falling out the window herself. He tightened his grip even more and held her dangling out the window with one arm.

"No, I don't think ye understand. I am going now with this gift and the Flag. Ye'll come back to me and fight or she will die." With that, he jumped backward out the window of the turret, landing like a cat on its feet, with Evie fighting his grasp and screaming for Evan.

Creighton fell to his knees while Lily sobbed. Evan was released by whatever force that held him. He rushed to the window and looked out only to see nothing.

"We need all the men we can find. The castle, the village and any damn man who is left standing at Dunscaith. We go to war now!" Evan roared.

"Roy, do ye realize he's calling the Fae Warriors to slaughter us? We have no way of defending ourselves from such," Creighton said, defeat in his voice.

"Oh the hell we don't. You heard him. Evie is the descendant of seven hundred years worth of Fae Blood. Blood that runs down the female line. Liam's mother was one hundred percent Fae."

Creighton looked like he had been slapped, and turned his head to eye Lily asking, "Lily, yer sister?" She covered her face and nodded.

"Why? How did I not know?"

"We have all the knowledge we could ever need," Evan paced the room staring at Lily.

Creighton continued to look upon his wife in shock. She looked up from her hands and nodded slowly to her husband, acknowledging everything Evan said as true. They were both descended from the Fae.

"Was it you that held me from Liam, Lily?" Evan stopped to ask her, eyes penetrating.

"Yes, it was. I did not want ye to die. There was no time to explain," Lily pleaded, wringing her hands.

Evan was furious, punching the wall. "Ye let him get away!? I could have ripped him to shreds right then!"

"No, ye couldn't have, Evan. Only a certain type of death kills the Slaugh. Ye can try all ye want yet he would return. And the Fae will fight on."

Creighton shook his head vehemently in disagreement. "He can be killed. It matters not what hell he thinks he'll unleash on us, if he dies with the Fae Warriors nearby, they shall become as neutral as they were to begin with. They only follow the leader who is there. If he is killed, the Fae will stop. For a full-blooded Fae ye should ken that, right?" Lily looked hurt at his anger.

"How do we kill him, Lily?" Evan demanded dropping to his knees in front of her. Lily's face twisted.

"There's a Fairies Blade, but it has been missing for at least a year. It is the same blade his father took his own life with. Only that blade shall kill Liam."

Evan's gaze met Creighton's. "But I thought he was murdered by you, Creighton?"

"No, of course not. I never meant him harm. He came to me after he realized what his son was. He had dreamt of the decimation Liam would inflict and began to research it. There was no way his mother should have given birth to a live child after death. His father spoke with healers, priests, witches, and in the middle, he found the truth. The Slaugh. He had come to me knowing it was only a matter of time before the killing started and he wanted to die. He knew the only way to stop the bloodshed was by dying on that damn blade and blessing it with his, the father's blood, still fresh. I wouldn't have anything to do with such heathen nonsense. I denied it. We fought about it and he tried to convince me to at least send him away; to send him to find Killie MacLeod."

Evan stopped breathing when he heard Evie's mother's name and looked to Lily. "Why Killie?"

"Because Killie was pregnant to the only known full-blooded Fae, seven hundred years from then. For Lochlann was my half brother, the product of a Fae male from the Realm, and my mother was a MacLeod … " Lily trailed off.

"So Evie is … "

"The closest to full Fae that he knew of," she concluded, looking down and closing her eyes.

"He originally wanted Evie's blood on this blade?"

Creighton answered, "He knew the killing would not start if he had the blood of a full blood Fae on the sgian dubh—or his own blood on it, blessed by a Fae. He could have stopped the massacre. Yet I being a fool thought he was a mad drunk and wouldn't help. Frustrated, he handed this knife to me to go find Killie and try to cut her unborn child, but threw himself upon it instead. His dying words were, 'Forgive me, I've borne a monster. Let my blood on this blade be the end of it.' Lily was there to hear it."

"Liam only saw the last part," Evan concluded.

"Aye. He came around the corner and only saw his Da dying at my hands. He pitched a tantrum, flung himself at me. The blade was lost in the shuffle and he was carted off back home to Dunscaith."

"Lily, did the blade get blessed when you were there? With Liam's father's last words?" Evan sounded hopeful as he asked her, holding her hands.

"I saw it happen and I quickly said a prayer over the dying man. I am not entirely sure that it counts as a blessing. But I did say words."

"Then we have to believe it worked. We have to find that thing and find Liam before he unleashes hell on Scotland."

"Where would we even begin to look?"

Evan paced the room while Creighton and Lily went over the night's events that happened so long ago.

Evan couldn't believe it. His wife was a direct relative from the Fae. It was now completely clear why Killie had put them through so much hell learning about the past. It was why she was so adamant about legends, myths and all things Scottish. It was why Evie had to grow up the way she did. He thought about Lochlann, Evie's father. He turned to face Creighton and Lily.

"How did Lochlann die?"

Lily put her hand on her mouth, trying to stifle a cry. Creighton put his hand on her shoulder and spoke.

"He was killed by Liam's father, we think. It's not entirely clear. With all we've discovered I'm not certain it wasn't Liam who killed him. All we ken is that after Killie left from being chased by Liam's father who just wanted to have or kill her, there was a struggle with Lochlann. Liam's father pushed him off the cliff overlooking the sea. His body was never recovered." Evan sighed.

"Was Killie here when it happened?"

"No, Lochlann sensed something was wrong, so he made her return to her own time. They were hand fasted the same day they found she was pregnant. Word got out and Liam's Da was incensed. I suppose he ken what a monster his son was, and knew that she or that babe would have the best way out of this mess. Killie went home to her own time the same day Lochlann died. She was devastated. She came back a long time afterward, right before you arrived. She said the end for us was near and she wanted to help. She brought back the photographs and baubles that Lily has, and told us to keep an eye out for ye. I never thought it would happen; I couldn't look at the pictures. When Evie arrived it never crossed my mind. Now I'm the fool." Creighton ran his hands over his weary face.

Evan recalled the day Killie died. It was a year before they had arrived. Samhain. The times when the veil between the living and the dead worlds was thinnest.

"Did Lochlann die on Samhain?"

"Aye, he did," Creighton responded, a bit confused.

Evan nodded. It was all making more and more sense. Killie had come back on the anniversary of Lochlann's death to give pictures of who to look for. Pictures of those who could save her future. Save the MacLeod and the MacDonald lines so that they wouldn't all cease to be ... *So that Evie and I could live.* Once her seed was sown, she could go be with Lochlann, in The Veil. That's why she was so serene in the clearing back home. She was done. She could go home.

Evan ran his hands through his hair. "How much time do we have?"

Creighton shrugged, crossing his arms. "Not much. I figure he's in a hurry."

"We have to find that blade," Evan said.

"I wouldn't ken where to start."

A thought struck Evan as he ran his hand across the only scar on his face. "What was Liam's Father's name?"

"Tarlach MacDonald. Why?" Creighton searched Evan's face for understanding.

Evan jumped up and ran to the door. He threw it open and ran down the staircase and through the hallways back to his chamber.

Lily and Creighton followed a little slower behind, unable to keep up with Evan's very long strides. They caught up to him as he was destroying his bed and surrounding tables.

"Evan, why are ye doing this?" Lily yelled, covering her mouth as she watched the man tear the room apart.

"When I arrived, I was in a huge fight with most of the men of Dunscaith. I got nicked in the face with a knife, a sgian dubh. I picked it up thinking it was a, uh, movie prop, a fake, but once I figured out I had been taken back in time, I kept it. I remember having it the entire time I was here. It had the initials T.M. burned in the handle. It has to be the Fairy Blade. It should be here!" He looked at the mess he'd made, pacing back and forth. "I usually kept it under my bed, and it's no here anymore." Evan rubbed his face again, trying to think of where it could be. "No offense, but ye dinna think any of the servants could have stolen it?"

"I dinna think so, son," Creighton said, not taking offense to the idea. He knew that Evan was desperate to find his wife, and to right the wrongs that Liam had thrown their way.

"What about Evie? The night she got lost in the woods. Ye said she destroyed things here. Is it possible she took it with her?" Lily asked quietly, putting her hand on Evan's arm to try and calm his nerves. Evan stopped and looked to her.

"It's possible, aye. We should check her room just in case."

They walked to the chamber next door and as he opened the door the smell of his wife permeated his senses enough to knock him off balance mentally. The rage resurfaced knowing that he no longer held her safe and he tore through her room looking for anything that would suffice in holding the knife. Coming up empty handed, Evan was lost. He punched the wall, bloodying his knuckles.

Creighton pulled him back by his arms, trying to restrain him. "She may still have it on her, Roy. Let's think of the positive. She might have tucked it away just in case. She knew someone was still following her." He patted the stressed man on the back as Evan's shoulders fell. He struggled to remember if she had picked up anything on their way out the bedroom chamber earlier. He didn't see her pick up anything but the serving maid had grabbed him too fast.

"Ye may be right. God, I hope yer right." He felt defeated.

Creighton saw the pain in Evan's eyes and took control. "Come; let's get the men ready to go to Dunscaith. The pass is cleared now of snow. If we push, we can be there by nightfall. We'll get any survivors and band together. We have to have faith that all is not lost yet."

Evan wished he could be so hopeful. Lily exited before the men and went in search of servants to pack food and water for their journey while Evan and Creighton alerted the clansmen of the plan to go to war … finally … war … but at what cost?

Chapter 24

I'm so tired. My limbs ache. I don't feel my feet anymore. I'm certain I have frostbite. These ropes are too damn tight for my wrists, and I'm bleeding now, great ... Wow, I've turned into a whiny woman. Oh, but no, he won't stop walking. If I had a rock I'd lob it at his skull. Nothing looks familiar out here...Which isn't saying much because I didn't get out too terribly far. Though the clearing we just passed reminded me of when I first got here. And now that I think about it, I wouldn't have remembered much of the scenery since I was upside down over Malcolm's shoulder ... so it's possible this is where I was ...

Evie perked up to pay more attention to her surroundings. She shuddered with anxiety as Liam pulled her along behind his horse, the rope that bound her hands pulled taut between them. She stared off to the side, taking in every detail of their surroundings, just in case she had to make it back alone.

Please let Evan have a plan. Let him be figuring this mess out ...

They began a steep decline down what seemed to be a cliff. Panic struck Evie as she saw the sea, and a small boat tied to a rock, partially hidden by trees . *He's going to take me off this island. Evan won't ever find my body at sea ...*

She dug in her heels and refused to go any farther.

"Keep up," he said, not turning around as he spoke. She dug in her heels harder and pulled backward, trying to stop him by force of fury itself.

Liam tugged at her rope hard enough to knock her forward, dragging her facefirst onto the ground. Her hands scraped along the ground, gathering rocks and dirt into her fists. He stopped after a few feet, hearing her curses behind him and jumped off his horse, huffing as if inconvenienced. He sauntered back toward her, and squatted down to the ground where she lay, struggling to get up. "Ready to keep up?"

Evie got to her feet and he rose to meet him eye to eye. "Go to hell."

Liam hit her across her face with the back of his hand so hard her lip split. Without making a sound, she slowly turned her head to face him and spat blood in his face. Liam grabbed her by the back of her head, wrapping the long braid of her hair around his fist. He pulled her close to his face and smiled devilishly, his eyes faintly glowing.

"Cheeky lass. Fiery soul. Would be such a waste to destroy it so soon. I have big plans for ye. It is hard to keep that in mind with ye acting this way." He leaned in, pulling her face up, and smelled her throat. "Though there are always other things that would suffice."
Rage filled Evie, and she raised her tied hands quick enough to knock Liam in the windpipe as hard as she could … *If they can't breathe or see* … He staggered backward choking and let go of her hair. She took that second of opportunity to shove her handfuls of rocks and dirt into his eyes. He grabbed for her wrists, trying to free them from his face. Evie pushed him backward and kneed him in the crotch. *Alright, Evan never said to do that but I'm pretty sure he'll forgive me …*

He dropped to his knees gasping for air while not knowing what to grasp first; his eyes, his throat or crotch. With Liam seemingly incapacitated, Evie grabbed the long rope, twisted the length around her, and began to run the direction she came. The tracks in the melting snow still visible enough to find her way back without getting too lost.

She stopped once she was out of sight in the woods and found a sharp rock to try and untie the rope. It was thin enough for her to scrape it until it frayed. She pulled against it until the rope finally broke free and rubbed her bleeding wrists. She tore off the bottom edge of her skirt, wrapped strips around them in makeshift bandages, and began to run through the woods toward the castle.

Liam recovered a short time after Evie's departure, his red eyes bright again from rage. He stood slowly, hating his mortal body for being so weak. He needed more souls to regain his inhuman strength. Regaining his posture, he began to smell the air for her scent. Finding the faintest whiff of her, he headed off into the direction she traveled.

∞

Evan rode hard down to the shore. It had taken him the rest of the day to ready the men to make the trip to Dunscaith. He steeled his nerves, though he was petrified for Evie's safety. He remembered the look on Liam's face as he tasted her skin in the turret room. The idea of him laying his fiendish hands on her made him want to scream. His face darkened in anger. He and his men made their way to the shore with no sign of passage from either Evie or Liam.

There were no tracks from this direction ... Maybe they went another way. I should have had more men to split up ... He pulled the reins of his horse to turn around and looked to Creighton, who was riding close behind. "Is there time to double back and check another route?"

Creighton looked around and to the position of the sun and nodded. "It's worth a try. I'll send men."

Evan cut him off. "No, I want to find the bastard myself," and sent his horse into a full gallop in the opposite direction.

Creighton continued to lead the clansmen to the seat and climb aboard the boats to go across the sea to Dunscaith, possibly for the last time.

He hadn't wanted to leave Lily, but she pushed him to do the right thing; above all, protect the Flag from evil. He had lived his entire life with the training for this moment. Lily had reassured him he would return. He had always taken comfort in her, yet he had a sinking feeling about this trip. Someone would not return, Creighton just knew it.

Across the way, Evan rode as hard as he could up the mountains looking for any sign of Liam and Evie. He glanced through the trees and the muddy snow that remained for any sign of tracks. He slowed his pace enough to see a shredded rope near a rock. He barely stopped his horse before he jumped off to investigate it further. Around the area he saw droplets of blood and fabric pieces the color of Evie's dress ... He looked around and found feet print small enough to be hers on the ground. Following it as far as he could to where as they ended—at the cliff to the sea. He said a small prayer as he looked over the edge, fearing to see her body lay upon the rocks below. Releasing his held breath, he made his way down to the shore from the cliff above, taking time to search his surroundings for signs of her. After the climb down, he made notice that her small footprints were gone, but larger footprints remained—fresh ones, and they stopped at the sea. Evan ran up the edge of the shore looking for a possibly discarded boat. Seeing none, he scaled the side of the cliff back up to his horse and made the furious trek back to where he last saw Creighton.

∞

It was nearing dark, but she was going to make it. The castle was in her sights. Relief overwhelmed Evie as she began to sprint toward the castle gates. She glanced around and was concerned with the lack of torch light and people milling around, but assumed they were probably still out looking for her. She decided to go directly to the solarium in search for Lily. Surely, she would know whom to contact to call off the search so they could regroup and rally the warriors for war.

Almost to the gates ... almost there ... almost to Evan ...

She felt her breath escape her. Something was choking her. Evie dropped to her knees grasping at her throat. With nothing visibly keeping her from breathing, she scanned the forest edge she had just escaped, seeing the red glowing eyes at a distance. He was smiling, standing at the tree line with his arms outstretched. She could hear his voice as if he were standing beside her.

"Come back to me and ye shall have another chance. Get any closer to Dunvegan and die now."

She seriously considered letting him choke her to death instead of having to grovel her way back to him for a breath, but the vision of Evan smiling at her, so relaxed and happy with her on the bed early that morning kept her from choosing any alternative. She'd grovel and beg and plead ... kill, maim, destroy; anything or anyone to be with him. She tried to gasp for air as she crawled on hands and knees back to Liam's direction.

"That's a good lass. Come back to me."

The air slowly returned to her lungs every movement closer she got to Liam, and the farther away from the castle. She was now coughing on the fresh air that flooded her as she reached Liam, kneeling at his feet. Evie sobbed at her loss. *Almost there ...* Liam patted her on the head like a dog.

"Yer life will be spared for now. Ye shall serve me well while I unleash the Fae upon the world. Yer fate shall quickly be sealed when the time is right, unless you choose to cross me again." He kicked her in the stomach and she fell over, retching in the grass. "Yer bloody betraying husband taught me that one. Perhaps I should show him how it feels through you. Or before you die, you can tell him. Wouldn't that be lovely?"

He still planned on killing her; she should have known that. Her fate was already sealed, he said. She was no longer in the purgatory or heaven she previously thought. She was destined to be in hell with this monster. Anger seared through her. She rejected the idea of dying before she decided it was time. She would not let go of her husband, her children, her life – for one man's evil greed.

She regained strength as the fury overtook the pain. Evie repositioned herself back on her hands and knees and scanned the forest ground. Twigs, sticks, and rocks surrounded her. She moved to a crouch and felt something pinch her inner thigh; a small knife tucked into the top of her garter. With renewed hope, she thought of how she could get it to it without Liam noticing.

Seeing that she had recovered from the kick, he grabbed her by her braid and pulled her to a standing position. "Now, we'll venture to Dunscaith and let the Flag ceremonies commence."

Missing her opportunity, she let him drag her all the way back to where she had escaped, near the cliff and the ultimate descent to the shore to quite possibly her untimely demise.

Arriving at the bottom of the incline where she originally had escaped, Evie was struggling to free herself from Liam's grasp. He kept pulling her down to him and time after time, she kept scratching, punching, and clawing her way out only to run a little bit away from the sea and fall underneath him again. She managed to knock Liam down and went for the knife, trying not to gain further notice of what she was doing. *Surprise attack if it all possible. The tiny thing would probably just piss him off but I have to try …*

Liam gained his footing as he grabbed Evie and pulled her back against his chest, pinning her arms down by her side with one hand, and wrapping the remainder of her rope around her. Evie fought him hard, kicking and biting whatever she could. Liam secured the rope around her as tightly has possible without the threads fraying and stepped back, looking at her.

"Wee evil sprite will learn. Ye cannae escape me, try as ye

might."

She spat at him and yelled. "How many times do I have to tell you to go to hell??"

Again the familiar pain came from across her jaw. This time was harsher and more debilitating than the first. She spat more blood onto the sandy dirt and tried to stop the stars in her eyes and the bile from rising in her stomach, yet consciousness escaped her. Liam picked her body up, threw it indelicately into the small boat, and set sail.

∞

Unaware if any of the other MacLeods reached the shore yet, Evan left the empty, lone boat on the beach and began hiking silently and quickly up the side of the trail to Dunscaith. When he approached, he saw immediately the destruction that Liam unleashed on the castle. Now in almost total ruins, he recognized the castle he was used to seeing in the postcards. Only a pile of rubble, covered over in moss and decayed beyond recognition over the next several hundred years, would remain. *So this is what happened …*

He looked around, not seeing anyone or any movement near the castle and stealthily made his way to the remains of the castle gates, not even aware of the discorporeal riders that were coming up from the same direction in which he arrived. He easily passed through the gates and began to look around for any signs of Liam or Evie.

Having spent so little time on the inside of Dunscaith's walls, compared to Dunvegan, it was a veritable maze of halls and stairs. He barely recognized it from the brief time he spent here. The place was barren and the insides destroyed from prolonged battle. Gone was the invitingly warm home he had arrived to not so long ago. It had been transformed into a horror movie. Great wooden furniture now lay in splinters. Tapestries were torn to shreds and burned. Blood stained the slate floor. The smell of decay and death overwhelmed Evan close to sickness. The slaughtered men and women weren't buried, but strewn in the hallways where they fell. Evan thought of how Liam regarded humans and safely assumed he thought of them as just food to consume; to discard like scraps. His heart ached for the families who had allowed this monster into their home; for the men who had called him as their chieftain, only to be led like lambs to the slaughter.

He made his way past the first turn in the corridor past the great hall and saw firelight glowing from a chamber up the steep stone stairs. He began to creep along the wall to remain hidden. An eternity passed as he made his way up to the fire lit room. Peering past the doorway, he frowned and his heart ached as he saw Evie. She was sitting on her knees, hands bound behind her back. She was too close to the fire, rocking back and forth maniacally. Her stare was unfocused and she muttered something under her breath. Her hair was matted into knots, her clothes dirty and ripped. Her eyes and cheekbones were multicolored and swollen from recent abuse and from crying. Her neck was bruising in the shape of a large hand, and her lip was freshly bleeding. Rage clouded his senses as Evan restrained himself from barging in and carting her off to safety. He knew Liam had to be close. There was no way he would leave her unattended unless it was a trap.

Evan scanned the room from where he stood. He recognized it as another entrance of Liam's office he sat in so long ago, when Evan found out about the Fairy Flag. He couldn't see anyone other than Evie from this angle, so he shifted his position to see inside and attempt to hear what she was saying, if it was anything coherent. The muttering grew louder and clearer as he strained to hear and understand.

"Cutter up high … He's on side … waiting for you all to die," Evan heard her repeat it over and over again. It made no sense. He wondered if she had beaten enough to detach her from her mind. Fury seared through his veins. He did not come all this way to have a monster destroy his family.

Evan moved closer still and looked into the room once more. It appeared empty from this angle but he couldn't be certain. He took a step into the room and paused. Evie glanced at his direction, still unfocused, speaking the words louder. "Cutter up high, he's on side, waiting for you all to die … " He looked around the room again and saw Liam facing a sideboard at the back of the vast chamber, hovering over a body. Evan focused on the man and not the face of his victim as he backed out of the room quickly. He crouched down at Evie's eye level and tried to will her to look at him. She clinched her eyes shut and shook her head vehemently and continued her chant eliminating the second verse, 'He's on side.' … The sideboard where Liam was standing. *That must have been 'on side.' All right, we're getting somewhere ...*

He kept in the shadow of the hallway out of Liam's sight, listening to the chant, attempting to decipher her code. *Cutter up high. Waiting for us all to die ... Cutter up high ...*

Evan exhaled slowly and rubbed his temples, trying to figure out what it could mean. She rocked up from her knees to her bare feet in a crouch. Her skirt moved to above her knees. She rocked continuously as her hem rose up her thigh with every movement. He thought she was going to stand up and take off at some point but she didn't. The material crept higher and higher still. Evan kept an eye on Liam, who was still concerned with the victim before him. He glanced down and looked at the face, and recognized him as the son of the MacDonald warrior who had stood up for him when he was staying here ... The young boy who had knocked me senseless and then apologized ... They had all stood for Evan that day and vowed to follow him. They pledged to help him against the MacLeods. Evan felt ill. *There is no helping him now ...* His heart sank for the young man and his father, who he had hoped had escaped. Evan vowed to make this right for the survivors, somehow.

He returned his gaze to Evie as she continued to rock, the material of her skirt now up to the tops of her thighs, exposing her milky white skin. Evan saw a glint of light on her inside of her leg and made a double take as he struggled to see the item. Tucked into the top of her stocking, dangerously high on her inner thigh was the small wooden-handled sgian dubh. He made out the initials of Tarlach MacDonald burned on the hilt. His mouth dropped open in surprise and looked to her face. Evie was now focused and staring directly into his eyes. She had stopped chanting and was just simply rocking back and forth with a look of determination on her face. Fresh tears began to fall as her strength faltered and she began to sob. Evan put his finger to his lips to try and quiet her. He had to think fast. He had to get her out of here. He mouthed the words, "Hang on, lass."

Looking to the back of the room where the old fiend stood, Evan wondered how long he had to surprise Liam and at least do some damage before Evan could get to the knife and gut him. Always having relied on his own physical strength, the idea of having to use a weapon was something he was uncomfortable with, but he knew it must be done in order to stop him. Liam would reign terror until the blade spilled his blood. Evan realized he only had limited time before Evie's sanity slipped away. Liam inhaled exaggeratedly and turned his back on the victim on the small table, suspiciously eyeing the room. His features were more drawn, his color ashen and yet his eyes were still a faintly glowing red. Evan backed completely out of sight, not wanting to draw attention to himself.

Liam walked to where Evie was and pulled her up by her arms, twisting them in an unnatural way behind her by the restraints, causing her to scream. He grabbed her throat and threw her to the nearest chair and returned to the fire place. Evan ducked out of sight into an alcove as Liam stalked to the entrance and looked around. Seeing nothing of interest, he sauntered back to where Evie laid crumpled and sobbing and picked her up from under her arms. He smelled her throat again as if he were about to devour her and she let out a hoarse cry. "Please just kill me now," she whispered as the man ran his hands into her hair and held her up by the sides of her head.

His breath was rancid as he spoke roughly. "As soon as yer husband comes, ye shall have yer wish and then some. But not a moment sooner. For now, we'll just enjoy each others' company, shall we?" He kissed her roughly, trying to drive his foul tongue into her mouth. She cried out and tried to free herself from him.

Liam pulled her back to look at her, his face mutating into Evan's features. She screamed out in terror, still shaking her head in retaliation. "Is this better, lass? Shall ye kiss the Ruadh Donas instead?"

Chapter 25

After what seemed like an eternity, the men and Creighton arrived on the shore. He immediately dispersed the orders to the men and they all headed for the castle. As they approached the massive stone fortress, they began to see the dark figures of men towering over the entrances and on what was left of the battlements. Mounted on large ethereal black horses encased in black plate armor, their eyes glowed faintly blue as their hooves radiated the same glow, resembling ice. Their riders were huge men with matching plated armor with spikes and points aimed to kill. They were inhumanly tall, and their long straight white hair was blowing in the faint breeze, their eyes glowing a matching bluish-white hue. Their faces were expressionless, their too pale skin perfect without any mar.

Only one warrior of the many who stood before Creighton showed any sign of disfigurement. The tallest, most muscular Fae in the front of the castle doors stared directly at him. His left eye glowed the blueish white, while the right one was faintly yellow. A silvery scar ran down from his forehead to his chin in a straight line in an apparent result of a battle.

Creighton knew they were outnumbered, not only in amount of men but by strength and size. Easily a hundred warriors strong, they sat atop their warhorses steeled and ready for combat. He knew there was no way they would defeat the Fae horde that stood before them. He advised the men to stay back as he approached the largest one in front with the scarred yellow eye. The warrior was expressionless as the chieftain moved toward him. The huge black horse he sat atop snorted blue flame and Creighton stopped, afraid to go any closer. The Fae warrior tilted his head to the side and waited.

He held Lily's face in his mind as a reminder of what exactly he was here for and stepped forward. Creighton cleared his throat and spoke. "I am Creighton MacLeod, chieftain of the Clan MacLeod. My family has guarded your gift of the Fairy Flag for hundreds of years. We come to seek the Flag to return it to its rightful home; before the hands of Liam MacDonald destroy peace in the human realm." He paused and held his breath, hoping it wasn't a lost cause. The entire world's peace was at stake. If Liam succeeded in taking Scotland to war with the Fae, their whole world would perish.

The Fae looked down upon the man, his face still void of expression. His voice radiated through the air as the wind, yet the creature's mouth never opened. "Human, you lost control of the Flag that was bestowed upon your family in kindness. You knew it held responsibility and understood of the consequences if it ever fell into anyone else's hands. The conditions were straightforward. Who holds the Flag commands it. Three wishes in its existence."

"Has the current holder set his wish in motion?" Creighton held his head up, bracing for the worst.

"We await his direction."

Creighton's hopes fell and fear gripped him. There would be Hell on Earth at Liam's command. They would not survive. He had failed the clan. He staggered a few feet backward and stopped. He regained his composure as he turned around and walked back to the waiting men.

"We will be going to war. Ready yerselves for anything." The men nodded and began to prepare for impending battle. Creighton knew there was no telling at this point what would happen in the coming moments.

∞

Evan saw his wife struggle against Liam and his temper soared out of control. In a blind rage, Evan burst into the room to where the two stood and ripped them apart, punching Liam in the face. Evie screamed and fell to the floor, watching the violence that unfolded around her. In a second, Evan took Liam by the throat, lifted him up far above his head, and slammed him down on the remnants of a nearby table. Liam fought back by using unnatural force to throw Evan back against the wall.

He crashed down onto the floor and was immediately back up and on Liam. "Fighting dirty are ye, Liam? Tsk tsk," Evan crookedly smiled as he jumped on him again.

Evie crouched in her position in the floor, unable to help with her arms tied behind her back. Liam and Evan wrestled and fought, while Evie scrambled to the fireplace and backed into it as far as she could to burn the ropes off her wrists. Screaming at the fire that burned her skin, she burned through enough to free herself. She grabbed the knife from her stocking and jumped into the fray, trying to break them apart. She only succeeded in getting herself knocked to the ground by Liam, who hissed at her while Evan took the moment to jump on his back. Evie threw the sgian dubh at Evan, who deftly caught it and stabbed Liam in the chest.

Liam fell to the floor moaning and clutching the wound gushing thick black ooze. He crawled to all fours, looked up at Evan, and chuckled. Evan kicked him in the face, causing Liam to fall unconscious on the floor. Bent over with his hands braced on his knees, he caught his breath and looked up to Evie, who was standing near the fire, holding her wrists. Evan went to her, hugging her tightly and kissing her face. He looked at her hands to judge the burns.

"Ye shouldn't have done that, lass. I could have handled him." He brushed her hair out of her battered face, taking assessment of her injuries. She looked around his shoulder to see Liam moving about on the ground. "Evan, I don't think this is over."

"I've seen enough action flicks to ken it's no over," he smiled and winked at her. The fight had invigorated him. He felt more alive than he had in ages. If he wasn't so concerned about the whole idea of dying and bringing Hell onto Earth, he could say he was having fun beating the daylights out of Liam, especially after the beating that he had inflicted upon Evie, judging by her current condition. He would happily spend eternity re-gifting those welts, burns and bruises. He had to give Evie credit for being so tough under the circumstances. He could tell her wounds were beginning to blister, yet she didn't seem to notice. In shock, most likely.

His thoughts turned to Liam. He was confused as to why the knife didn't take him down as Creighton and Lily had expected. He was now concerned that the blade had not been blessed properly and that they would be stuck with the fiend for all time or until they died, whichever came first. He gripped the sgian dubh handle tight as he slowly turned his head to look over his shoulder and watched

Liam slowly rise to stand. He slid Evie behind him with one hand as he turned around to face him again. He was covered in the blackish ooze yet the once open wound under his throat seemed to have healed. Evan's mind raced as he realized whatever Fairy magic was supposed to occur hadn't.

"What is it, Evan?" Evie asked, putting her hand on his arm, but winced at the pain it caused and pulled it back.

"Nothing, apparently. I had a theory but it's been debunked. There's been a change of plans." He looked back to Liam as he heard him laugh wickedly at the matched confusion on their faces.

"Oh, so ye thought that wee knife would kill me, aye? So gullible are ye to believe such nonsense from a couple of old MacLeods. There is no death fer me at the hand of Ruadh Donas. But as soon as I give the command to the waiting Fae outside, yer death will come swiftly. I promise." He bowed deeply for dramatic effect.

"Oh, is that so? Let's test that theory," Evan growled, freshly annoyed, and jumped agilely over the broken wooden table to grab Liam by the throat, knocking him off balance. Both Evan and Liam fell and crashed into what was left of the stained glass window. Evie barely heard herself scream as she saw the two men fall from the tower.

∞

The MacLeods stood toe to toe with the mounted Fae, waiting for any sign of Evan or a sign of advancement from the opposing side. Creighton paced back and forth, speaking with his men. As he walked slowly back toward the front of the clan, he saw a flicker of light from a room at the castle tower. He stopped walking and tried to focus. He attempted to get closer to the building but the Fae were too attentive. As if they had heard his thoughts, they closed rank to disallow the movement. Creighton moved as close as he could get and again tried to focus on the room, mentally preparing himself for what was about to come. He heard screaming and the men behind him began to ready themselves; claymores, swords, daggers and bows in hand awaiting a sign.

Glass shattered from the room's window and two men fell from the tower room. Creighton held his breath as he recognized the shock of red hair from one of the men. The two men were grappling in mid air as they plummeted toward the ground.

∞

Evie was barely aware that the screaming voice in the room was her own as she watched them plunge toward the ground, two stories below. Standing in horror, she saw her life stop in time. She was suddenly numb, unable to move. The entire moment looked as if she were seeing it through someone else's eyes ... *This can't be my life. He can't be gone ...*

Shaken from the temporary shock, Evie turned and ran from the upstairs tower room, down the winding stairs and through the maze of halls to the outside courtyard, stopping as she saw the huge Fae warriors atop their steely black mounts. Her heart lurched. They were just as the portrait in Lily's solarium. She also saw the MacLeod men and Creighton beginning to approach the castle. The Fae had yet to receive any orders from Liam so as neutral as they were, they still attempted to stave off the angry and concerned highlanders. Evie ran to search the ground where the two had fallen out the window and found them still punching, choking and grappling for dominance. Evan maintained the upper hand, even though Liam was determined to use his inhuman strength and arrogance to best him.

Evie, thanking the stars that Evan was still alive to fight, ran as fast as she could toward Creighton, who met her halfway frantically yelling. "He's no going to beat him like that, Evie. They'll fight for days." He grabbed her by the upper arms and shook her. "Do ye ken where the knife is?"

Evie looked confused and remembered the knife she had tucked into her stocking. "Evan has it but we tried to stab him and it didn't work. Liam said it wouldn't kill him! Evan got so mad he pushed them both out the window. I don't know what for, I thought he was dead." Evie shook her head and let the fear wash over her as she relived the moment upstairs in her mind.

"Nay, lass, don't doubt him. Evan was thinking on his feet. Now we all can help him out here instead of in the castle. He landed directly on top Liam when he fell out that window. He never missed a second of pounding on him as they landed either. But we've got to get the sgian dubh from him. Ye have to be the one to kill Liam if we want the bloodshed to end."

Evie's face blanched as she shook her head furiously. "There's no way, he's too strong."

Creighton dropped his voice lower and stared deep into her

brown eyes to try and calm her. "Lass there's a lot that ye dinna understand right now but trust me, ye have to be the one. Ye are the only one who can save us all now. Quick, before Liam gets enough breath to command the Fae, we have to get that knife." He ushered Evie toward the two men across the courtyard, looking out for the Fae who were beginning to circle their warhorses around the two fighting men.

Evan managed to roll Liam over into a strong-armed move, which the fiend was unable to escape. He pulled Liam to his feet and held him with one forearm digging around his throat and Evan's other hand pushing the side of Liam's head sideways against his own neck, still holding the sgian dubh. "Ye will die this day, Liam, if not by my hand, then by another."

Evie ran to Evan's back and all but shouted, "Where is it, Evan?" Liam growled and fiercely tried to escape Evan's grasp, but Evan just threw both his legs around his and brought him back down to the ground with a resounding 'thump.' So many years of wrestling were finally becoming useful. So many years of training for this very thing were finally coming to fruition. "It's against this useless bastard's throat," he growled into Liam's ear.

Evie dove for the knife and Evan loosened his grasp for a split second to give her control. Liam took that second to elbow Evan in the stomach and free himself. Evan rolled over with the wind knocked from him and dropped the knife while clutching his gut. Liam lunged for it at the same time as Evie. He turned on her before she could escape his raised hand and knocked her down. He then twisted his head around to face the Fae and screamed, "As I command, kill them all!"

Chaos erupted around them. The Fae warriors, now with a direct order, kicked their horses and began to run toward the MacLeods at a full gallop. Creighton and his men stood at the ready for the battle of their lives.

Liam growled as he dodged Evan's fist and leaped over Evie's sprawling form. She looked up at his now alarmingly red glowing eyes, paralyzed with fear as he grabbed her by the hair and pulled her head back. He smiled wickedly as he stabbed her in the chest just below her collarbone, releasing her head to fall back on the ground. He crouched over her body, snarling like an animal, taking deep breaths while his eyes rolled in his head. In shock of the blinding pain, she grasped the wound, pulling back a shaking, bloody hand. Anger and horror both took her over as Liam laughed hysterically so close to her face she could smell the death emanating from his breath.

Her limbs were heavy as she fought to maintain consciousness. Her head lolled to the side as she watched Evan grab Liam from behind and began to punch him repeatedly, yelling at her to get up. *I hear you, Evan. Just give me a minute. I'm not done yet ... movie ain't over ...* Evie closed her eyes for a moment in attempt to regain strength, her body rebelling at any attempt to move. She heard the fighting between the clan and Fae behind her and a wave of calmness overflowed her. Evie opened her eyes and watched the heinous battle unfold before her while she laid in a pool of her own blood. She tentatively put her hand on the ground to push up and winced at the pain.

Gotta finish this ... up to you ... Evie pushed again, grinding her teeth at the shooting pain in her shoulder, chest, and arm and stood swaying. Slowly, she stumbled to the discarded knife on the ground. She bent down to pick it up, almost falling over. Picking it up with her hands trembling against the handle, she righted herself and staggered to where the men were fighting.

∞

Evan tried not to show any sign of noticing Evie's approach to Liam as he kept beating the fiend with his fists. He knew it was pointless but had to render him useless somehow in order to weaken him enough for Evie to kill him.

He let the fury over take him as he thought of Evie's wounds. They were not in a place for medicine. There was no penicillin. There was no emergency room. She had already overcome death once before and it petrified him to think they would have to go through it yet again at the hands of this monster.

He worked Liam over and over, their strength equally matched. Evan knew what move he would make at every point, simply because Liam had learned every single one from him. He knew the strategy and he was not apparently smart enough to waiver from that. *Which is a blessing ...* He glanced to his wife as she walked closer. Evie's face was so pale. Her lips were beginning to turn gray, her eyes glassy and unfocused, yet she remained upright and unfaltering in her quest. Evan's heart stopped for a second as Liam's expression turned to recognition and whipped his head around to face what Evan had been trying to avoid. He knew she would not be strong enough to drive the sgian dubh into the fiend. Liam pulled himself from Evan's grasp and turned around smiling as he saw Evie clutching the Fairy Blade in her small shaking fist.

The fighting escalated behind them. As the Fae jumped down to fight the clan, their horses faded into mist. The MacLeods were holding their own against them, far better than Creighton had honestly expected. The sounds of steel on steel, the sound of men ranging from battle cries to death throes echoed off the walls of the once majestic castle.

Creighton found himself face to face with the Fae leader, the scarred yellow-eyed creature matching his wisdom of war blow by blow. Taken by a surprise hit from Creighton's hand, the leader's sword was knocked free and landed in the dirt beside them. Creighton dropped his own and put up his fists as he was recently trained to do, and waited. The Fae looked perplexed and tilted his head in confusion.

"Why do you not pick up your sword, MacLeod?" his voice whispered through the air, again without any sign of movement from his mouth.

"Because that's how I fight, Riordan. Evenly." The Fae closed the gap between the men instantly and picked Creighton up by the throat and yelled, his voice causing thunder to crash around them. "How do you know my name, mortal!?"

"Yer family … is my family," he choked, gasping for air. Riordan the Fae dropped him to the ground and listened intently now crouched down beside Creighton, pulling a dagger out of his belt, holding it to the old man's chest.

"If ye had listened, ye would ken," the chieftain gasped. "Liam's mother was Ivy, my wife's sister. Yer half sister … Lochlann's half sister." He pointed to where Evie, Evan and Liam were struggling and finished. "Lochlann's daughter is the girl. She's yer niece." He sat back on his elbows gasping for air, waiting to be run through with the intricately serrated blade that was held high above him.

Riordan stood slowly and faced the fighting threesome across the field. A loud ominous horn sounded and the entire Fae army stood motionless, waiting for instructions. The MacLeod clan that remained stood at the ready, confused at the abrupt stop in action.

The scarred yellow-eyed Fae's voice once again permeated the wind as it blew around them.

"We leave this place at once. The Fairy Flag returns to MacLeod. This is family. I have overridden the command of the Flag and it shall not be counted."

One at a time, the Fae began to dissipate into mist until there was no one but the clan, Creighton, Evan, Liam, and Evie, still fighting for her life. Rain began to fall heavily as the entire Fae army was gone.

Liam snarled at Evie as she walked up to him slowly, infuriated by the warriors' disappearance. "Ye little wretch. I should have killed ye first."

Evie strained to focus, her eyes still unwilling to cooperate to see Liam's face. Feeling as if she were in a dream, she lifted her arm holding the sgian dubh and weakly stabbed at him. Liam dodged easily, laughing at her feeble attempt. She raised it again and he turned to face Evan, exposing his back to her, obviously uninterested. "Ye people sicken me. There's no way out of here alive, now or ever. I shall have the Flag, I shall command again and the entire realm full of souls shall be mine. If I have to kill all the MacLeods to have the Fae do my bidding, consider it done."

Evan took two steps toward Liam and pushed him backward with all his force. Evie, who struggled to stay upright behind Liam, caught the fiend in both arms and with a last surge of energy, she grabbed him by the hair, pulled his head back, and slit his throat from one ear to the other as they both fell backward to the ground.

Liam gurgled and flailed, unable to breathe. The blackish ooze began pouring again from his body at an alarming rate. Evan grabbed Evie from under Liam, cradling her in his arms as he ran them both away from the fiend who was still gasping for his life. He met up with Creighton and motioned for the entire clan to head for the shore to leave quickly.

Evie was still bleeding and now gray-skinned, laying still in Evan's arms. A fresh rain masked the tears now falling from his face as he collapsed on the sand. The rain came down hard as he furiously repeated the motions of CPR. Creighton watched in horror as Evie's face became ashen and her lips blue. Evan would not relent. The wound in her chest was bleeding too fast. Every breath he gave her caused more to gush out, yet he refused to quit. Creighton bowed down to grab Evan's arm, trying to still his actions but Evan turned and pushed him off, quickly returning to Evie's aid. He took her pulse … nothing. He fell onto his hands and knees, screaming. "We won, dammit! We beat him! Ye cannae leave now! We've come too far. Please! If there is any such thing as a fairy tale let this one end the way it's supposed to! I cannae go on without ye in it!" He sobbed as he moved her body to lie in his lap, cradling her head. Rocking back and forth, he cried into the rain as it fell over them.

The earth shook and the sky darkened. Sparks of light began to flash in mid-air like fireworks. Clansmen pointed to the lights as Creighton put his hand on Evan's shoulder. Creighton put his hand to his mouth in disbelief as he watched Evie's deceased father, Lochlann, materialize out of the rain that fell, as a puzzle put together with the drops. Walking forward with his form shimmering with every step, he slowly made his way to Evan.

Creighton backed away and Lochlann placed a watery gray hand on Evan's shoulder. He looked up to him in total helplessness and stared at the apparition in confusion.

"Is this my daughter?" The voice that spoke was watery and ethereal. Evan could only nod in disbelief.

He bowed down to her face and touched it lightly with his fingertips, leaving her face wet and flushed with color where he touched. He brushed her hair from her face leaving a freshly wet pink mark in its wake. Evan looked at Evie as the rest of her face began to retain the color of the marks from her father. "May I hold her?"

Evan stood, carefully cradling Evie in his arms and held her out to the watery man, unsure of if he were dreaming or if he had finally lost his mind. Lochlann held her like a baby with her body floating in his aqueous arms. "I never got to see her." He ran his hand over her face, causing more color to return to her wet skin. "Beautiful just as her mother. Such a strong warrior woman." He looked down upon her with a look of pride. He kissed her on the forehead. The color began to return to her face and raced down her neck and into her chest. The wound beneath her collarbone closed with his touch, leaving a silvery scar in its place.

He held her out to Evan again, who took her into his waiting arms. "Take care of my daughter, Evan MacDonald … forever and ever," he said as he walked toward the water's edge and entered. With every step, his form dissolved back into the sea from which he had perished so many years before. The rain stopped as mist ushered onto the shore.

Evan stood, stunned at what had just transpired and looked down at Evie. She was staring up at him, her brown eyes wide in surprise. "Did you get the son of a—" she asked hoarsely.

He dropped to his knees and crushed her body to his in an embrace with a mixture of laughter and tears. Evie wrapped her arms around his neck and held on until he calmed down and looked at her. He brushed a lock of hair from her face. "Aye, lass, we got him." He felt Creighton's hand on his shoulder and looked up. Tears had filled the old chieftain's eyes as she reached down to grab Evie's hands in his. "Och, lass we thought ye were gone."

"Gone? What do you mean?" Evie looked to them in confusion.

Creighton kneeled down in the sand and patted her leg. "Ye almost died. Liam had stabbed ye with the Fae's blade. But it was your blood on that blade that made it possible to kill Liam."

Evie blinked in confusion, then looked down at her chest. The small silvery line that remained was already beginning to fade. "But, how did I not die?" Evan took her hand and pressed it to his heart. "Yer father came to the rescue."

"My father? He was here? How?" More confusion swirled in her head as she attempted to stand. Evan jumped to his feet and caught her as she toppled over.

"Aye he was here, sort of in spirit, I suppose. I'm not sure," Evan said, scratching his head. "He appeared out of the rain and healed ye. Then he faded away into the ocean."

Evie looked out to the water, wishing he'd return to meet her. She sighed and turned to Evan. "I want to go home. Take me home, Evan."

Creighton nodded to the clansmen who had gathered around them and they all headed for the boats. Evan took Evie by the hand and they walked together in silence.

Chapter 26

$\mathfrak{T}$heir return to the castle was bittersweet. Evie entered the through the portcullis hand in hand with Evan. There was a mixture of sadness for the fallen warriors and the relief knowing the Flag was back in the hands of the MacLeods and a world war would not erupt between the Fae and the mortals. The clan greeted them with hugs and handshakes through the tears of sadness. So many warriors had fallen at the swords of the Fae. They knew throughout the clan that it was unavoidable. They knew the Fae warriors were born to protect those who held the Flag in their possession. It just so happened, the possession was Liam's. Unfortunately, he had made the command and started the war. Evie and Evan had heard the outcome from Creighton's perspective and were thankful the Fae named Riordan had cut the battle off before more precious lives were slaughtered.

Lily joined them in the great hall as they all took their seats for a much-deserved meal. She immediately flew to Creighton and threw her arms around his neck, knocking him backward a few steps. Watching the couple reunite caused Evan to squeeze Evie's hand. She looked to him and smiled. Creighton kissed Lily on the forehead and whispered in her ear; words only meant for her. She kissed him back and removed herself, straightening her gown. She wiped the tears from her face and smiled, relieved and relaxed knowing her husband had made it home safely.

Turning to face Evie and Evan, Lily could tell by just looking at them—they wanted nothing more than to just be alone. They were weary and huddled against each other as if they were the only beings in the room. Lily took note and hurried their meal along and about midway through ordered servants to have Evan's room prepared with a bath so they could rest.

A weary looking Evie turned to Lily when she finally sat down beside her and put her hand on the older woman's hand. "Tell me about my father." Lily blinked in surprise and she sighed.

"Lochlann was a very good man. He was very saddened when yer Ma left us. He was beside himself." Evie stopped her.

"No, I want to hear about him as a person. What was he like? What did he look like? What kind of life did he lead here?" Her eyes were pleading. "Just give me something to remember him by."

"Yer father was a prankster. He was forever causing us all grief. I swear they traded his hide with Loki's himself some days. He was a thoughtful man and a very good provider in the short time yer mother was here with us. He loved her dearly and was shattered when she had to return home. Lochlann was a warrior, through and through. He fought and served the Fairy Flag for nearly a hundred years before he gave up his immortality." She saw Evie's surprise at the last bit and patted the back of her hand. "It is all right, lass. He wanted to be with Killie more than anything. It brought ye here. The magic is powerful in ye. I can see it. Ye look a lot like him in his mortal form."

"So what did he look like in his immortal form? Like the Fae we saw at Dunscaith?" Evie looked to Evan and back at Lily again.

"Aye, well, if they were fair-complexioned and white haired, yes. He was the same. They tend to be about the same size. Huge. Gargantuan, even." She winked at Evan, who smiled tiredly and took a drink from his tankard, lifting it up in a toast to her.

"Not a thing wrong with gargantuan, my lady," he replied.

"Och, no, nothing wrong with it. We always figured the taller they were, the more pure of Fae blood they were. Though I don't know what happened to ye," she laughed, sizing up Evie.

"Was he in the portrait in the solarium?" Evie asked, remembering way back to the first time she saw Lily, alone in the room addressing the canvas on the wall. Lily took a deep breath and smiled softly. "Yes, that was yer father and his two brothers; Riordan and Collum. Lochlann is the one standing in the portrait."

"Are they still alive?" Evie tried to remain focused, but with weariness and now a full stomach, was beginning to fall asleep. Creighton interrupted to answer, waking her up with the change of voice.

"Aye, Riordan is still alive. He was leading the Fae today at Dunscaith. Collum has been missing for quite some time." He finished the bite he was eating and drank deep in his tankard. Evie shifted to look at Creighton, now fully awake. "He was there? My Uncle?"

"Yes, lass, he was there. He was the one who ordered the Fae off us. He was the one with the yellowed eye and scar," he motioned to his face, showing Evie where the scar ran from his forehead to his chin. "While I was fighting him, I explained who ye were, and he rescinded the command. He disna want to hurt family. He'll catch hell I'm sure from the Realm, but it was for the good of them and us."

"How did he get that scar?" Evan asked, now curious. Creighton finished his drink and shook his head slightly. "That's a story for another time." He returned to his trencher and didn't look up again. Evie pouted and asked, "But what if we don't have time later?"

Creighton peered up from his plate and winked at her. "Lass, haven't ye figured it out yet? We make time." She smiled at him and watched as she was bombarded by clans' folk wanting to know the battle was won.

Evie, without direct conversation to keep her awake, began to nod off, and leaned into Evan's side. Lily motioned for them to leave and go up to their chambers to bed. Evan excused them, picked up his wife, and ascended the stone stairs to their chamber.

∞

Evie had a hard time not falling asleep in the tub, and Evan had to wash her hair for her, ridding her of the dried blood and dirt from earlier in the day. He was thankful that she would now have no burns or stark reminders of her time in Liam's castle – as they were now like her collarbone; merely thin, unnoticeable silvery lines where the burns once were. He managed to get her clean and out of the tub without drowning, and she got dressed. Dozing, Evie watched as Evan took his own bath, and then joined her in the oversized bed.

"Think we'll go home soon?" Evie asked, nuzzling against his bare chest. He grumbled and wrapped his arm around her, pulling her closer, closing his eyes. "I dinna ken, lass. Maybe soon? Maybe later? Maybe never?" The last words fell off his lips almost in a longing tone. Evie caught the change, propped up on her arm, and stared at him.

"Would you stay here?" Evie asked, a little tentatively.

He opened one eye and looked at her quizzically. "It depends. Are ye staying with me or going back to Virginia?"

"I'm not going or staying anywhere without you," Evie said, tracing his chest slowly with one finger.

He closed his eye and grinned slowly. "That answers yer question."

Figuring the conversation ended, Evie lay back down in the crook of his arm and closed her eyes, giving in to her exhaustion. She finally had all her answers. Her heart knew peace as Evan held her. The mysteries surrounding her mother's death were finally out in the open and she could relax. For the first time she felt the weight of the world lifted from her shoulders and breathed her first breath, free of sadness or confusion. She lay in his arms and smiled. Her mother could rest now with her father. She could now rest with Evan.

He shifted and she opened her eyes to find him above her, his long red hair tickling her face. "What?"

"Don't 'what?' me, woman," he said, poking her in the ribs, causing her to giggle. She rolled away from him and closed her eyes, still smiling. "We don't have time for this. And I'm sleepy."

Evan leaned his head down and growled mischievously into her ear. "Then I suppose we need to make time as Creighton suggested, aye?" Evie smiled as he kissed her neck, tracing his tongue along her jaw line, to kiss her behind her ear. Her mouth dropped open and she turned to face him, wrapping her arms around his neck bringing him closer to her. "Aye, I suppose you're right," she whispered, giving in to pleasure over sleep.

∞

The next day they awoke late, and found their food waiting for them in the chamber. They leisurely ate and went downstairs to begin their day. Evie found herself shooed from the kitchens to rest. She wandered into the courtyard and settled on playing with the children as she picked through her herb garden, looking for any new plants from the new spring crop. Evan left to meet with the men in the lists, leaving her there to enjoy while he went to speak with Creighton and address those who fought with them on the field at Dunscaith.

The day went by as Evan kept an eye on Evie's whereabouts in the garden and the courtyard. Time passed quickly as they went about their normal routine until it was time for the evening meal.

Heading back toward the castle, Evan noticed the wind change direction abruptly. New spring leaves began to fall. Evan looked to the sky and watched it change colors; from blue and clear to cloudy white and then to heavy gray. The difference was almost immediate. The temperature dropped and the hair on his arms began to stand on end. His heartbeat quickened and he began to frantically look around the courtyard for Evie. Unable to find her where she had been all afternoon, he broke into a run through the portcullis. Creighton and Lily spotted him and began to run after him. Calling her name, thunder began to crash. *Not again, please.*

"Where did ye see her last, Evan?" Creighton called, catching up with him.

"She was in the courtyard. I saw her playing with one of the children when I saw her wander closer to the gates. I turned to answer a question from the men and she was gone." Something was nagging at him. Something was wrong. He knew the threat of Liam was gone but there was something very bothersome in the woods.

"Lily, did ye see her wander off?" He asked, running his hands through his hair with worry. Lily, the last one to arrive outside the gates shook her head. "No, son, I went into the kitchens." She wrung her hands nervously. "She hasna been gone long. Perhaps she's just gone for a walk?"

Evan knew the answer was all wrong. "Not without telling someone." Then as he turned around to face the woods where he found her almost dead, arrow shot in the back, he saw a flash. His heart stopped as he focused. Through the trees was a familiar flame, spiraling above the trees like a cyclone.

"Oh, God, no," Evan managed as he broke into a full run toward the woods with the chieftain and his wife following.

They entered the edge of the woods to find Evie collapsed at the edge of the flames, her eyes open and fixed, with a slight smile on her face. Lily gasped and Evan ran to her, picking her up while fearing the worst. "Not again, please no." He shook her shoulders and tried to get her to focus on his face. "Lass, are ye there, can ye hear me? Please, Evie."

She slowly looked to his direction and put a hand on his face.

"Hey, our ride is here."

"Ye scared the bajezus out of me, Evie. What happened?" He yelled, the color returning to his paled face. She sat up in his arms, staring again at the cyclone.

"I saw it in the courtyard. It just flew up out of nowhere. The weather changed as soon as I saw it, clear as anything. I had to follow it. I feel like a mosquito and a bug zapper. I can't pull away."

Evan had to admit, the flames were mesmerizing. She turned back to him and her eyes began to tear.

"We have to go back, Evan. It's time. Our family, they're waiting for us," she said faintly. Evan pulled her up to meet his gaze and patted the side of her face. "Are ye well, Evie?" Still dazed, she looked at Evan, her eyes glazed over with tears. "Our kids need us, Evan, We can't stay here. They need us."

"I ken, lass. We'll get there but not now. We have to finish what we started." Evan stared out at the tornado like flame in the middle of the woods and closed his eyes against its fury. "Not now, Evie, fight this. We have to finish here. We'll go home soon."

Evie started to fight his embrace."What if it doesn't come back, Evan, what if we miss this and we're stuck here? We have to go now!"

Lily saw the struggle, heard Evie's concerns, and started toward them. "Evie, lass what's amiss?" She crossed into the woods, her gaze returned to the flames, and she knew instantaneously. The flame had returned just as she expected. She placed her hand on Evan's back and said quietly. "Evan, it is all right to go home now. We are safe here. Liam's destroyed. We burned his body and his ashes were scattered throughout the mountainside. Go now. Be with yer family. That is what this flame means. Someone has figured out the puzzle. They await yer arrival. They've sent the flame for ye."

Evan was confused. "What do you mean? Someone has figured it out?" Lily smiled softly. "Liam wasna lying when he claimed he summoned ye. What he dinna ken was that I was also summoning. With two rituals going on at the same time, it pulled ye both. I knew it was only a matter of time before Liam lost his hold on who he was. The signs were here before ye came. I ken how to summon ye, with the centuries of training I was given by my parents, and their forefathers and mothers, the Fae. I summoned for Evie. Liam summoned at the same time and it was coincidence and fate and destiny that ye both came at the same time." She watched as Evan's face turned from confusion to understanding.

"So yer saying that someone at home, possibly one my children, has figured out how to summon us back home?" Evan asked, confused.

Lily smiled softly and nodded. "Yes, someone has figured it out."

"So that means that ye were the one who summoned Killie here so long ago? She didn't come on her own, ye summoned her?"

Lily put a hand on his face, nodding. "The first time yes, but that's a story for another time, son. Ye need to go home."

Evan was torn. He wanted to stay here with his wife, the wife who loved him and who came to him freely, the Evie who laughed and loved and was by his side through it all. The one who made love to him so easily even under false pretenses and who had absolved him of all his sins when he revealed himself.

He was scared to go back and have the bustling life they led corrupt their love again. He knew his family needed him. Someone was calling them. He knew Mason, Keiran and Leeann waited for them. He had to go back. But he found so much here. He looked down at Evie's face, now streaked with tears, still staring off into the dancing flames.

"Evie, what do ye wanna do?" he asked her, finally.

She turned her head to face him again and cried, "I want to go where you go, Evan. I don't want to be without you ever again. But I want to see my kids."

Evan smiled down at her, and kissed her softly. "Then let's go home, lass."

∞ ∞ ∞

Elysabeth Williams

Photo by Donna Lynn Photography

Elysabeth Williams showed a passion for storytelling and writing at an early age. Then in 2006, she was given the opportunity to write music reviews for an online magazine since music had always been a large part of her life. Still not sated, she dabbled in short stories over bedtime with her daughter.

In spring of 2008, she received the push she needed to make her writing and publishing dreams come true. While having coffee with a friend, she was reminded of her love for writing. When she mentioned how she used to write, she was told very profoundly, "You're still a writer—write!" After the epiphany, Elysabeth sat down, wrote her first novel, and has been writing ever since.